# Inked Together

## Book 1 of the Inked Together series

Diane Michaels

ArrowHeart Press

Copyright © 2021 by Diane Michaels
Cover images from DepositPhotos

**ArrowHeart Press**

First paperback edition: March 2022

ISBN 978-1-7374156-1-9

# CONTENTS

# FRIDAY

# CHAPTER 1
## VIOLET

It's nothing but armpits as far as the eye can see. I always arrive early for our daily meetings, only to have the latecomers push in front of me until I'm standing behind a wall of the tallest members of my division. At least the meetings are first thing in the morning, when everyone is freshly showered. Later in the day, I'd be up to my nose in armpits.

Ben Harris ambles over to the scrum at the pace of someone who hasn't learned to tell time. His limbs are loose, and his expression untroubled. He gives a quick rake of his fingers through silky chestnut hair to sweep the strands from his blue eyes and nods at me. "S'up?"

I retract, flustered. "I'm, er… yeah… I'm chilling."

Not true. I can simmer with the best of them. Stew, fret, or plot a project down to the tiniest detail. But chill? Ben's the chill dude in the office, and since he almost never acknowledges my presence, I'm definitely not in chill territory at the moment.

He gives me a thumbs up and scoots to the left flank of the group. I should follow him. For practical—rather than stalky—reasons. I'd have a fighting chance of seeing my boss and the sales board.

Or I could stay put. It's safer to stand behind people who are at least a foot taller than me, using them to shield my view of my chalked-in name wallowing in the swamp at the bottom of the board.

"Hey, thanks for coming, Ben. Let's get the ball rolling." Instead of criticizing my colleague's tardiness, Derek, my boss, sounds like he's happy his best bud has arrived. "Last day before the long weekend, folks. Clients might check out early. You should count on talking to a ton of voicemail accounts today. Imagine your contacts listening to your message first thing on Tuesday morning. Labor Day means the unofficial end to summer. They might be bummed to be back in the office. The coffee won't have kicked in. Keep the sales pitches fun; leave them a message they'll want to return. For calls to existing clients regarding a problem, keep your conversation solutions oriented. Business has its ups and downs. Make sure you're part of the ride up."

It wouldn't be a morning meeting without Derek's elevator puns. A bit too on the nose, considering we're in the elevator service management business. He expects us to pepper our conversations with similar phrases. *Give the clients a little lift*, he'll say.

Or an inexplicable case of seasickness.

It wouldn't be a typical morning without my boss assigning me the lamest leads, either. Once he has handed plumb assignments to the rest of the team, he informs me today I'll be chasing month-old dead leads in a town with few high rises.

I hide my frustration in my response. "Thanks, Derek," I say with perky enthusiasm.

"Violet, are you here?" Derek asks.

I jump and raise my hand. "I am, and I said I heard you."

The men in front of me turn around and scowl.

Derek says, "No need to be angry. Since I can't see you, how would I know you're here? Please tone down your attitude on your calls this afternoon. Perhaps a pleasant demeanor is the secret ingredient you're missing when you try to make a sale."

His joke receives a hearty laugh from choice members of the team. At least it's a few decibels shy of the one they had shared in my second week on the job a few months ago. Derek had forced me to turn the space in front of his desk into a runway where I modeled an outfit he described as "nun-adjacent."

I'm not saying my Pam Beesly-inspired wardrobe of cardigans and A-line skirts is sexy, but I had considered my outfit to be cute and professional. His hint that shorter, tighter skirts could play an outsized role in propelling me to the top of the leaderboard incentivized me to change my style to its current, genderless state. I suspect my boxy gray suits might not be entirely responsible for landing me at the bottom of the rankings every day, though.

After the meeting, I approach my call list with the intention of proving I have what it takes to make it in sales. Whenever someone's voicemail answers, I paste on a smile, convincing myself the client is currently unavailable because they are engaged in a conversation over a long-simmering dispute with their elevator service contractor. I leave messages, hoping my pitch will be the elixir to make the world right again.

At twelve-thirty, without having made a single sale, I race out of the office. Friday lunches with my two best friends are the sprinkles on the sundae of lunch breaks, and I'm more than ready to milk the sixty minutes of freedom for all they're worth today. I sacrifice a couple of them to wait for Anja in front of our favorite deli in downtown Jersey City. She is half a block away and coming in hot.

"You haven't been waiting long, have you?" Breathless, she swoops in for a hug. Her long, blond hair tickles my cheek.

"A minute or two, tops. C'mon. Tracey's already found us a table." I hold the door, and we go inside.

"I'm sorry I was late. I meant to leave earlier, but—"

"No need to explain or apologize. I know you. We've been friends since sixth grade."

She hugs me again after placing her order. "Lucky me. I knew you were a keeper when you shared your slice of cake with me at lunch the first day of middle school."

"And I'd still offer you half." I tap my credit card against the reader and grab my sandwich, water, and bag of chips from the clerk. I wave the chips at Tracey, who's sitting in our usual booth in the back. Her red hair is a beacon, pulling me to safety like a lifeguard.

"How was your morning?" I ask, scooting in next to her.

"Full of banking goodness. And yours?"

I tuck my stick-straight, dirty blond hair behind my ears and sigh. "The usual."

Anja sits on the opposite side of the booth. "I hate that your job makes you unhappy. Is three months in too soon to quit?" she asks.

I rub my clammy hands against my thighs. "I wouldn't want to disappoint my former boss by giving up immediately. She recommended me for the promotion. Also, I want to prove I don't actually suck at sales."

Tracey wiggles a pickle at me. "You don't suck at your job. You just haven't had the chance to succeed, thanks to the head of your department being a tool. A normal boss wouldn't turn making a new employee fail into his favorite daily activity."

"I suppose. Enough about my sad-sack job. How's life in the classical music world, Anja?"

She sets her tuna wrap on her paper plate. "The new season begins in a couple of weeks. I'm drowning in proof copies of our artists' program biographies and press materials."

"I'd trade with you any day. Creating content would be a dream. I wish I had waited for a position to become available in my company's communications department," I sigh.

"I'd love to swap lives with you. Being one of two women on a team with eighteen men would be a dream come true."

Tracey snorts. "Still boy crazy after all these years. Violet, any of your coworkers worth introducing to our friend?"

I shrug. "A bunch are older and/or married. And the five or six single guys who think Derek walks on water are... Yeah, no. They're a bunch of jerks."

"Even the guy you baked cookies for?"

Ben is the only member of the team who was nice to me after I transferred from payroll at Heading Up into sales. Besides the time he did a favor for me, for which I thanked him with the cookies, we don't interact much. He might not be cut from the same cloth as the office sycophants, but he hangs out with them because he's also one of Derek's stars. He's pretty blasé about his status, though. Tons of sales or none, he's fine with wherever he lands on the ranking chart. Me, the day I reach number one, which he did today, I'm dancing on top of my desk and gunning staples into my chest.

"Hello, Violet?" Tracey taps the crown of my head.

"What? Oh, sorry. Ben's okay, I suppose. I'd introduce you to him, Anja, but he and I aren't friends."

She shimmies her shoulders. "Do you have any company events where you can invite guests? It would be a more natural setting for an introduction."

"None that I've been invited to."

Tracey steals a potato chip from me. "Don't bother asking me to come if things change. I don't want to meet your boss. Should you ever invite me to be a plus-one at a company event, I will spontaneously remember I had agreed to parade through Journal Square dressed in a balls costume to promote testicular cancer awareness the same night."

"You and me both. I wish I had a better sense of who Derek was before I took the job. I couldn't tell you what kind of warning Helen should have issued, though. To the best of my knowledge, she doesn't have a file full of complaints about him from members of his team. My former boss would have protected me if she did. That's the whole point of human resources, isn't it?"

Tracey puts up her dukes. "I have to retract my previous proclamation. Take me to your next meeting. The second your boss treats you unfairly, I'll bring a world of hurt down on him."

"While I love having you on hand to defend me, I'll deal with Derek in my own way, thanks."

Anja sets her can of soda on the table with a bang. Thankfully, it isn't full enough to explode. "Violet, you're the last person who would make an impulsive decision. But something tells me no amount of insightful planning will improve things at work. If you can't figure out a way to enjoy your job soon, you'll need to bite the bullet and devise a simple exit strategy."

I scratch the back of my neck. "I don't know…"

Tracey wraps her arm around my shoulder. "We're behind you one thousand percent. We'll help you however we can in your job search."

Anja nods. "Now is the perfect time for a project. September marks the beginning of the school year. Let's pretend we're about to enter our senior year again and swear to make this year ours. Violet, you need to turn things around in sales or find a better job. I need to find a decent man. And Tracey…" She bunches her lips.

Tracey shrugs. "I don't know. Maybe it's time I get back out there."

I clutch her arm. "You mean, like, dating?"

"Yeah, sure. But I don't want to talk about it. Anja, you can mark me down for your pledge. Just promise you won't push me."

"No problem. I'll be hoarding all the men until I find The One, so you're safe for the moment. Can I get an amen?"

I purse my lips and wrinkle my nose. "Fine, RuPaul. I'm in. Now, for a more serious question. Who wants to split a brownie with me?"

Easy for Anja to create the pact. She looks like a mermaid, minus the tail, and never has trouble meeting men. And when Tracey sets her mind to something, she accomplishes it. Me? I had counted on the promotion I received in June to be the start of my actual adult life, but I haven't been able to make anything happen with it. Derek might give me the crappiest leads, but other people in the department manage to take dead leads and breathe life into them. Blaming my boss won't improve anything for me. It's my responsibility to find the elusive path to success.

Fun. Deciding to change my life will require chocolate. Lots of chocolate.

## CHAPTER 2
## BEN

I take my time returning to my cubicle after lunch. Friday afternoons before a long weekend should be illegal. I don't mean afternoons specifically. It's the working part I could do without. Who's at their desk the day before Labor Day weekend? This morning Derek had yammered on about leaving the sorts of voicemail messages clients will want to hear first thing on Tuesday morning before the coffee kicks in. Messages from me, a guy who wishes he were anywhere else, won't make anyone glad to be back at the office.

I've saved (or procrastinated making) the most important call for this afternoon. The new owner of a major hotel within walking distance of both the office and my apartment replaced half the staff recently. Derek believes the guy running the operations department might be ripe for the picking. The hotel is the sweetest lead to come through our department in the last few weeks, and it's mine because I mistakenly had a good day yesterday, landing myself at the top of the leaderboard.

Life's about balance; I work hard enough to keep the commissions rolling in, but not so hard I have to actually… work. Major clients don't often go to contract following the first meeting. Or even the second. I should be stoked with my new lead, but it might be more bother than it's worth.

Peter, a member of Derek's inner circle, slaps me on the shoulder on his way to his cubicle. "Congrats, dude. Drinks tonight?"

"Sounds great. Oh, but I can't. I have an appointment."

"Nice! Is she hot?"

Inwardly, I cringe. "Hot in the sense that it's next to impossible to book an appointment with her. She's a tattoo artist."

"Dude. Bet some fresh ink is the killer edge a guy needs to be on top of the food chain around here. I should come with you."

I inch away from him. "I doubt they take walk-ins. Next time, okay?"

Peter bobs his head. "Yeah, next time."

I've had top sales in the office twice in the year I've been here. The atmosphere can be kind of competitive, which isn't my scene. Most of the guys are cool, but I have the impression their friendliness relates to their hopes of siphoning someone's success via osmosis.

Violet is the rare person on our team without a weird agenda. I had helped her a couple of months ago. The next day, she left a plate of homemade cookies on my desk. Before I could thank her, a few coworkers surrounded me and ridiculed me for attracting her attention. They were cruel, mocking her for wearing pants instead of skirts and looking like an awkward boy. I had laughed, uncomfortable and unsure of how to defend her. By the time I thanked her, she had closed herself off. I figured she wasn't interested in being friends, so I've since kept my distance.

I glance through the opening of my cubicle into hers. Without noticing my attention, she grabs a fistful of her hair and holds it against the front of her shoulder. From the way she keeps squinting and making her eyebrows squirm, she must be engaged in an epic battle.

Violet's always at or near the bottom of the leaderboard. I suspect success in our office has a lot to do with Derek. For whatever reason, he has taken no interest in her as an employee. If she were a guy, I'd encourage her to hang out with the gang on Tuesday evenings, but there's a major bro factor going on. It can't be easy for her. Julie, the only other woman on the sales team, seems to weather the overabundance of testosterone. She'd be the better person to offer Violet advice.

Time to get to work. I study the files for the hotel. The facility has several elevators plus an escalator. Hotel guests put more wear and tear on equipment than office workers, which means the elevators require more servicing. A contract with all the bells and whistles would yield a huge commission.

I plant my feet on the desk and dial the number. A woman with a dusky voice answers. "Operations."

"Good morning. I'm calling for Alex Jiménez. Is he available?"

"Alex is available."

I wait to be transferred. She stays on the line. "Are you transferring me?" I ask.

"No. I'm Alex."

Strike one against me. "Oh, I'm sorry. My boss told me you were a… You know what? It doesn't matter. This is Ben Harris from Heading Up Elevator Service Maintenance."

"Hmm. HUES-M." She breaks into a throaty laugh.

I could listen to her laugh for hours, but since I don't know why she's laughing, I find it unnerving. "Excuse me?"

"I'm a sucker for an acronym. Bad habit of mine, searching for them whether or not they exist. Your company's doesn't form an actual word."

"Oh, of course. That's because with ours, the H is silent." I cock my brow, waiting for her to figure it out.

"Uesm… Got it. Use 'em. Hmm. I don't advise you share your joke with potential clients."

"You're right. It's my boss's joke. Sorry."

"No problem. I'm guessing you called me to sell me something, right?" Her voice strikes a perfect balance between being slightly cheesed with our conversation and enjoying herself, nonetheless.

"I'm guessing you picked up the phone, hoping someone would sell you something."

Oh, that laugh. That sweet, sweet laugh!

"It's like you're reading my mind. Give me your best elevator pitch."

"I pitch elevators for a living. You sure you can handle it?"

"Bring it."

I put on my serious sales voice. "I understand the Christopher Jersey City has undergone staffing changes. Are you new to your post?"

"I am. They brought me over from their hotel in Morristown last month."

"Congratulations on the promotion. It is a spectacular property. Perhaps you haven't had the chance to dig through the mess of files you inherited yet, but do you know if the hotel deals directly with its elevator service contractor, or are you in need of a management solution?"

"While I'm still familiarizing myself with the operations and can't say for sure, I believe my predecessor dealt directly with the contractor. Let me guess: you're going to tell me of a better way." She laughs through her nose. It still sounds delightful.

"My company's elevator pitch is a single sentence: Our product is time. You strike me as too savvy to fall for it, though."

"Perhaps not; time is an enticing commodity."

"What would you do with extra time?"

"I envy people who put their feet on their desks and enjoy of cup of coffee. Perhaps even with some biscotti."

I guiltily slide my clodhoppers from my blotter, taking half the office supplies on my desk with them.

She asks, "What was that crash?"

"Guy in the next cubicle. He's learning how to pace and talk on the phone. Keeps knocking over the walls between us. I'll deal with him later. What's your favorite flavor of biscotti?"

"Chocolate, of course. What else do you offer besides empty calories and time?"

"An interface between the hotel and your elevator service contractor. We will analyze past service records to determine whether your contractor overcharges you, provides more servicing than your equipment needs, or had your predecessor sign a disadvantageous contract. Our services free you from scheduling routine maintenance or being present during service calls. We read the compliance codes so you don't have to. Well, unless you enjoy a little light reading. Truly engrossing stuff. Should your equipment require modernization, we'll make recommendations. Many of our additional services pay for themselves. Even seemingly honest contractors squeeze extra dollars from their clients. I won't let it happen on my watch."

"You said your name is Ben?"

"Yes."

"Okay, Ben. I'm intrigued. Come to the hotel on Tuesday morning at eleven. Someone will show you to my office. Bring glossy brochures. I love me a nice packet of materials. Now, for a guy who promises to sell me time, you've taken up more of it than I have to share. I'll see you on Tuesday."

"Yep, and I'll come bearing biscotti."

I toss my phone onto my desk and bend over to retrieve my stapler and its pals. Yeah, I'm kind of okay with my new lead. A contract might come with a ton of work, but I wouldn't hate staying in touch with Alex in the process.

# CHAPTER 3
## VIOLET

Post-lunch, with the odds of reaching a living person (who preferably will not summon Beelzebub to mount a defense against the rude caller daring to sell something) equal to me establishing a colony on Venus, I prepare for hours of fun with voicemail. Today is not the day to focus on my pledge to Anja. Not that I don't take it seriously. A sure-fire way to get my juices flowing is to present me with a goal and the opportunity to create a detailed plan. Should it involve charts, graphs, and a glue gun, even better.

I crane my neck around the wall, sussing out the activity of the nearest team members for sources of inspiration to use during my next round of sales calls. Peter stares at his screen. To the uninitiated, his scowl indicates he has found language in a client's service contract that isn't in their favor. His expression doesn't match his actual activity: placing bets on the weekend's games. He makes his sweet commissions thanks entirely to Derek's perception he's a killer salesperson who deserves the best potential clients. Let's see him hit the daily top five with my stack of leads.

Over in Ben's cubicle, I stare into his sole, namely the underneath of the toe of his left sneaker. His feet have settled into their favorite home atop his desk. I would give my crafting corner—hmm, maybe just my pinking shears and three bottles of puffy paint—in exchange for his sense of ease with a client.

Since he's always in the top ten, his casual approach to sales is worth borrowing. I wrap my hands under my right calf to hoist my foot onto my desk. My shoe lands with a clunk. I dig my heel into the desk's surface to counter the rotation of my chair, fighting with everything I have to keep my right foot in place while I lift my left leg. Thank goodness I'm wearing pants. I'm not here to put on a show.

My left foot has taken its job of holding me in place more seriously than I had realized. After I lift it, my chair scoots away from the desk and into the file cabinet beside me. The wall shudders.

"Hey, Violet. I'm working here!" Ricardo, my neighbor, invisible due the partition, is a stickler for a quiet environment.

"Sorry. Chair mishap. It won't happen again."

Whoever invented putting feet on desks must have had a beef with people under five-ten. No, under five-five. Ah, what does it matter? The world isn't built for a five-foot-one-inch woman.

I roll my chair back into position and plan my approach for the rest of my calls. Maybe where I've gone wrong with my job is coming across like a person whose boss has ground her to a pulp. The disappointment from another bad stack of leads must seep into my voice. Time to switch things around and invent new personas for my calls.

For the first pitch of the afternoon, I settle on a stoner, the daughter of the CEO. She might join a protest against the evils of capitalism later, but not until she finishes playing this dope game on her brand-new system, complete with a state-of-the-art gaming chair. In other words, like, I have to make the call, but I couldn't care less about it.

The phone rings twice, three times, and I gird myself to talk to another machine. "Hello?" a gruff voice says.

"Oh, ah… He-ey. This is Violet, from Heading Up. How's it going?"

"What is it? I ain't got a lot of time."

My jaw, which spends a fair share of the workday clenched, marries my surfer girl accent with a wicked case of Locust Valley Lockjaw. "Exactly. Who does? And keeping track of things that aren't even your job, you know, dealing with your elevator service contractor or whatever, can be such a drag."

"I can't understand a word you're saying. Sounds like you have a mouthful of cotton balls. I gotta go."

Click.

Forty-three calls later, give or take, I have not made a single sale or appointment. The humans who had answered the phone received my pitch with patience and grace. Yeah, right. And the people who had begun their long weekend early will listen to my messages at a later date, wondering why they were the lucky recipients of calls from a constipated Barney the dinosaur, Meryl Streep on shrooms, or Dora the Explorer during a bipolar episode.

Anja's right: I need to focus on either improving my sales record or finding a place where I'd be happier. I slap my palm against my head, realizing I have wasted my chance to practice my sales pitch this afternoon. Instead of trying on ridiculous personas, I should have honed my message and the delivery.

Well, duh. I've found the missing ingredients. Setting and implementing goals are my strengths. I need to Violet the heck out of my sales calls to move ahead at the company. And if I can turn my plan into a crafting project…

# CHAPTER 4
## BEN

I ditched the office at four-fifteen, grateful Derek didn't see me leave. Having done the bare minimum, I saw no reason to pretend to be busy. Not when I had better plans.

I've doubted whether I am worthy of an appointment with Saffron, a world-famous tattoo artist, since she announced openings in her schedule for this week back in April on Instagram. Inklyn is a studio for people who take their tattoos seriously. And Saffron? I mean, she's a legend. The pieces she posts are works of art. She's a magician at blending colors and creating textures. Most of her clients ask her to design their tattoos. She free hands a lot of them, too. What right do I have to walk in with my own design?

I might have flipped over the news of having my name drawn in a lottery, but I have considered canceling the appointment a few times since. My conversation this afternoon with Alex, my new lead, has erased my doubts. I'm pumped. I deserve a tattoo.

My first tattoo is a souvenir from a drunken night during spring break. Name a clichéd stupid guy activity, and I majored in it in college. My tattoo is a tiger, mid-roar, stuck a bit off-center on my left shoulder blade. The good news is I didn't spend the rest of vacation nursing a festering wound like one of my buddies, and the ink has faded into a yellow and blue blur.

Once, when I was goofing off at work, I drew a circle of squiggles radiating from a central point on my calf with a whiteboard marker. I messed around with the design on paper later, turning it into a 3D sun. The rays emerge from the center close together, appearing like they're in the foreground near the center before they undulate and recede as they spread apart. I redrew a neater version of the initial sketch before sending the design along with my application for an appointment with Saffron.

You wouldn't expect to find a world-class tattoo studio behind Inklyn's Journal Square storefront. A simple red neon sign flashes "tattoos," and a poster advertising a band's upcoming gig at a local bar is taped on the window. The place I received my tiger had more appeal than this hole in the wall. But I open the door, and there she is. I can't believe Saffron Meisner is standing at the reception desk, waiting for me.

I save myself from fanboying by greeting her from the doorway. "Hey, I'm Ben, your five o'clock."

"Welcome to Inklyn. I'm Saff, and this is Roy. He'll check you in."

The edge of her jet-black bangs is sharper than a razor. She wears a black T-shirt and black jeans. Veins of black and gray ink snake along her right forearm, turning her pale skin to a block of marble. I am not cool enough to be here.

"Thank you for selecting me. It's an honor."

"The honor is mine. I like your design."

"Thanks. I drew it."

"I like it even more." She tucks her tablet under her arm and beckons me. "We're good to go. Follow me downstairs."

DIANE MICHAELS

A metal spiral staircase leads to the basement. In contrast to the stark, nearly empty reception area, the studio is hopping. Artists hunch over clients seated in each chair. Tattoo guns whir, blending with the heavy metal soundtrack booming through the speakers.

Saff leads me into a back room with three chairs, two of them empty. She points to the middle chair. "Have a seat. Which calf are we looking at?"

I slap the center of my right calf. She opens her tablet and compares my design to the canvas I offer her.

"We could put it dead center and keep it symmetrical or…" She swipes to a second page. "Whichever you want."

She holds the tablet for me. On it are two sketches, showing renderings of a calf from the back and the side. The center of the sun sits toward the right edge, and the rays, shorter than they are on the rest of the circle, wrap around the leg.

"Wow. Yeah, that's cool. Maybe a bit bigger than I expected? I was imagining it to be five inches long. But I definitely want your version."

"I'll print it out smaller, and we'll transfer the pattern onto your calf. If you don't like the size or placement, we can change it."

I relax in the chair while she goes to the printer. The shelves on the wall behind me display dozens of bottles of ink in every color imaginable. Next to me, a rolling metal tray covered in plastic wrap holds white condiment cups (that I hope are not for ketchup or relish), tongue depressors, a razor, and a can of shaving cream. The tattoo gun lies on its side, ready to tear into my flesh. My heart stutters for a second.

Saff returns and shows me my sketch, rendered in purple ink on paper. "Is it okay?"

I raise my thumb from my fist.

"Good. First things first, we have to remove the jungle growing on your leg. Find a comfy position, and I'll shave you."

Guys normally don't get excited about shaving their legs, but having your tattoo idol lather your calf with foam... Yeah, add having my leg shaved to my list of favorite experiences. She braces my leg with her left hand and drags the razor in no-nonsense strokes along my calf. She might mean business, but it's impossible not to have other ideas. Men are pigs. Sorry.

After rendering the area smooth as an easy-listening playlist, she scrubs the skin and affixes the transfer onto my calf. "Check it out. The mirror's around the corner."

I walk over to the mirror and stare at my leg from a couple of different angles. Okay, this is going to be totally epic. I kind of want to scream like a little girl, the excitement is that intense. But Saff doesn't need to meet my inner freak. I return to my chair with a touch of swagger and nod. "Looks cool."

"Excellent. I went ahead and chose a black ink for you, a sample I received earlier today of a deep, true black. I've heard rumors about the product, but since it's next to impossible to snag it, I didn't believe it existed until the bottle arrived. The coverage is better than anything on the market. The ink is vegan, organic, and will stay black, black, black if you treat it right."

She holds the bottle in front of me. The brand is Mystic Mate, and the color's name is double black. "Sounds great. Happy to be your guinea pig."

"Perfect. We'll start you out face down. Should you want to change positions, just holler. I figure we'll be at it for three hours. Last chance to use the bathroom, call a friend, or change the design."

"I'm ready. Let's do this thing." I immediately cringe. She doesn't need to meet the amped up version of me, but that's who she's tattooing today.

# CHAPTER 5
## VIOLET

Somehow, I make it to five o'clock. I race from the office to the Grove Street PATH station and emerge into the mayhem of Journal Square. I have eighty-seven-and-a-half blissful hours before I have to return to the office. Best of all, Monday is the big day.

The Hoboken Historical Society is hosting events over the weekend, culminating in a tablescape contest. I had never heard of such a thing until last year. The competitors' displays brought together elements of crafting and precision in a way that spoke to my inner creative rule follower, inspiring me to enter this year.

The theme is tea at Downton Abbey. I have spent five months studying previous winning designs and fabricating the decor for mine. Everything is ready, but I plan to practice setting the table twice a day tomorrow and Sunday. No way I am leaving anything to chance.

I had asked Tracey and Anja to assist me at the competition. My idea backfired. Because I had pitched the contest with such enthusiasm, they decided to enter the competition as a team, which left me without an assistant.

They're probably right to assume that if anyone can set a table with a single pair of hands, it would be me.

On the walk home, I try to imagine a first-place ribbon pinned to my backdrop, but shards of a day spent pitching to the voicemail accounts of disinterested parties keep infiltrating my reveries. I suspect my problems at Heading Up run deeper than whether I sound like me or a deranged cartoon character during a pitch. What I need is for Derek to miraculously decide to invest in me. Fat chance he'll change, though. I have to face the decision Anja held me to earlier today and prepare to fall in love with my job or to quit. Or… Maybe *I* need to change on a fundamental level.

My revelation regarding the root of my problems lands on my brain with a disorienting thud. Since walking often clears my head, I pass my apartment and continue to the end of the block, hoping I'll stumble on a solution. A woman exiting the tattoo parlor on the opposite side of Summit Avenue draws my attention to her. Half her hair is turquoise. The other half has been shaven clean. Leopard spots cover her scalp. A few are the same shade of turquoise as her hair and outlined in black. The rest of the spots haven't been filled in.

A tattoo. Huh. I bob my head, which might read as a rhythmless woman inappropriately grooving to an imaginary reggae soundtrack. My eyes flick to their upper corners. I am the last person anyone would expect to have a tattoo. However, a tattoo could be a talisman, a means of kick-starting my inner badass to turn me into a rock star at the office. And I bet an hour or two in a tattoo artist's chair is more comfortable—cheaper, too—than multiple sessions with a shrink.

I press the walk button and wait for the sign to change. Tattoo or not, I'll always be a rule follower. With a forceful inhale, I enter the studio, still undecided about whether to go through with my just-hatched plan. Behind the register, a man with shaggy black hair and all the tattoos—seriously, is there ink left for the rest of us?—has his elbows planted on the counter. A woman my height with messy blond and pink hair and cherry blossoms cascading down her left arm hoists her bag over her shoulder.

"I guess I'll call it a night, Roy," she says. "Unless we can move one of next week's clients to tonight." She notices me rooted in the doorway. "You here for an appointment?"

"No. I was just passing by."

"Do you want a tattoo? I'm available. The client who should have been here until closing couldn't take the pain. She left before I could finish."

"I… uh…"

"Relax. The process isn't scary. Unless you plan to tattoo your scalp. Is this your first?" I nod. "Upper arms are a decent choice." She extends her hand. "I'm Amelia. Welcome to Inklyn. Do you have a design in mind?"

"I'm Violet. No… uh, yes. Maybe… I don't know… Would it be weird to get a violet?"

"Dude, nothing's weird to me. I've inked pictures of genitalia onto shoulders. Heck, a couple of brave souls have laid out their junk for me to beautify. Besides, I specialize in flowers. I love doing violets. Here. Follow me downstairs. We'll find a picture that speaks to you."

My stomach quivers. I gulp and try to calm my nerves. Sure, a tattoo is permanent, and I'm laying a massive amount of responsibility on it to inspire me to change. But is it that big a deal? The way my body quakes, you'd think I had agreed to enter a Faustian, life-changing bargain.

I grip the metal pole at the center of the tightly spiraled staircase, descending with far more tentative steps than Amelia. The noise and brightness of the basement knocks the breath out of me. It resembles a construction site filled with people wielding miniature jackhammers that they dig into their clients' skin. Everyone in the room is male. I don't belong here.

Amelia disappears into a room in the back. I wind my way through the chairs, taking surreptitious glances at the tattoos in progress. The clients aren't howling and squirming with pain. They remind me of patients getting their teeth cleaned, only the hygienists have taken a detour and are working on their shoulders or backs or whatever instead of their mouths.

The back room has a quieter vibe. Amelia shuts the door behind me. The lighting is dim except for the spotlights shining on the bodies of the two clients in the room. I hop onto a black leather chair, dangling my legs over the side with my back to the other clients. Amelia rolls her chair next to me and hands me her tablet, opened to a page filled with a dozen sketches of violets.

"Maybe we'll put it someplace where I could hide it." I peer over my shoulder and push the fabric of my sleeveless top aside. "How about here?" I press on my shoulder blade.

"We can put it wherever you want. I won't lie to you: it can hurt like a mofo to tattoo right on the bone. To hide it on a fleshier spot, we could go with your thigh. But why hide it? Better question would be why you picked today to get a tattoo?"

My chest rises. "I'm having work issues. My boss gives me the absolute worst assignments. He'll help anyone else in the office succeed except for me. To him, I'm either invisible or an easy target for ridicule. He makes his point with such frequency, I've started to believe him. A tattoo could remind me I can—and should—be bold."

Amelia presses her lips together. "Dude, I hear what you're saying. You and me, we're the same height, and we're chicks. We don't exist unless we demand people make room for us. If you want to attract attention, hiding won't cut it." She circles her fingertip on my upper arm. "Put your tattoo where you can see it. Remind yourself you deserve to be seen."

I stare at the spot she had pointed to before examining the choices of flowers in front of me. Most are single blossoms or delicate clusters, perfect replicas of my namesake flower. One design, a spray of three flowers blooming above angry, imprecise black stems, stands out from the rest. The flowers are smudges of purple and pink with yellow centers. They're the total opposite of me. I am the queen of coloring within the lines. The rebel blossoms amplify what Amelia had said to me, though. I didn't come in here to keep being me.

"Is this design okay?" I hunch my shoulders, struggling to hand her the tablet.

"I love it! Dude, if you don't pick it, I'm choosing it for my next tattoo." She leans across my chair to show the tattoo artist behind me the tablet. "Saff, how jealous of me are you that I get to ink this design?"

I turn, scraping my teeth on my lip. My tattoo has a public life before the first drop of ink enters my skin. The woman takes the tablet and moves to the side. A man lies face down on the chair. He looks familiar....

"Ben?" I ask.

He turns his head. "Huh?"

"Ben, it's me. Violet Pensky."

He scrunches his face. "Violet from Heading Up?"

"Yeah. How random is it to run into each other?"

"Wow. You're the last person I would have expected to see here."

I can't let his remark offend me. My friends and family members would have said the same thing. "I've taken myself by surprise, too. Coming in for a tattoo is a totally spontaneous decision."

"Cool. We'll have to compare tats later."

I sit straighter and smile. It shouldn't mean anything to me, but I appreciate that he didn't challenge me to explain why I'm here. I doubt he's like the rest of my team. I should talk to him more often or bake him another batch of cookies. The existence of a friendly face in the bullpen could make the difference for me believing I belong.

His artist returns the tablet to Amelia before rolling Ben onto his belly and firing up her tattoo gun.

Amelia expands the image on her screen. "I'm thinking three inches, top to bottom. Should take two hours, tops."

I span my thumb and middle finger to measure the design and place them on my upper arm. "Wow. Um, okay."

She sends the design to the printer and leaves me staring at my arm while she collects the print. I'll never again be exactly the same, which is the most simplistic statement I could make. Still, my skin pricks in anticipation.

Amelia returns and prepares to alter me, or at least my upper left arm. After a few passes with a razor and a thorough scrubbing, she transfers the purple outlines of the flowers onto my skin. I crane my neck over my shoulder. It makes sense to have the design on me, like it should always have been there.

The other tattoo artist swivels toward Amelia with a bottle in her hand. "The stems would be gorgeous in this ink. Check out the insanely deep color. The coverage is out of this world."

Amelia leans over to examine Ben's calf and then studies the label on the bottle. "I've never heard of the brand. Mystic Mate? The name's sort of cheesy."

"Who cares? It's a sample someone sent me. Best black ink I've ever used. This is my first go with it, and it won't be my last."

"All right, I'll give it a try."

Amelia pours the ink into a small white paper cup and dips her tattoo gun into it. "Violet, I'll ease you into the process. First, I'll run the gun to get you used to hearing it. Then I'll do a three-second pass on your arm. Take a breath before I touch you and exhale slowly while the needles are in your skin. Okay?"

Tension prevents my shoulder blades from laying against the back of the chair. Despite the armrest under my left arm, I tense to take full responsibility to hold it for Amelia.

"Dude, you are one uptight chick. It will be a lot easier on you when you relax."

"Okay."

I meditate on the cyclical nature of the whine from her tattoo gun and inhale on her command. The needles are way less painful than I had imagined. In fact, a pleasant tingling sensation radiates from the point of contact. Before I've finished counting to three, the buzzing subsides. "That's it?"

"Uh, huh. It wasn't so bad, was it?"

"Wow. No, it's more bearable than I had expected."

"Then let's get to work."

Initially, I struggle to wrap my brain around the notion of me sitting in the chair and having an army of tiny needles invading my skin. My mom is... I can't guess what her reaction will be. Or my friends'. But I feel more like myself while Amelia hunches over my arm and injects ink into me than I have in a long time.

She is chattier than I would prefer, but since all I have to do is lie still and wince occasionally while she toils, I play along. She's different from anyone I know. None of my friends would dye their hair shocking pink, get a tattoo, or be into roller derby. I feel cooler and tougher simply by listening to her story.

"Violet," she says. "I've been mulling over what you said earlier about being seen. I had the toughest time getting a tattoo studio to hire me. It's a man's world. Thankfully, I met Saffron. I wouldn't trade working for her for anything."

"My boss is way into the male culture, too. It might be better for me to work for a woman. But I don't want to quit until I've figured out whether I'm part of the problem. It would help if I could understand how my boss sees me rather than rely on my own perceptions."

"Excuse me?" Amelia turns off the gun.

I say, "I wish I could see myself differently."

The tingling in my arm intensifies. Wait. Mine isn't the only voice speaking. Ben matches me syllable for syllable. I turn to my right and say, "Jinx!"

Ben isn't next to me. Instead, I face a stranger who is having his chest tattooed. Amelia must have spun me around. I swivel my head to the left. She's on the opposite side of the chair next to me, tattooing...

Me?

# CHAPTER 6
## BEN

Yes, there are worse things in the world than lying on my stomach while a tattoo goddess works her magic on my calf, but I'm bored and dying to see her handiwork. Saffron switches off her gun for a few seconds, and I stretch my neck, trying to catch a glimpse of the tattoo. I see too little of it to be meaningful.

"Shoot. I wish I could see myself differently. Do you have a mirror handy?"

Violet and I speak simultaneously. Oddly enough, she also said she wanted to see herself differently. Odder still, it was her voice asking for a mirror, not mine. I turn to the left to speak to her, but she's gone. And so is her chair.

I flip my head to the right. Saffron has her back to me, tattooing a man's calf. Hey, wait. She stole my design and is putting it on some other guy. "Excuse me," I say.

Oh, this is getting weirder. Violet said the same thing as me again, except I didn't hear my voice along with hers.

Ow! A bee stung my arm. I bat my hand to swat it away.

"Sorry. But give me a warning next time. You don't want me slipping with the needles buried in your flesh." The chick with the bright pink hair—Amelia, I believe—holds her hands in the surrender position.

I glance at my left arm, which is not the arm I left home with. Years of biceps curls, gone. My arm is skinny as a—

Holy f*&$! I'm not me. I'm…

Violet?

I whip my head to my right and gape at a person who looks exactly like the guy I saw in the mirror a couple of hours ago. The eyes staring back at me are wide enough to pop out of their sockets. We both point to the other and then ourselves.

"Violet?" I ask.

Amelia says, "Not yet. I'll finish with the black ink in a couple of minutes and switch to the pink and purple. I've heard people say they can feel the different colors going in, but I don't believe it."

The me who is not me nods his/her head. I flick my right arm to the side and drop my jaw. "What do we do?" I mouth with exaggerated movements.

Violet shakes her head. My head. She holds a finger to the lips attached to the head. She's not wrong. We can't say anything until we understand what happened. How would we explain to the tattooists there's been a bit of a mix-up?

What if one of them cast a spell? Could either of them be a witch? Definitely don't want to say the wrong thing to her. I'd hate to discover she knows worse spells than this.

If I had the magical powers to swap people into other bodies, I'd boast about it. Yet neither woman is paying the least bit attention to anything besides the patch of skin under their tattoo gun. Is casting spells so commonplace, they don't care anymore? *Poof! You're a two-headed donkey. Now, what's for dinner?*

I have to find the bright side to my predicament. For starters, I can see my calf better from here. Oh, god. This is my fault. Didn't I wish I could see myself differently? Man, had I known my wish would be granted, I would have wished for something better. Hmm…

I could have wished to hook up with Alex from the hotel. She sounds hot. Her laugh sure gets the motor running, and she has a super chill, easygoing nature. I could have wished we'd have a connection at our meeting on…

Yo, how long is this swap going to last? I can't live my life inside Violet's body. I'd have to be her, which means I can't go to my meeting on Tuesday if we're not back to normal.

Wait a second. Since I am Violet, I reside inside a female body. Do chicks stare at their chests all day? Asking for a friend, 'cause no way am I sizing up Violet's boobs at the moment. I have no opinion regarding the tempting view I've stumbled upon. That said, I imagine walking around with a pair of gorgeous, perky breasts within arm's reach would leave me too distracted to accomplish anything. My right hand agrees. It slithers along my belly, hoping to cop a quick—

A judgmental cough interrupts me. Violet wags a finger at me. "Nah, uh." Her eyes tell me she ain't fooling. I drop my hand.

She and I are now connected. I can't process what that means because we don't know each other. She's not really part of our team yet. I don't remember her ever coming to our weekly post-work hangs at a local bar on Tuesdays.

She's pretty in an understated way. Her usual work attire is slacks and a jacket, like a uniform. She's intelligent and has made me laugh before, too. And the cookies she baked to thank me for a small favor I did for her might be the one genuine, caring gesture anyone at the office has ever made.

I guess the situation means I've signed up for a crash course in all things Violet, which intrigues me. I can tell she's kind. And tough. She seems to take Derek in stride. I never would have pegged her as the type to get a tattoo. That she wants it on her upper arm instead of on her ankle or a tiny design on her inner wrist tells me she has self-confidence. All are attractive qualities that go very well with her br…

*Bad, Ben. Look away from the chestal region!*

I crane my neck to mark Saffron's progress. The sun tattoo is nearly complete. I compare it to Violet's tattoo on my current arm. Since Amelia is shading the third flower, we are both nearing the finish line.

The daring but artistic design Violet chose impresses me. The colors bleed like a watercolor, and the linework is intentionally ragged.

I rake my fingers through my new crop of hair, which is sleek and soft. She doesn't wear her hair in a fancy style. It hangs straight, like dirty-blond fringe to just below her shoulders. I pull a handful of hair under my nose and take a sniff. Instinctively, I close my eyes and smile. It has a subtle, flowery smell that makes me want to lean in and sniff it again.

"You ready to see it?" Amelia asks.

I let go of my hair and peer at my upper arm. "You're done?"

"Yup. You remember where the mirror is?"

I check on my calf first, still in its chair to my right. Saffron leans away from it and angles her head. "I'm finished, Ben. Go check it out."

Violet and I rise slowly from our chairs and eye each other suspiciously. I nod and lead us to the mirror.

She jerks her head toward me once we're around the corner and out of earshot of the tattoo artists. "What's going on?" she asks.

"I'm clueless. I wished I could see myself differently. Maybe something happened when I spoke?"

"I wished for exactly the same thing at the same time. I've been playing the moment over and over in my mind. Something fishy had to have happened when we made our wishes. One second, I was me and the next, I was looking at me. Did you have a weird tingling sensation?"

"Yeah, the whole time. Now that you mention it, it grew into almost a mild electrical shock the moment I made my wish."

She nods. "How do we turn back into ourselves?"

I shrug my shoulders. "We'll figure it out."

"We'll figure it out? Dude! I've never been turned into another person. This isn't normal."

I jab my thumb downward. "We have to act like it is. Lower your voice. You're being... I don't freak out over things."

"Excuse me for freaking out!"

"Let's be on the lookout for clues regarding our situation before we go nuclear. In the meantime, turn around. I want to inspect my tattoo."

She spins and crosses her arms. "Well?"

I want to run my fingers across it, but her calf is not mine to touch. "It's pretty awesome. How do you like yours?"

She wraps her hands around my arm. My skin melts from the warmth and strength of her palms.

*Get a hold of yourself! It's wrong to get hot and bothered by your own hands touching your arm.*

A flicker in her eyes makes me wonder what she's experiencing. She bites her lip. "Wow. I... Yeah, I love it." She rolls my arm inward, raising her brow. "Nice. Do you have plans later?"

I do a double take. "Why?"

"Yo, focus. We have to sort out this mess. I live a couple of minutes away. Come to my place, and we'll make a plan. For the moment, return to your seat and act normal. I'll meet you outside the shop after we pay."

"Okay."

We must look suspicious AF because neither of us can master walking in someone else's body. I owe Violet a huge thanks for wearing sneakers instead of a pair of high heels. Nothing would give away my newbie status in the body swap universe more than falling flat on my face.

Saffron pulls a piece of paper from a small box and unfolds it. "The aftercare instructions for the new ink differ from what we recommend. Usually, we suggest wearing the bandage for only a day. Bear with me, because the instructions are written in an ominous rhyme, which I guess is on-brand for a product named Mystic Mate. *Never shall I see the sun until one hundred sixty-eight hours are done. Let me hide beneath my cover so I can shine when the week is over.* They go on to say to wash it with antimicrobial soap, pat it dry, and to apply the aftercare cream of your choice in dim lighting after sundown each night."

Amelia grabs the paper. "Someone's taking themselves *way* too seriously. I agree about keeping your tats out of the sun, though. Once they heal, don't be stingy with the sunscreen. You want the colors to stay true. Honestly, it's not the worst thing to try it their way. Call us in the event anything gross happens to them."

Amelia and Saffron coat our tattoos with goop and tape bandages over them. Saffron hands Violet two extra bandages. "Amelia, give your client extras. The originals might not last the week."

I shove mine into Violet's purse, and the four of us head upstairs. Saffron leads us to the checkout counter. I fumble through Violet's wallet and pull out a credit card. She shakes her head. Oh, I had picked her debit card. Even the tiniest things will be weird until we reverse the spell. I hope I don't destroy her life while we wait for the week to end.

# CHAPTER 7
## VIOLET

What the actual hell? Will I be stuck in of Ben's body for the next week? And he in me? I never had reason to distrust him prior to tonight, but watching his hand reach for my boobs right after the switcheroo opens an entirely new vein of problems I hadn't considered. Not that I've ever considered the way to handle our current situation before tonight.

We exit Inklyn without either Saff or Amelia showing any signs of being hip to our predicament. I raise my head to check in with Ben, but instead of seeing him, I take in a view of the spire of the church across the street framed by the velvety blue twilit sky. Duh. He's shorter than me now.

I bend my neck and center my gaze on my face staring up at me. "I live just down the block. Follow me." The light turns green, and I cross Summit Ave.

"Slow your roll. My legs are too short."

Tell me about it. I've always wanted to be taller. Wishing people wouldn't treat me as an insignificant, weak female creature is another favorite fantasy. I somehow doubt Ben has ever wished to be a pipsqueak of a woman. While things suck for me at the moment, I wonder whether they will suck more for him while we are in the wrong bodies.

A maternal urge swells within me. I need to educate him on myriad topics related to being a woman. I hope he has patience, because I have at least three separate lists and graphs I have to make for him tonight to explain navigating the world in his current state of being.

I lift the latch on the gate in front of my house and lead Ben down the flight of stairs to the right.

"You live in a basement apartment?" He doesn't appear impressed.

"Uh, huh. My father insisted I choose a place with affordable rent. And this is what I found. Welcome home."

The ceilings are lower in my apartment than they are in the upstairs units, but it has never been an issue before. I duck my head to clear the doorway. I have a couple of inches to spare, but an intense sense of claustrophobia descends on me from the loss of the extra foot of headroom that has prevented me from minding living in a Violet-sized apartment before tonight.

Ben enters my living room and swivels his head, taking in his surroundings. "Your home is much nicer inside than I had expected. You have great taste."

I had labored over the paint colors two years ago to the point where I might now be forever banned from shopping at the Communipaw Avenue Sherwin-Williams. The blue in the living room is a stand-in for the sky, which, despite the tiny windows ringing the apartment, is all but absent from view. And the buttercup yellow in my bedroom is worth having had to return two different gallons until I found the perfect shade.

"Thanks. Have a seat. We have a lot of ground to cover. Are you okay with wine? What am I saying? Your tastebuds love the pinot noir I have open. By the way, you can't stand commercial lagers, Scotch makes you cough, and you must stay far away from tequila. Trust me when I tell you it's for your own good."

"Now I'm dying to know what happens if I drink it. But I'm fine with wine, I suppose."

I debate whether to invite him on a tour of the kitchen, but anyone with a sliver of logic and knowledge of the alphabet could find their way around my cabinets. No need to dawdle. To keep things moving, I plan to speed walk across my living room to grab the wine, but blessed with his legs, it takes a mere five giant steps to propel me to my destination. I invert two glasses, thread them between the honking man fingers of my left hand, and palm the bottle of wine before returning to the living room.

He scoots from cushion to cushion on the couch, searching for a comfortable position.

I point to the corner of the couch. "Put the pillow behind you. Your feet will hit the floor."

He tucks a brown and cream striped pillow into the small of his back. "My legs haven't dangled over the edge of a seat since I was seven. Now I understand why women have an unholy love affair with decorative pillows."

I, meanwhile, worry my knees will put out an eye. Seated next to him on my undersized couch, I resemble a parent attending back to school night in a kindergarten classroom, sitting in furniture scaled for the tiny tots. I pour us glasses of wine and gulp mine before Ben wiggles himself forward on the couch to reach his.

"Sorry. I should have waited for you. I have dreamed of this glass of wine since the moment we switched bodies. Your guess is as good as mine for when the nightmare ends, but my gut tells me we're stuck like we are until eight o'clock next Friday night."

"Why eight?"

"That's the time they put on the bandages."

His eyebrows dive into the bridge of his nose. "Wouldn't it make more sense for the spell to end exactly a week after the switch?"

"The rhyme specifically mentioned lying underneath a cover for a week. We have to take it literally. Sorcerers and witches are sticklers for literal meanings." I eye him from the corners of my lids. What if he goes off script? "You have to promise me you will obey the instructions to the letter. No way am I spending the rest of my life as you. No offense."

"Oh, you don't have to tell me. I can't be a girl forever."

"You're a woman."

"Same difference."

I cross my arms and tuck my fists under my armpits, which, being damp, ruins the mood I meant to set. I quickly remove my hands and rub them on the plaid shorts I'm wearing instead of glaring sternly at him in a he-man pose as planned. "No, it represents a major difference. I'm twenty-six. Girlhood ended years ago. Look, women get less respect than men. Don't go around making things worse by calling yourself a girl."

"Duly noted. What else?"

"You wanted to touch my boobs before."

"Um, yeah. It seems like the biggest perk of being you, having a pair at my disposal."

"They are *my* breasts. Touching them without consent means you are touching me without consent."

He shifts his jaw. "Oh, no. I wouldn't take advantage of you. Ever. I'm sorry. It didn't occur to me." He presses his lips together and stretches them into a slight smile. "I give you blanket consent to, um, you know…" He eyes my crotch.

*Ew!*

I slam my hands into my lap. "Ow!"

Not only do I learn how delicate the contents of my lap are, but I also discover my laugh, which sputters from my other mouth, is offensively shrill, bordering on maniacal. I wish I would shut up.

He slaps his hand on his lips. "Lesson number one: the family jewels require tender, loving care. Guard them with your life."

"I won't make that mistake again."

"You probably will. If it happens in public, pretend it doesn't hurt. And definitely don't pass out from the pain in front of the guys at the office. I'd never live it down."

"I thought I had a handle on the rules we need to follow, but the list keeps expanding." I drum my fingers on the coffee table. "We definitely have to switch apartments. My neighbors will freak to see a man going into mine."

He pulls his lower lip into a frown and nods. "Not a common occurrence, I suppose." His eyebrows dance rudely.

"I've hit a dry spell. But that's none of your business." I set my glass on the table hard enough for wine to slosh over the rim. My concern regarding his answer to my next question takes priority over my urge to clean the spill. "You don't have… a girlfriend, do you?"

"If your love life is none of my business, why ask me about mine?"

"Come on! This is totally different. You were teasing me. I'm asking because if you're in a relationship, we're screwed. We can't hang with people who know us well."

"Relax. I'm single."

I leap from the couch to get a rag. "Good." I put his mile-long legs to work, fetching a cloth and returning to the living room in no time flat.

While swiping the cloth over the wet surface, my mind whirs as it confronts the enormity of the task at hand. "We should keep our phones but only use them to text. Under no circumstances can you answer a call."

"You're saying we can't tell anyone what's going on?"

A vein pulses in my forehead. "We have to keep our predicament between the two of us. We should swear to keep our secret." I hustle over to the bookshelf.

*Bible, bible…* The closest to it I have handy is *The Scrapbooking Bible.* I pull it from the shelf and set it on the coffee table in front of Ben. "Left hand on the book, right hand in the air."

He snorts. "We're swearing on a crafting book?"

"Deal with it. Now, repeat after me. I will not tell a soul that I am not me."

"What about people without souls?" My eyes stab his. He takes his left hand from the book for a second to surrender. "Fine. I will not tell a soul that I am not me. Are we done?"

"Almost. I will respect the body I occupy."

He swivels his head from one side of my chest to the other. That is, the chest he's wearing. "Oh, I respect it all right."

"Come on! I'm being serious."

"I... What was it again?"

"I will respect the body I occupy."

"I will respect the body I occupy."

I remove my hand from the book. "Okay. What are you doing this weekend? The only thing I have going on is a tablescape contest on Monday."

"A what now?"

"Table setting. I've designed... You know what? We'll discuss the event later. I need you to be available from early Monday morning into the afternoon."

"Okay. My friends and I were thinking of hanging out tomorrow, maybe shooting hoops on Sunday, but I can cancel everything."

"Yeah, you don't want me playing sports." Although I'm itching to see if I inherited any hand-eye coordination along with his body. That would show Mrs. Geary for betting I'd spend my entire life with black eyes, considering the number of times I got whacked in the face with a ball during gym class.

I clap my palms together. My goodness, I have ginormous hands. The things I could accomplish with them...

*Not now, Violet. Gain control over the big picture and experiment with these mitts later.*

I say, "We have to hammer out the rest of the details. The next week is going to be tough. We need to prepare."

"Do we, though? How hard can it be? We have the same jobs, and we both live in Jersey City. Let's take it as it comes. I need your phone number. I'll write down my address, give you my keys, and we'll check in with each other later, 'kay?"

How hard can it be? I want to scoff at him. But striding through the world in a man's body might offer a few advantages. Perhaps acting like a different person could, too.

# CHAPTER 8
## BEN

"I'm feeling lightheaded. And a bit nauseous." I grip the edge of the couch cushion to stay upright. "Could it be a side effect of the, er, curse?"

Violet sucks in a deep breath and bolts upright. "Oh, it's my fault. I didn't eat dinner. Your sugar levels might be crashing. Give me a second." She heads into the kitchen.

I'd be lying were I to say the next week doesn't intimidate me. Instead of dreaming of fondling my boobs, I should have considered the basic challenges of dealing with a borrowed body.

Oh, man! What about…?

A host of bathroom-related questions flood my brain. Great. Now I have to pee. Springing from the couch does nothing to help my dizziness. I take sluggish steps to the kitchen. "Um, Violet? I need the bathroom."

"It's at the end of the hall."

"Yeah, but how should I…?"

She takes a labored breath. "Hmm. Sit, and it will happen when you're ready. Wipe front to back and wash your hands, please. Oh, and remember our pledge: no peeking or touching or paying any attention whatsoever to my lady parts."

"I just need to take a leak. You're safe with me. Wait. You're not having your…" At the age of twenty-six, I'm still as uncomfortable about the female reproductive cycle as I was in junior high. "Do I have to worry about tampons?"

She presses her palm to her forehead and exhales through pursed lips. "Thankfully, no." She hands me a glass of orange juice. "Drink this. I'll have snacks ready for you."

I swear no beverage has ever been so magical. Every cell in my body dances with joy while I gulp my way to the bottom of the glass. "What did you put in it?"

"Nothing. My body… Your body needed sugar, and orange juice is the best delivery system. I'm not diabetic or anything, but keeping a regular eating schedule is important. Stress plus hunger is never a good thing for me."

The orange juice reminds me I came into the kitchen to solve my bathroom issue. I've faced portable johns at a crowded music festival late in the day with less trepidation than I experience on my trip to her bathroom. What sort of mishaps will I unleash while using her, er, equipment?

I flip the switch in the bathroom. The ancient turquoise and black tile is hideous, but the place is cleaner than a hospital. The sink isn't coated in soap scum or the dregs from my razor. I sniff the gleaming white towel hanging next to the tub. It smells like an ad for laundry detergent. Unlike the toilet bowl in my bathroom, I can't guess the age of the porcelain by the number of rings.

Well, here goes. I stand with my calves grazing the can and unzip my pants, revealing the first mystery: Violet is a sensible, cotton panty-kind of gal. With my pants at my ankles, I drape a hand towel in front of me as a modesty screen and take a seat. And… Okay. It's different, but I can hack it. Once I'm done, I get in and get out with the TP and cover the naughty bits before anything distracts me.

I toss the hand towel on the floor and head for the door. Oh, right. My hands. I retrieve the towel and sling it over the towel bar next to the sink. Violet's soap dispenser matches the toothbrush holder, and a field of flowers wafts from the soap. Fancy. After drying my paws, I try to adjust the towel to make it neater. I should have paid attention to how she had it before. Doesn't matter. I have the entire week to figure out how to be Violet.

She waits for me in the living room. Cheese, slices of salami, and crackers sit on a wooden board. "Let's get some protein in you."

Who has grownup food sitting around the house on a random Friday? At my apartment, I'd have little more to offer a guest than half a takeout container of rice and a box of cereal. I snag a handful of cheese and meat and shove the food into my mouth. I could have succeeded with my old mouth, but the new one doesn't open wide enough. Hunks of food drop into my lap and onto the floor. Nothing prettier than a dainty woman eating like a cave dweller. I bend over to retrieve two pieces of cheese from the floor and pop them in my mouth.

Violet chokes on her wine. "Dude!"

"What? Five-second rule, right?"

"So help me, my body had better not contract every known illness while you're wearing it."

"Relax. Everyone eats a pound of dirt each year."

She draws backward. "Doesn't sound legit."

"It was my mom's favorite health tip in my childhood."

"My mom would have cut off your hand the second you ate floor food." She picks up a solitary cube of cheese from the tray, using her thumb and middle finger. Manners fit for a queen are ridiculous on my original hand. "Are you feeling better?" she asks.

"Yes, thanks. I should probably hit the road... Wait, I'm already home. Let me grab a couple more bites, and then I'll take you to my apartment."

She swings her head from side to side. "I can't let you come back here on your own."

"I'll be fine. I always walk alone at night."

"Not when you're built like me."

I open my hands, palms up. My fingers are as slender as pencils. I bet they've never been in a fistfight. The old version of me would never send a woman into the night alone. But the woman I'm offering to protect is living inside a body few people would mess with. "It seems wrong, but I see your point. I'll text you the address. My keys should be in the inside pocket of my jacket with my wallet. Oh, and sorry in advance for the mess. I hadn't expected company tonight."

She stuffs her hand in the pocket, pulls out the wallet, and reaches for her purse on the chair next to her. "Neither did I. I'm sure your apartment will be fine. I'm going to take my debit card. It might be hard to pull off using each other's credit cards. Here, why don't you grab yours?" She tosses me my wallet. I miss. I never miss an easy catch.

"Do you belong to a gym?" I ask.

"Yes, but I don't go very often. Here's my membership card. I go to the Journal Square branch. How about you?"

"I work out three or four evenings a week and on the weekends. The fitness center is in my building. Here's the keycard. You need it to open the door to the gym."

"I'd go more often if mine were as convenient. I'll try to take care of your body the best I can."

I shrug. "Whatever's good for me. Look, we're in a messed-up situation. You and I, we're not well acquainted. I'm sure it will be weird, but we'll make it through the week. Good is a high enough bar for me. We shouldn't aim to be perfect at living someone else's life."

She rolls her lips. "Perhaps you know me better than you think. I don't want to harm your body. And I'm nervous about what could go wrong with mine. I definitely don't want people to be suspicious of us. So, yeah, I want to be you the best I can."

"Don't sweat it. Call me in the morning?"

She presses herself upright and stuffs my wallet into a jacket pocket. "Anything else you need to know? The sheets are clean. Huh. I suppose it won't be weird for you to use my toothbrush. I mean, you'll use it in my mouth, right?"

"I hope you don't stay up all night dwelling on toothbrushes and what have you. It's all good." I wolf down one last chunk of meat and stand.

I meet her at the door. We stand toe to toe, avoiding each other's eyes. She says, "Well, have a good night."

"You, too." I should hug her. But weird. Who else besides us could ever experience giving themselves a hug? I stretch my hands toward her anyway. She responds in kind, and we embrace. While hugging myself with her arms is bizarre, for the first time since the swap, I feel ten times less alone.

# SATURDAY

# CHAPTER 9
## VIOLET

I squint and fight the process of waking. Slivers of light sting my eyes, and I rub my fists against my eyelids. It feels like I'm pressing bowling balls into my sockets. I pop my eyes open.

"Whose hands are these?" I ask myself.

Oh, wait. I'm still Ben.

It's nine-fifteen. I haven't slept past eight in years. Probably has something to do with crawling into bed at two-thirty last night.

Ben's apartment is far more luxurious than mine. It has a stainless-steel fridge with French doors, polished concrete floors, exposed brick, windows larger than a beaver, and not even a hint of nineteen-fifties' era turquoise tiles. His housekeeping skills? I couldn't go to bed last night until I had addressed a handful of health code violations.

I hoist myself into a seated position and lean against the wall. An obstacle course of discarded clothing covers the bedroom floor. The sheets are clean, thanks to a late-night swim in the washer, but they're the only part of the room I had tackled before bed.

I slept in the same T-shirt and pair of boxer briefs Ben had worn yesterday. I run my hands down my thighs—his thighs. They're rock solid, and I am dying to get a decent look at them. No, Violet. Bad. I shudder, imagining Ben standing naked in front of a mirror, taking a tour of my body.

I've distanced myself from his body so far. He might kill me for this, but last night I discovered that going to the bathroom becomes less scary when I sit instead of stand and maneuver his manhood with a giant wad of toilet paper to avoid touching it. I'm ready for another round of destroying the universe, one roll of toilet paper at a time, which motivates me to get out of bed.

It's a mystery that a man who has three empty bottles of all-in-one shampoo/conditioner/body wash in his shower can sit atop the leaderboard at work. How can someone who can't close the cap on a bottle close a deal?

I stare at my face while I wash my hands. Is it vain? Invasive? Since I don't plan on covering the mirrors for the next week, stare I shall. Ben is a handsome dude. I've known it from the day I started at Heading Up.

More than his appearance drew me to him. He doesn't move around the office on a wave of arrogance the way several of the men in my department do. During my second week, he had volunteered to accompany me to an evening meeting with a client in Irvington after I had mentioned I wasn't familiar with the neighborhood. I hadn't meant to ask for his help. At the meeting, he and the client established a rapport, but once the client signed the contract, Ben made sure Derek counted the sale as mine. No one else at the office had done anything remotely nice for me. Or has since.

After I left cookies on his desk, I overheard a few coworkers making fun of me while leaning over the walls of his cubicle. I'm pretty sure Ben didn't say anything mean, but I didn't hear him defend me, either. In light of his behavior and friends, it has seemed safer for me to keep my distance from him.

I brush sleek chestnut-brown strands of hair out of my eyes. In the bathroom's dim light, the blue of his irises reads kind of watery. A bulb in the light fixture is out. I'll bring a chair in here later to…

Hold on.

"I'm tall!" I dance around the bathroom gleefully when I discover I can reach the bulb without assistance. Fingers crossed, Ben stores spare lightbulbs on his highest shelf. I race throughout the apartment, test-driving my wingspan on every shelf in the unit even after I locate the spare bulbs (found in his pantry next to a can of soup). Everything in here is within arm's reach. I am in heaven!

And pantless. I'm standing in the kitchen in my drawers. Guess I don't have a choice about examining my legs; they are bare, and the lights are bright enough to illuminate a Broadway stage. I lower my gaze and smile.

Well done on the legs, Ben.

My fingertips trace the definition between the front and back thigh muscles. I double back and run the palm of my hand against the front, tightening the muscles to enhance the experience.

I step my right foot to the side and peer over my shoulder at my calf. Lengths of white tape secure the black plastic bandage over the tattoo. The bugger responsible for our mess.

I wish I could see mine.

Instinctively, I rub my left biceps on the spot where my new violets are blooming on my real arm. My hand lingers. His biceps is a work of art. I'm dying to sneak a peek at his chest.

In my bedroom on the other side of Jersey City, the closet doors are mirrors. His are painted gray. I close his bedroom door. No full-length mirror behind it, either. The mirror above the sink in the bathroom is the only one in the apartment. He must not be as vain as I had assumed.

I swear I will behave around his body. The best way to honor my pledge is to cover my tempting flesh. I rummage in his dresser for a pair of shorts in case I want to work out after breakfast. The closest to clean is a pair of heather-gray drawstring shorts crumpled into a ball at the rear of a drawer filled with shirts, socks, and sweaters. I smell many loads of laundry in my immediate future, emphasis on smell.

Weekends, I often make eggs or pastries for breakfast. I close my eyes, picturing the oranges and cranberries I bought on Thursday with the intention of baking a loaf of quick bread today. Let's see what my consolation prize will be.

I open the fridge. Does he even eat? He has eight bottles of hot sauce, two open ketchup containers, and a crusty jar of mustard sitting on the shelves of the door. The main space houses three bottles of beer, a box of Chinese takeout, a bruised apple, and a carton of milk. I take a whiff of the latter. It nearly fells me.

I haven't switched places with a man; I've switched with a cliché. From treating his luxury apartment like a trashcan to stocking his fridge with useless items, he's the living embodiment of the young bachelor. Meanwhile, he has moved into a sanitary, well-appointed apartment with enough food to last a month. Will my apartment—not to mention my body—survive a week under Ben's care?

# CHAPTER 10
# BEN

I hate myself for waking up early this morning. Day one of a long weekend should involve sleeping late. I tried to sleep in until at least nine, but my body spent from seven until eight poking my slumbering consciousness and cursing it for being lazy before I finally surrendered.

I'm sure Violet's sleeping habits play a role in why she never comes in late. Since my commute is shorter than hers, I have no excuse for my flexible approach to the start of my day. In fact, with twelve hours' experience of being Violet, I realize that she, not me, has the discipline to sit atop the leaderboard at Heading Up.

I kick yesterday's clothing away from the bed to clear my path to the bathroom. I had planned to go to bed fully dressed—I mean, who is strong enough to hide under the covers with a pair of breasts, there for the petting?—but I unearthed a pair of pajamas from under her pillow. Designated sleepwear. What a concept.

The discards from Violet's outfit that I've strewn on the recently vacuumed carpet look lonely. I could dump the contents of her closet onto the floor to make the blouse, pants, and bra appear less exposed. It would represent a major departure in her design style, though. Her closet is more organized than a tour of an Iranian nuclear facility. The pants hang together with other pants, and the color-coordinated blouses are balancing on their hangers by both shoulders. Mind blown.

I peer into the two hampers in her bedroom. One is for underwear and T-shirts. The other must be for dry-cleaning. I toss the blouse in with its mates and lay the pants over the top of the dry-cleaning bin like she had done with her suit jacket before she left last night. Now I understand why she wakes up early: treating clothing with respect is far more time-consuming than throwing everything on the floor.

No way I'm spending my day tidying. A quick breakfast, and then this dude in women's clothing is hitting the gym. What to eat? I wish… I'm banishing the word *wish* from my vocabulary. No more unintended transformations for me.

I'm going to miss the convenience of having a coffee shop in my apartment lobby. Wait a second. I live in a home where orange juice, cheese, and meat miraculously appeared last night. I bet Violet's carton of milk hasn't yet expired. Hopefully, she has cereal.

I find not only cereal stored in plastic containers and marked with the variety of cereal contained within, but also a veritable smorgasbord in her pantry. I'm pretty sure a choir of angels sang while I opened the fridge. Fruit, yogurt, milk, and more sit in orderly rows inside. If I had this much food at home, no way I'd be as skinny as her.

I wrap my hand around my upper arm to measure her biceps. A bandage crinkles in my palm.

Oh, yeah. The tattoo.

I'm surprised it doesn't itch or sting the way my first tattoo did. I'll take a peek under the wrap when I clean it after sundown.

The idea of removing the bandage tenses every muscle in my core. I'm sure Violet will nail the crap out of caring for my tattoo. If anyone is going to screw up, it will be me.

# CHAPTER 11
# VIOLET

"'S'up?" A man jabs his fist at me after I enter the elevator on my way to the building's fitness center.

I nod at him. At the last second, I realize I'm supposed to tap my fist to his. He makes explosion sounds while spreading his fingers. I imitate him. By all appearances, I seem to have survived my first-ever fist bump.

"I never see you this early. Yo, new tat?"

"Yeah. Got it last night."

"Cool. Can I see it?"

I palm the bandage protectively. "Once it has healed. The tattoo place was super specific about keeping it protected."

"A friend of mine practically needed his arm hacked off because of an infection. Better to wait. You headed to the gym?" I nod. "Wanna workout together?" he asks.

"I, uh, thanks, buddy." Ooh, I hope *buddy* isn't off brand for Ben. "I'll hit some reps a bit later. Gonna start slowly with cardio." Man, I'm killing it in the gym lingo. Or killing Ben's image.

"Cool. Hit me up if you need me to spot you."

The elevator stops on the third floor. Mystery man waits for me to exit. I had intended to let him go first to lead me to the fitness center. I pull the "oh, my lace is coming loose" move on him and bend over to fiddle with my sneakers in the hallway. He walks to the right and slides his card into the reader on the wall next to a glass door twenty feet away. I hustle to catch him before the door closes.

The room is small. Nobody waits at the door to check us in. Rolled towels sit in cubbyholes at the entrance. I grab a towel and wrap it around my neck, which I believe is the sporty way to handle things. Glancing at my workout mates, I alone hold that perception.

I toss the towel over the handle of an elliptical machine and hop on, a familiar part of my routine on my rare visits to the gym. My feet spin out of control on the lowest setting, because my Herculean thighs beg for a challenge. I stab the resistance button until I find a comfortable setting. Even then, I pedal faster than I would at the height of my normal workout. The experience is like switching from a kneeling scooter, the sort people with a broken leg use, to a Ferrari.

It takes twenty minutes to break a sweat, an occurrence which I regret the second the funk from under my arms reaches my nose. My inherited armpits make a strong case for why men should shave their pits. I dab at my neck with the towel and scan the room, hoping no one will notice me while I compress the towel between my arm and my torso on each side to sop up the mess. Maintenance complete, I toss the soiled rag into the bin and snag a fresh towel.

My fist bump pal is on his back on a bench, hoisting a bar above his chest. He slams the bar into the holders and rises into a sitting position. "Ben, want to work in?" I take a second before registering I am the Ben in question. I tap my chest, and he beckons me. "You normally start with two-fifteen, right? I'll grab another fifty pounds for you."

"No need. I'm sure your weights are fine."

*And I'm sure I will be crushed underneath the bar within the next ten seconds.*

Since I can't guess which muscles I need to stretch, I speed dial my way through a handful of possibilities. The last one might have been a move borrowed from the Hokey Pokey.

Ever the weightlifting pro, I lay my towel on the bench, smoothing it within an inch of its life. A final flourish of my fingers to get them psyched for their role in preventing the death of Ben, and I wrap my hands around the bar. I press it to lift it out of the metal pegs and then lower it until my wrists rest on my chest. With an exhale, I force the weights away from my body.

The bar is lighter than Styrofoam. Holy cow, I'm strong! I waste ten reps and drop the bar into its holder with a satisfying clang.

My buddy scowls at me. "Dude, that was a jerk move."

I hold the bar to hoist myself upright. "What?"

"You should have just done your normal weight instead of showing off."

"I wasn't…" No, I should keep my mouth shut. He thinks I'm Ben. If I use my words to explain myself, he'll grow suspicious.

I hover over him while he does his next set. Would Ben heroically lift the bar one-handed were his friend to lose control? Like discovering I could reach items on the top shelves, I have an uncontrollable urge to test the limits of my strength.

He hops off the bench. "All yours."

I head to the weight rack and take far too much pleasure in carrying a twenty-five-pound weight in each hand back to our bench. Even with the added weight on the bar, I sense during my next set I could handle more. How much can Ben lift? And how many sets should I do?

I'm grateful his friend isn't trying to engage me in a conversation. Ben doesn't strike me as the chatty sort, either. I don't talk to people at the office, but with my friends and family, I'm fairly talkative. If someone wants to discuss crafting or baking, forget it; I'm unstoppable.

I shadow my workout partner over the next half hour. Once we finish, we exchange another fist bump and head into the elevator. "Good workout. Thanks for inviting me," I say.

The elevator doors open a few floors above the fitness center. "No prob. Same time tomorrow?"

"Sure."

We both stand, staring at the doors until they close. "Ben, that was your floor," he says.

Shoot.

I guess I'm lucky I have him to remind me, because I totally forgot where I live. "Lifting brain."

*That's a thing, right?*

He chuckles. "Been there." He steps into the hallway after the doors open again and wraps his arm around the wall to press the button for the sixth floor. "See you tomorrow."

"Have a great day."

I wish I didn't smell like an abattoir. Kind of a catch-22. I desperately need a shower, but Ben doesn't have any shampoo. Only problem is I can't bring this stench into public to buy a replacement bottle. Shopping will have to wait until after I...

... Face my naked self for the first time.

No way. I'm wearing underwear and a pair of sunglasses. Oh, and rubber gloves for cleaning the private bits.

# CHAPTER 12
## BEN

Leggings should come with an instruction manual. Has anyone ever died while putting them on? After a ten-minute struggle, I have inserted my right leg through the mirage of a leg hole. I fall twice while wrangling the left leg into the beast. Righting myself, I check out the results in the closet mirror.

The front has a few extra sags and bags, and I'm enduring the mother of all wedgies. I pull the waistband away from my bellybutton, exposing the product information. I'm no expert, but my guess is I've put the leggings on backwards. And backwards they're staying.

My facetious plan to add Violet's wardrobe to the lonely items I had chucked on the floor last night comes to fruition. I hold every T-shirt she owns against my body in my search for one capable of hiding my wrinkly groinal region. I finally hit pay dirt at the bottom of a shopping bag stuffed at the back of her closet.

In the mirror, the green Pensky Family Reunion 2009 T-shirt swallows my torso, and my arms stick through the sleeves like toothpicks in a trucker's mouth. I gather my hair in my hands, pulling it into a ponytail. The sight of my chest rising under the loose-fitting shirt distracts me.

*Focus, dude!*

Hair elastics are almost as challenging as leggings, but I wrestle most of my hair into what I'm allowing myself to believe is a ponytail. I bat at the lumpy bits scattered around my skull and call it. Anything neater is above my pay grade.

I contemplate possibilities for my workout as I walk to the gym. Violet's muscle mass hasn't benefited from her workout routines. I'm tempted to be a beast every day this week and set her up to build on my foundation, but I'd hate to injure her.

The man at the front desk of the gym doesn't make eye contact when I hand him the membership tag to swipe. "Thanks, bro," I say.

He furrows his brow and shrugs. "Have a good workout."

I'm guessing Violet isn't the sort of person who calls a guy *bro*.

This place is gigantic. I'm envious of her for having tons of equipment at her disposal. I could join a bigger gym, but why bother? Mine is convenient.

My feet lead me in the direction of the free weights out of habit. I pass the class studios on the way. A stunning woman stands outside the second room. The apples of her silky smooth, light brown cheeks shine alongside her smile. Instead of flirting with her, I should ask for pointers on corralling hair into a perfect bun like hers.

"Care to try the barre workout today?" she asks.

"What, drinks and lifting?"

She tilts her head and laughs. "Not that kind of bar. Ballet."

I peer into the room. Two women wearing leggings (facing the right way, I assume) and little black skirts are stretching their legs by resting their feet on the wooden bar running the length of the mirrored wall.

Violet has the tiny, lithe body of a ballerina. I bet she'd dig taking the class. "Yeah, I'm in. But I'm a total beginner. Is it okay for me to join?"

"Absolutely. You'll catch on right away. We start in three minutes." She tilts her head. "What happened to your arm?"

I glance at the black bandage poking out the bottom of my sleeve. "Oh, I have a new tattoo."

She scans me from arm to hair and then along the length of my body. Her gaze shifts, becoming more distant or disinterested.

I slip away from her into the room and stuff my pocketbook into a cubbyhole before picking a spot against the mirror a few feet away from the other two women. With my hands wrapped around my thigh, I hunch forward to raise my leg onto the bar. I don't expect to be able to lift Violet's short leg the full height. Surprisingly, it offers less resistance than mine would. My ankle settles onto the bar with only a minor burning in my inner thigh muscles. Turns out, I have flexible lady legs. I straighten my back and lean forward, touching my fingers to my toes.

By the time the instructor returns, four more women have joined the class. Mental note: look into the class schedule at my building. Even housed in a woman's body, I'm a fan of the male-to-female ratio. And each woman is hotter than the next. If I have a knack for ballet...

Nope. My other body isn't made for stretchy activities.

The instructor flicks on the sound system, and tinkly piano music flutters from the speakers. She asks us to stand in first position. Heels together, toes out. Again, my legs take the instructions more seriously than I had expected, pointing nearly to the sides. When I bend my knees, they track right over my toes.

"I thought you were a beginner. You have a gorgeous turnout," the instructor says to me.

An unnatural amount of pride swells in my chest, which is especially confusing since I don't understand her compliment. Perhaps I've learned the best pickup line ever. Or would women think I meant something ruder?

The compliment gives me the confidence to apply myself to the class. Turns out, my body doesn't need this man brain of mine to tell it how to soar. I suppose throwing a great pass or making an epic dunk has a certain flow to it, but no athletic endeavor has ever infused me with such a sense of grace. Bass-ackward leggings, T-shirt the size of Toledo, and lumpy hairdo aside, I feel pretty and strong. And grateful to occupy this body.

# CHAPTER 13
## VIOLET

"Are you a ballerina?" Ben asks.

His call caught me while I was dripping shower water onto the bathmat in front of the mirror while I wore a towel wrapped around my waist. "No. Are you a caveman?" I swear the amount of stubble on my face has doubled in the last three hours.

"I apologized for leaving the apartment a mess last night." His tone defensive sounds unnatural on him.

"I'm not asking about your apartment. How often do you shave?"

"Oh, yeah, don't bother shaving over the weekend unless the stubble irritates you."

I press the pads of my fingers against my fledgling beard and slide them toward my chin. The sensation of the stiff bristles bending under my fingers is addictive, and it soothes the mild itch. "Why'd you ask me if I was a ballerina?"

"I took a ballet class at your gym. Your body knew all the moves."

I have noticed barre classes on the schedule, but group classes and I don't go together. The other women come in

61

with full faces of makeup and trendy leggings. I make the choice not to fuss over my appearance, but sometimes people can lead me to believe I chose wrong.

"I took ballet for eight years as a kid. I even graduated to the pointe class, but my teacher was never going to pick me to be Clara or the Sugar Plum Fairy."

"You lost me on the last sentence."

"Pointe is where you go up on your toes, and Clara and the Sugar Plum Fairy are the lead roles in *The Nutcracker*."

"Who cares if you were the star? Was it fun?"

"I found it fulfilling because I function best with rules and goals, both of which ballet has in abundance."

"But what about the sense of painting flowing lines in the air when you move your limbs or the weightlessness in your leg as you stretch it high before your muscles and gravity have their say?"

I remember girls in my class smiling a lot more than me while they danced. I've never been the sort whose body could carry on without her. My brain prefers to be in charge. It often locks my body in a prison of tension. "I should try the class in the future."

"Do you want to go with me tomorrow? They're offering it again at ten."

I conduct a one-handed port de bras, pushing my left hand forward, opening my arm into second position, and floating my hand to my side. Ben's muscles fight with my mind, and I huff at the lack of grace I observe in the mirror. "You're not built for ballet."

"That's kind of harsh. I could learn, and I figured because you're an expert, it would make it easier."

"I'm sorry. I shouldn't have said you couldn't do it. I bet you could learn."

"Do you always give up before trying?" he asks.

"What? No. I'm super motivated. Once I have a goal, nothing can stand in my way." The mirror reflects my eyes shifting and my eyebrows doubting me. "I try lots of things. The contest on Monday is new for me. They'll probably award first place to someone who has been doing tablescapes for years, but it doesn't deter me from wanting to do my best."

I hear myself on the other end of the line, making a brief humming sound while exhaling through my nose. It comes across both as a signal to close the conversation and as a bit judgy. It must be a reflex even Ben, who I'd never peg to be judgmental, can't control.

"My bad," he says. "I don't know why I asked. Even though Derek keeps saddling you with sucky leads, you haven't quit. It shows your dedication."

I haven't quit *yet*.

"Thanks. While we're talking about the gym, I worked out with a friend of yours this morning. Didn't get his name. Short blond hair, chiseled jaw—"

"I couldn't tell you who I know with a chiseled jaw. Guys don't describe each other that way."

"Okay, let's see. He did a press thingy lying on his back with, hmm, one hundred sixty-five pounds?"

Ben's laugh pierces my ear. I pull the phone away.

"Shane. He's a good guy."

"So, you've memorized how much everyone can lift, but you can't describe their faces? For the record, you have a chiseled jaw." My fingertips take another romp across the landscape of the lower half of my face. I creep myself out when my eyebrows raise appreciatively. Could anything be weirder than being attracted to yourself, even if it's not actually you?

"You have a thing for chiseled jaws?"

The laugh coming through the phone resembles a demented clown with ill intent. Note to self: enroll in a class to fix your collection of noises and verbal ticks once you're back in your body.

I say, "I don't care for where this conversation is headed."

"You have nice eyes."

*Well, that's a different direction for our conversation.*

I jut my head toward the mirror, examining the vibrant blue eyes staring back at me. "They're gray and beady."

"No, they're calm and deep."

"Eyes are the window to the soul, Ben. You're seeing yourself behind mine. My eyes tend to be intense because I'm usually hyper-focused, hence them being beady."

"You're saying I'm calm and deep?"

"I don't know about deep, but you're calmer than me."

"So, relax."

"I can't relax on command."

"You can. Just stop caring."

"Like, I shouldn't care about anything?"

"Yup. Sort of. I mean, I care about people, and I'm always glad to do right by a client, but I'm okay letting things happen however they're meant to happen without my input. Trying to succeed puts a lot of pressure on something that probably doesn't need to be perfect. And should Derek notice me killing it with every client, he'd always expect me to bring my A game. The job's okay, but I don't want it to take over my life."

"We're built differently. Each assignment I receive, I imagine the best possible outcome and strive for it."

"Is that fun for you?"

"At first."

"And after?"

At some point with each lead, the frustration mounts because I've yet to realize anything close to my expectations. My job is an exercise in futility, but until I made the pact with Anja yesterday, I hadn't been paying close attention. Something has to change. Give me a client on par with Ben's new hotel, and I bet I could sell a bigger contract because the outcome matters to me.

I say, "I enjoy the challenge."

"You do you. Speaking of which, what do you have planned for my body today?" The lilt in his voice tells me he's smiling, like smiling in a way that should have me worried about what he plans to do with mine.

"I'll go on a grocery run, wash a few loads of laundry, introduce your furniture to a dust rag—"

He yawns loud enough to rattle the light fixture. "Boring! Take me out for a spin. You can legally walk around topless, for instance."

"Do I detect a hint of jealousy now that you can't?"

"Hey, I've found a cause to care about. I could campaign to free the girls. What do you think?"

"I think you're obsessed with boobs."

"And you don't have a proper sense of appreciation for them. Can I say you have the most uninspired collection of bras?"

"No, you may not. I'm starving, and since your kitchen offers nothing for me to eat besides condiments, I need to keep moving."

"You definitely earn points for caring about food. Thanks for stocking the fridge for me."

"Enjoy. Talk to you later."

"You got it."

I had planned to call Ben after lunch with a list of tasks and rules for him. Our conversation instead morphed into the sort I'd have with… with a friend. Except for all the talk about breasts.

Maybe it's better I'm getting to know Ben. Self-preservation might be why I've resisted talking to him at the office. I suspect I've shortchanged myself because of it.

# CHAPTER 14
## BEN

I had been wondering about the sore muscles in the back and neck I had inherited since we switched bodies. Initially, I'd written them off as a byproduct of Violet's last workout before the swap. I've since decided they're self-inflicted.

At the office, she reads kind of negative and aloof, like she has an axe to grind but hasn't yet addressed whatever's pissing her off. It might be because she closes so few contracts. Sure, it might also be because of the teasing she endures from some of our coworkers. I've figured by not joining in their conversations, I could be one of the good guys. But my silence doesn't help, either.

Maybe I can make her life easier. If I handle her leads the way I do mine—by doing nothing besides schmoozing with whoever's on the line, she might rise higher on the leaderboard and earn a bit of respect. Yeah, I'll make it my job next week to position her higher so she can put her determination to better use after we switch bodies.

In the meantime, this body needs to lighten up and have fun. I'm taking myself to my favorite bar tonight to seduce a man into buying me drinks. But not dressed in used workout clothes facing the wrong direction.

I sniff under my arm. "Pretty impressive, Ben. You don't smell like a barnyard even after working out."

I should still take a shower, but it will be damned near impossible to behave myself. Warm water, soap, and a woman's body? Sorry, but I'm only human. It's a fantasy in constant rotation in my mind. That and watching a woman get off while sitting on a dryer.

Huh. Technically, I wouldn't be touching myself if I sat on top of her dryer while it was running. Enough, Ben. Not touching myself is probably how I need to handle the shower, though. Violet has a pair of yellow rubber gloves slung over the edge of the kitchen sink. Wearing gloves plus showering in the dark should do the trick.

I go into the kitchen to retrieve the gloves. And check on the dryer situation while I'm at it. My washer and dryer live in a closet in my kitchen. No way a woman would want to amuse herself in this particular fashion in my apartment since the top of the dryer is a good six feet off the ground in its spot atop the washer.

Violet's kitchen doesn't have any closets in it. I open the rest of the doors in the apartment but don't find any hidden appliances. There goes that fantasy.

And the shower fantasy needs to go the same route. I unearth a one-piece bathing suit in her dresser to wear over a pair of underwear. The battle with the leggings is nothing compared to the effort of inserting myself into the spandex bear trap of a bathing suit. At least I put it on the right way.

Fifteen minutes later, with my G-rated shower complete, I wipe steam from the bathroom mirror with my forearm. I tighten the belt on my robe and wrestle a towel around my wet hair into a shape I'd generously call a turban. Points to Violet on her well-stocked shower. I sampled the full collection of products. To be safe, I plan to avoid bees until the fields of flowers anointing every square inch of me calm down in the scent department.

The little I know about women is they have beauty routines involving hair and makeup. In order to score free drinks tonight, I'll need a lot of help figuring out how to style my hair and paint my face. I should check YouTube to see if anyone has ever posted a how-to video for a man new at being a woman.

Famous last words. Nothing prepared me for the experience. If it weren't for my body screaming for food (I promise I won't forget to eat lunch again), my initiation into makeup tutorials would have stretched far longer than the two hours and twenty-three minutes I spent glued to my phone. Am I the last person on earth to learn makeup videos are a thing?

Drag queens guided me on the intricacies of contouring, and Staten Island Italian ladies taught me to apply eyeshadow while using the brush like a windshield wiper. Everyone made a big deal about blending. In the end, I put my trust in an Eastern European woman who resembles Violet. She took her clean face to glam (vocabulary word of the afternoon) in several steps I believed I could copy.

My knowledge is going to go to waste. Violet's makeup collection comprises a tube of mascara, two lipsticks in shades I've never seen on her lips, and tinted zit cream. But she's pretty. She doesn't need a face full of heavy makeup.

I consider myself lucky to have inherited her hair. Despite the neglect I showed it while watching women and the occasional man transform their faces, it dried on its own to hang straight and shiny. I can't resist dragging a handful under my nose and taking a whiff like I did at the tattoo parlor yesterday. Perhaps because I have her sense of smell, not mine, I decide I hadn't lived until discovering tea roses today. I might stay home tonight and get high from sniffing my hair.

In my mind, I had pictured myself wearing a cute, sparkly dress, the kind that ends mid-thigh. Violet's wardrobe is deficient in the sparkly, short skirt department. I settle on something close, a sleeveless dress with a low enough neckline to offer a peek at the cleavage. It might be a bit long in the back, but it shows a healthy amount of leg in the front. Thanks to its girly flounces, I'm pretty enough to score a free drink or two.

After dinner and a generous pour of wine, I stick Violet's house key, my debit card, a tube of lipstick, and some cash into a pink plastic case I found in the bathroom. The fact that Miss Neatnik has misfiled a pocketbook far from the collection on the shelf in her bedroom closet gives me hope she isn't too far gone. The case doesn't have room for my phone, so I stuff it in my bra. It's not the most comfortable place for it, but you can't see its outline under the dress's frills. One last twirl in front of the mirror, and I declare myself to be the belle of the ball. Here's to you, Violet Pensky!

# CHAPTER 15
## VIOLET

I t kills me to text Tracey and Anja that I won't be able to join them for a drink tonight. I've never needed to see them more than I do now. If anyone could give me sage advice about living in a man's body, it would be my squad. I swore to Ben I wouldn't reveal our secret to anyone. But wait a second: who says I can't say hi to my friends while disguised as Ben?

Tracey and Anja have never met him. By insinuating myself into a conversation with them, I can soak up their awesomeness while pretending to be a single man who's rather easy on the eyes (that part won't require any make-believe). I doubt I'll have to worry about Tracey, because she isn't ready to jump into the pact. So long as I don't appear flirty when I talk to Anja, I bet I can pull it off.

They're meeting at the rooftop bar of a waterfront hotel a few blocks from Ben's apartment and down the street from his new client. He has the world at his fingertips, doesn't he? It's yet another way he doesn't know how much more challenging life is for the rest of us.

Which is unfair for me to say. I'm unfamiliar with what it took for him to get where he is. Or what battles he still faces.

Work is the sole cause of my defensiveness, but the sour mood it conjures has begun to infect the rest of my life. The next week should be a vacation for me. Everyone at the office will treat me the way they do Ben, which is far better than they treat Violet. I need to enjoy it while it lasts and thank him for the opportunity.

I studiously arrive at the hotel twenty minutes later than my friends had said they were meeting. It's quite an operation to orchestrate a random arrival time since being punctual is my jam. I could have been here forty-five minutes ago, but I had to force myself to kill an extra five minutes in the apartment followed by a slow stroll through the three floors of amenities in his building. After adding eight blocks onto my five-block commute, I let the elevators at the hotel leave without me four times until I deem it time to head to the roof.

I spot my friends by the railing overlooking lower Manhattan, and my heart leaps. To gain courage before I pretend to meet two lovely strangers, I stop at the bar to order a drink. I'm sure Ben's tastebuds would enjoy a beer, but I have an itch I need to indulge.

I tap the bar to attract a bartender's attention.

"What can I get you?" she asks.

"A margarita."

"Frozen or on the rocks?"

Since my uncivil divorce from tequila in college, the promise of swimming in the icy waves of a frozen margarita without repercussions is beyond tempting, but I doubt a drink bedecked with a paper umbrella belongs in the hands of a manly man. "On the rocks."

I pull out enough bills from my wallet to cover the drink and a generous tip and exchange them for the glass the bartender slides to me. I take a greedy sip through the tiny straw. Ah, bliss! And then panic. It must look ridiculous for a man who can bench press over two hundred pounds to siphon his drink through a squirrel-sized straw.

I leave the straw and my napkin on the bar and make my way toward my friends. Tracey leans forward in her seat, enthralled by whatever Anja is saying. Anja twirls her straw. Her eyes stray from Tracey's and meet mine. She tucks her blond hair behind her ear. I think she's interested in meeting me. But is she interested for the wrong reasons?

"This must be where all the fun is happening," I say, leaning against the railing next to her.

Shoot me. Seriously. If a man said that to me, I'd break into an uncontrollable laughing fit.

My friends haven't had enough to drink to give me a proper sendoff. They snicker politely and ignore me.

Anja continues her story. "So then I said, 'Do you honestly believe I want to eat it after you picked a hair off of it?' I can't believe how bad the service has gotten."

I nod. "I know, right?"

Tracey glares at me. "Move along. Nothing to see here."

Anja's eyes scan the length of me. She appears willing to give my embarrassingly awful attempts at a conversation a pass, the opposite of what she should be doing. The smart thing would be for me to leave.

I come around to the front of their table. "Can I buy you the next round to apologize for my intrusion?"

"Like a free drink would change my opinion of you. Would you leave us alone, please?" Tracey's eyes narrow, sending a chill along my spine.

Meanwhile, Anja's eyes widen. "Awesome! Violet came." She stands and waves frantically.

I turn toward the bar, only to be blinded by a pile of hot pink ruffles. Cue the flashback to the hideous dress I had to wear to my sister's wedding. The woman in the dress has a black bandage on her left arm, and a pair of flaming red lips leap out of my former face.

# CHAPTER 16
## BEN

My phone is doing some serious damage to my left boob, but even this clueless dolt knows better than to dig around in his bra in a crowded bar. I perform a stealth maneuver, pressing my forearm against the offending hardware while twisting my torso to the right. The phone moves a millimeter, but not in the right direction.

A woman by the railing seems to be directing air traffic based on the frantic way she's waving her arms. And I swear she's looking straight at me. Although I'm sure we've never met, were I wearing my usual body, I'd introduce myself in a flash because she's gorgeously endowed with long, blond hair, a healthy dose of curves, and a high-beam smile.

I scan the bar in case I'm misreading her. Nobody around me responds to her. I face her again and notice someone else gesturing at me, albeit more subtly. I'm feeling rather popular until I realize who it is.

Violet race walks toward me the second she catches my eye. "What are you doing here? And what are you wear…" She lowers her gaze to my left hand. "Wait. Why are you carrying my tampon case?"

I stare at the plastic case I'm now tempted to drop upon hearing the dreaded T word. "This isn't a pocketbook? I needed a small bag for my keys, and it matched my dress. I guess that explains why I found it in the bathroom."

"We have a lot of fires to extinguish, and your clutch is the smallest of them." She glances over her shoulder. "Did you notice anyone waving at you?"

"Probably my biggest regret of the last twenty-four hours is not being in my own body to introduce myself to the woman with blond hair."

Violet wags her finger at me. It's not a good look on my body. "Anja is off limits; she and Tracey are my best friends."

I consider trying the finger wag move on her. "Are you crazy? You're the one who made me swear on a scrapbooking book I wouldn't tell a soul we had swapped bodies."

"I haven't said a word. They texted me about meeting for drinks. My plan was to enjoy a night with my friends vicariously. Unfortunately, they don't like you. Well, Anja does, but Tracey's devising a way to push you over the railing without it appearing to be deliberate."

"What did I do to earn a potential case of death?"

"You came across as kind of slimy. I didn't mean to. No way did I want to appear to be making a move on anyone."

"This is getting interesting. What happens if a woman comes on to you tonight?"

"I… I, um… Hooking up with *any*one is the farthest thing from my mind." She gets an eyeful of my cleavage. "What exactly did *you* have in mind?"

"For all the drinks I've bought women over the years, I thought I'd turn the tables."

"While wearing that dress plus my face? Your chances of scoring are less than zero."

I wrap my hand around her biceps to reassure her. The contact generates a jolt of electricity along the bare skin of my arm, making me lose my sense of composure. I swallow hard. "You're wrong. I've spent an embarrassingly extensive amount of time staring at you—at me—today. And watching makeup tutorials. Don't ask. But all the women and the occasional man slathered on tons of creams and powders to cover their skin. Yours has a natural glow to it. And your pores—I am now an expert on pore size, by the way—are possibly the smallest on the planet. You don't need their goop; you wake up pretty."

She rakes her teeth on her lower lip and takes a step away from me, shifting her eyes to her feet. "Guys like you don't buy women like me drinks. I'm the wingman. Men with no game get stuck with me, and even they don't show an interest half the time."

"Don't settle for the wingman. Choose the man who interests you. You want to see how it's done? I'm thirsty."

"I can't say I'd ever want to watch men hit on me from afar. Besides, my friends are probably wondering why we're ignoring them."

"It's all good." I stare at the plastic container in my hand. "You don't want me slapping your tampon case on the bar to pull out my cash, do you?" I flick my eyebrows at her. She shrugs, defeated, and takes the case from me. "Give me a minute," I say. "If I don't score, you can be a gentleman and buy me a drink."

I throw my shoulders back and toss my hair. Two guys on the far side of the bar have lined up shots. I shimmy toward them and slide between them. "So many shots! I bet you wouldn't miss this one." I run my finger around the rim of the glass on the end.

"Not if it's going between your pretty lips." The guy to my left slides the glass in front of me. He glances at me from the corners of half-closed eyes. I grow queasy under his leer.

But it is a free shot. I chug it, wincing from the burn of the tequila. "Thanks."

A second shot appears in front of me, courtesy of the man to my right. "It's only fair you sample mine." The tip of his tongue darts between his lips.

I chug it and slam the shot glass on the bar. "Thanks. Well, I'd better be getting back to my friends."

Dude on the right grips my wrist. "It doesn't work that way. We bought you drinks. You have to stay and talk with us for a while."

I try to wrest my arm from his hand, but he's stronger than me. This has stopped being fun. I lean away from the bar to search for Violet. She is three feet behind me, balling her fists.

"I... My friends are waiting for me. Let me reimburse you for the shots." I point to the "pocketbook" in Violet's hand. She approaches the bar, never taking her eyes from the man holding me captive.

"I don't want your money. Gimme a kiss." He unclasps his hand from my arm and pulls my head to his. I'm powerless to escape. He's too close for me to inflict much damage with a headbutt, but I should try.

"Ow! Who the hell are you?" His hand grabs for his eye.

Violet is holding a Thor pose, the pink plastic case a thunderbolt in her hand, ready to hit him again. "You don't get to ask the questions. Hands off my sister." She holds her palm to me and slips my hand into hers. "You okay?" she asks me.

My heart races, and I struggle to catch my breath. "I am now. Let's get out of here."

We rush away from the bar into a wall formed by the two women I had noticed earlier. They're taller than me by several inches. The redhead reels me into her chest. "Violet, we were so worried! What has gotten into you tonight? If you're hard up for cash, we would have bought you drinks, honey." She tips her head, sniffing my face. "Please tell me you weren't drinking tequila."

"Only two shots." With my adrenaline on the decline, I realize I might have to blame my dizziness and nausea on the tequila. Oh, and the large glass of wine I drank earlier is probably having its say, too.

The blond-haired beauty wraps her arm around my shoulders. "I held her hair the last time, Tracey. It's your turn to be on puke duty."

The women squabble over who should take me home. Violet steps into the circle. "I'll take her home."

The redhead shoves her aside with her elbow. "No way. She probably approached those douchebags to escape you. You're done here. Shoo!"

I reach for Violet's arm. "Wait, you guys. I know Ben from work. I trust him."

The woman with the blond hair holds her finger in the air. "You're the guy she baked cookies for?"

Excuse me? Violet's friends know about me? Huh.

I grin at her. "He is *that* Ben."

Violet shuffles her feet and avoids my eyes.

Tracey crosses her arms. "Anja, not now."

I'm dying to know what that means.

Anja shrugs and runs her finger over my bandage. "What's going on here?"

"Oh, I got a tattoo yesterday."

"Show me!" she says.

I fiddle with a loose corner of the tape on my bandage. "I haven't cleaned it yet. It's probably still nasty and raw. I'll show you after it heals."

The redhead purses her lips. "Something's going on with you, Violet. Tattoos, tequila, and voluntarily wearing a Mardi gras float in public?"

"I'm just…"

*…completely confused about who I am?*

Violet takes a step forward. "Violet had a rough week. Our boss hasn't shown her any support. She told me yesterday she wanted to be someone different in hopes it would make Derek change his mind about her. I think it's cool she got a tattoo. It's pretty: a cluster of violets."

"*You've* seen her tattoo? Maybe you two are friends, but right now, she should be with the people who know her best. You need to leave and let us take care of her."

It makes sense for her friends to be protective of her. Between the vulnerability I'm experiencing in the aftermath of my encounter with the jerks at the bar and the tequila shots, I can't trust myself not to spill the beans about who I really am. Thanks to the Violet immersion I've experienced over the last day, though, she's the only person I want to help me find my way home.

"You guys, you're the best friends a gal could have, but you should stay. You were having fun before I messed everything up. Ben can take me home. And if he tries anything with me, you have my blessing to throw him off a tall building. Okay?"

They speak to each other with their eyes and shrug. The redhead tucks my hair behind my ear in a kind, nurturing gesture.

She says, "Be safe. Keep my contact card open on your phone and call the second the situation doesn't seem right to you. Promise?"

"Promise."

Anja hugs me, and perhaps I enjoy it more than she—or Violet—would want me to. "We'll see you bright and early on Monday."

"Monday?"

The redhead gives her head an exasperated roll. "Holy cow, Violet. How many shots did you have? The tablescape contest, silly."

"Oh, right. How could I forget? Yeah. See you Monday. Ben, you ready?"

I can't read what's happening behind Violet's eyes, but at least she hasn't abandoned me. Once we're in the elevator, my stomach becomes host to a surfing competition. I grip the walls and say, "I'm not feeling so hot. Could we go to my place? It's closer."

She shakes her head. With a wan smile, she says, "Fine. But I won't hold your hair when you hurl. Remember: I warned you to stay away from tequila.

# SUNDAY

# CHAPTER 17
## VIOLET

The only thing more disorienting than waking up in someone else's body is waking up in said body in an unfamiliar location. Morning hits hard even though I had but a single drink last night and went to bed before midnight. I blame the coarse fabric of the cushion I used as a pillow and that I'm twenty-five percent larger than the couch on which I slept. Why exactly did I sleep in Ben's living room?

I pad across the kitchen floor and stand in front of the closed bedroom door. The local Geiger counters must be going nuts from the snoring coming from the other side of the door. I open it a crack. Ben, tiny as he is at the moment, sprawls across the mattress like an NBA star.

Oh, right. Tequila and my former body don't mix.

I've bounced back fairly quickly from two shots of the devil's blood in the past. His head and stomach will be tender, but not so tender that food is out of the question. I am hungry enough I could swallow his couch and be ready for a three-course meal. Being twice my usual size means eating twice as much. I suppose I'll tire of Ben's insatiable appetite, but at the moment, I'm itching to cook up a storm to feed my new hunger.

I'm elbow-deep in pans of challah French toast, scrambled eggs, and bacon when Ben rises from his slumber, hair sticking out every which way and with gallons of drool caked to his cheeks. He's wearing one of his button-down shirts, which hangs to his knees.

I smile at him. "Good morning, sunshine."

Oh, I suck.

He disappears into the bathroom with a grunt.

I pour us each a glass of orange juice and move the glasses to his ridiculous kitchen table, better suited for a bar than an apartment. It is small, square, and stool height. Because bachelor.

By the time Ben trudges into the kitchen, I've plated the food and poured us each a mug of coffee. His is black, per my personal preferences. Meanwhile, Ben's mouth can't stand coffee unless it has a splash of milk and two sugars. I add two pain killers to his place setting and take a seat on the stool closest to the stove.

He tries to hop onto his, but no go. Pulling it away from the table, he climbs it like a ladder. He grasps the table to swing the chair in place, rattling the dishes from his effort.

I pretend I hadn't watched his performance, instead saying, "My prior experience with hangovers tells me you'll feel better after you eat. The water I made you drink before bed helped, right?"

He stabs at the eggs. "Yeah. But who gets a hangover from two shots?"

"A one-hundred-pound woman who matched a rugby player shot-for-shot in college." I take a bite of the French toast. "I won, by the way. Nine to his eight."

A bit of life creeps into his cheeks. "Boyfriend?"

"It had been my plan to hook up with him, which is why my flirtations involved dousing my liver in lighter fluid. I wanted to impress him. I didn't."

"I'm surprised you had it in you."

"Had what?"

"Fun."

"I'm fun." I doubt his vocal box has ever made some of the noises that I've forced through it since Friday night. Nor should it. I wish I could retract my last sentence and the defensive way I uttered it.

He rests his elbow on the table and his chin in his palm. "I guess I haven't seen your fun side."

"You don't know me."

"True. How come you never join the team after work?"

My fork drops with a clatter on the plate. "With Derek?"

He buckles with surprise. "Uh, huh. Every Tuesday." His eyes calculate whether he should have made the confession.

"No one has ever invited me to come along. Does Julie go?" Julie is the only other woman on our team.

He sucks on his bottom lip. "Huh. I don't think so."

"That's Derek for you. He probably invited her when she was new because she's pretty. But if everyone in the group acted like a bunch of bros at the bar, a chick, especially one with a fiancé, wouldn't be into the scene."

"I've never given it much thought, but yeah, I get the impression he's a different boss to you than he is to some of the guys, me included." His hands flop against his chest. "Is it a drag to have him for a boss?"

I've decided not to explain my point of view to Ben. Let him go in next week without my prejudices. He's likely to succeed because he'll still be himself, a man capable of closing the deal.

"I'm lucky to have the job, and I want to succeed at it."

"If it doesn't work out, you could always open a breakfast restaurant. Your cooking is amazing."

"Thanks, but I don't plan on quitting my day job."

Not until I've had a shot of doing it in a man's body

"Good." His smile seeps into me, warming me to my toes.

# CHAPTER 18
## BEN

I've never made breakfast for an overnight visitor to my apartment. And officially, I still haven't. Am I the guest in this situation? I'm losing track of who I am.

Well, I know I'm a man who shouldn't have bought my bar table. A person of Violet's stature would need a year's residency in Cirque de Soleil to conquer the stool. A more suitable outfit would help, too. I'm always a sucker for a woman wearing one of my dress shirts over a pair of panties. The way I climbed onto the stool at breakfast while swaddled in a too-large shirt couldn't have been sexy. Not that I wanted to be sexy for Violet.

I want to be something for her, though. She deserves mad props for a thousand different reasons. First, my apartment hasn't been this clean since my realtor showed it to me. I'd better learn a few good habits before Violet discovers the pigsty I've made of hers. Her gourmet breakfast is righting the wrongs of last night, too. Which brings me to last night: she punched a guy to defend me. It's probably the coolest thing anyone has done for me in ages, but I'm mortified to have put myself in a position where I needed defending.

"So, about last night." Humiliation prevents me from meeting her eyes.

"We're cool."

"I'm not. I embarrassed myself in front of your friends. Please forgive me."

"I've texted them, saying I'm going through some stuff. They're more concerned about what the jerk at the bar did to me, or you, rather than about you showing up dressed like a toddler on the pageant circuit."

"A toddler carrying a tampon case purse."

She chortles. "You definitely need a few style pointers."

"I suppose. I didn't find anything in your closet resembling what a woman should wear to a bar on a Saturday night."

"And what were you looking for? A costume suitable for a Cardi B video?"

"I don't appreciate you making assumptions about me. It matters less to me what a woman wears than the attitude she projects. After soaring through ballet class yesterday morning, I wanted to wear clothing that expressed how I felt in your body. Feminine, confident... Your pantsuits made me slump and stare at the floor."

She rolls her eyes. "I wouldn't wear my work clothes to a bar. A pair of jeans and a nice shirt would be fine. Entering a bar boobs first and asking randos for free drinks will get you in trouble. As you've now learned."

"I screwed up. If you hadn't been nearby to rescue me, I hate to imagine what would have happened. Thank you."

"You're welcome, although I regret reacting with violence. That's not who I am. Lesson number one for being a woman: in the corner of your mind, you always have to remember a man might hurt you. Maintain a guarded demeanor until you know someone well. You can relax a bit when you're out with friends."

"How can you hook up with a guy you've just met if you don't trust men?"

She bends her finger over her lips. "You need to read the signs. Two guys with a line of shots on the bar? Yeah, you don't want to have anything to do with them."

"Your friends didn't trust you in my body last night."

"I know. You'd think I'd be an expert in the field of male creepiness, but I failed to present myself as the sort of man a woman would trust. Tracey rejected me the second I spoke to her."

I push my hair behind my ear. "Women don't reject me. I thought it was because I'm a handsome devil."

"A little self-absorbed, are we?"

"I'm joking, but I'm not."

"Explain, please."

I adjust the hem of my shirt lower on my thighs. "Some men are all about their moves. Not me. I see a woman who interests me, I approach her. No games or formulas. We talk, nothing more."

"You remind me of Derek. Oh, sorry. Let me try again. You don't deserve such an insult. I'm talking about his business advice. Once, I made the mistake of asking him for help with my contracts, or lack thereof. First, he criticized me for having to ask, and then he mapped out a ridiculously simple plan, like by following his three easy, but vague steps, I'd be the queen of commissions. No one can sell to the voicemail of a client who wanted to have nothing to do with the company a month ago. Something else has to be in play. It's easier to close a sale from a strong lead. And it's a lot easier to be confident when everyone likes you. I guess I don't come across as likable on my sales calls."

I take the death plunge from the stool, maintaining a shred more dignity than I had on the climb onto it. After dumping my dirty dishes in the sink, I lean against the counter and say, "I like you."

Her eyes melt, which has the same impact on my heart. With a shy smile, she says, "I… That means a lot to me. You're nicer than I had given you credit for being."

The gooey moment slams into a wall. "Making assumptions is a habit of yours. Just stop. Let things happen on their own."

She processes the comment for a second. Her eyes grow quizzical. "So, when you sidle up to a lady, you don't assume she'll throw herself at you?"

"I walk over to her because she smiled at me. Her reaction tells me she wouldn't mind me coming over to say hello. Whatever happens next is a series of reactions. Nothing's planned or calculated. I'm cool regardless of whether we click."

"Let me try. Smile at me the way women smile at you."

It's weird making a move on a person wearing my face and weirder still to do it on command. I picture the last woman I brought home to my apartment. What had captured my attention was the way her smile originated in her eyes.

I mimic her expression by tilting my head, observing Violet out of the corners of my eyes, and the moment I can confirm she is watching me, I widen them and part my lips like I'm about to ask a question.

She hops off her stool. "Let me try." She licks her lips and sucks a noisy breath through her nose. She stares at me accusatorially and waits to tilt her head until she does a move with her mouth that would make mothers rush their young children into safe spaces.

I hold my hands to my face in mock horror. "Dude… ah… no. What was going on in your head when you looked at me? Were you planning to abduct me? Or serve me for dinner?"

"Yes, that's exactly what I wanted to convey." She slaps her napkin onto the table. "I give up. Let's wash the dishes and get on with the day."

"In a second. I might have solved your problem. You didn't have any motivation, aiming your smile at me, or rather you, in the full glory of a hangover."

"Thanks. It sure gives me a boost to learn I'm an uninspiring sight."

"You've misread me. You're a healthy heterosexual woman. Right?"

I'm not winning any points with her this morning, judging from the way she scowls at me.

"I am…"

"Let's take the show into the bathroom and try some moves on our reflections. You need a good-looking man to inspire you."

"Again, your plan reeks of self-absorption." She presses the backs of her fingers against her lips. A hint of a smile, one that would stand a good chance of bringing me to her side were we in a bar as our former selves, stretches under her fingers. "But who knows?"

The words on the tip of my tongue could not be more unadvisable for the guy stuck in her body as a result of a stupid wish. But I can't stop myself. I wish I could know what she's thinking and hope it's the same thing as me.

# CHAPTER 19
## VIOLET

The threat of dismemberment wouldn't shake the truth out of me, but Ben's suggestion of flirting with my face—his face—in the mirror isn't the worst idea. I study his blue eyes, gauging their adjustments while I shift my point of view from disgruntled to intrigued. They're at their most engaging when I relax. The instant before I let his lips form a smile, the muscles in his cheeks contract, pulling the grin into his eyes, which lowers the lids and makes the corners crinkle. I turn my head away by twenty degrees and find my gaze in the mirror. Yeah, I'd let this man buy me a drink.

Meanwhile, he amuses himself by puckering, posing, and piling my hair on top of his head. I peek at my other self. Ben has found an aspect of my face I've missed before. Coaxed out of hiding by his easygoing nature, I appear less closed off. Maybe this is what inspired him to tell me I was pretty last night. My stomach jumps and twirls at the notion of him being attracted to me.

Applying a romantic context to Ben while standing side by side in the mirror and meeting the wrong reflection disorients me, though. I step aside and press a loose bit of tape from his bandage against his arm. "I'm afraid it won't stay put. The tape has lost its sticky."

"It got wet in the shower yesterday, and I took it off to clean the tattoo before I went out last night. The goop they told us to put on it probably bled into the tape, too. I mean to find a solution."

"We have to fix the bandage before it falls off and…" My stomach ties itself into a series of knots when I imagine Ben exposing the tattoo to sunlight. "You can't screw this up for me!"

He rolls down his sleeves and backs away from me. "Trust me, okay?"

"Sorry. I do trust you."

I cock my head when I hear my phone ring in the living room. I run to it and flip it over. Mom. Without thinking, I answer the call. "Hi, Mo… Mrs. Pensky. It's… Adam, Violet's landlord. Since I was closer to her phone, I answered it." I tip my head back, my heart pounding despite the last-second save.

"Nice to say hello to you. How are you?"

"Fine. And yourself?"

"I'm well, thank you. Your voice is huskier than usual. You sure you're okay?"

"I'm fine. It's just a morning thing. My allergies are acting up." I don't know whether Adam suffers from allergies. Next time I see him, I'll shove a bouquet of goldenrod and dandelions in his face to check.

"Is Violet available? We were worried because she usually calls us by now."

"Oh, uh, yeah, she's here. It's my fault she didn't call. Charles and I invited her upstairs for breakfast. Let me get her."

I tiptoe into the bathroom. Ben is still messing around with my hair. I hold the phone behind me and whisper, "I made a mistake and answered a call. It's my mom. Say hi and ask her if she and Dad are going to see the grandkids today."

He clenches his jaw and puffs his cheeks before taking the phone. With a squint at me, he says, "Morning, Mom. What are your plans for today?" He correctly assumed my mother would take her time answering his question, thus allowing him to chat with me simultaneously. "Who did you tell her you were?"

"Adam." I hold my finger to my lips to remind him to speak quieter.

"Adam, huh? A dude your mom knows. Do you have a secret you're not…? Mom, that sounds great. Wish I could join you, but Adam and I have plans." His eyebrows waggle. I slash my hands in opposing directions. "Uh, huh… Right… No, everything's fine. I've never felt better. Did I tell you I got a tat—"

I tug his hand to pull the phone away from his head. Covering my mouth, I speak in a stage whisper to pretend I'm in another room. "Violet, the food's getting cold."

Ben gnaws on his knuckle. "Sorry." He brings the phone to his ear. "Mom, I hate to do this to you, but I have to run. Have fun with… uh… Have a great day." He ends the call and glares at me. "The rules—*your* rules—state we weren't supposed to answer our phones. You busted my chops over a bit of loose tape on your tattoo's bandage, and yet you're the one who keeps breaking her rule about interacting with family and friends."

"I forgot. Every Sunday morning, I call my parents at nine. They'd file a missing person report if they didn't hear from me by lunchtime. Why were you going to tell them about my tattoo?"

"Wouldn't a woman who calls her parents at a set time each week be the sort of dutiful daughter who tells her mother everything?"

I roll my eyes. "I'll tell her. Eventually. But not until I can show her in person. When I'm in person. Will you tell your parents about your tattoo?"

He shuts the light in the bathroom and enters the kitchen. "I don't need to rely on mutilating my body to disappoint my family."

"How can you be a disappointment? You've told them about your new hotel client, right?"

"They wouldn't care. Unless I was a Senator or CEO of Goldman Sachs, they'd consider me a failure."

"Ooh, harsh."

It also explains why he is a highly functional slacker. What's the point of trying to succeed if his parents have never supported him?

"No big deal." He pushes the handle of the egg pan, which still sits on a burner. "I suppose we should clean the dishes. Unless you'd be cool stacking them in the sink and ignoring them?"

Every hair on my body wants to stand on end from the horror of the suggestion, but I can't throw that kind of energy at him. "I'd prefer to tackle them now. You're more than welcome to help."

"Of course, I will. I could stand to learn a trick or two from the master. Lead the way."

# CHAPTER 20
## BEN

I had expected Violet to have a stroke after I mentioned leaving the dishes in the sink. She proved me wrong by not criticizing me. Housework's not the worst when someone who gets her rocks off from it takes the lead. And honestly, I wasn't in a rush to leave, which meant I had to lend a hand.

She's different away from the office. The same walls exist around her, but I'm beginning to understand why she built them and how I might help her knock them down. How I might want to help her destroy them.

I've met plenty of interesting women, and sure, the women I take home also happen to be beautiful, but I swear I pay attention to more than their bodies. Something's different with Violet, though. I listen to her without equating what she says with the person I see speaking to me, and at the same time, I gain extra insight into who she is by experiencing the world in her body. Where I used to think she was unfriendly, I now understand why she's wary of letting in people, especially men.

She hands me a plate to load into the dishwasher. "Are you feeling more like yourself, whoever that may be?"

"I'm several stages ahead of where I was earlier this morning. Might have to take things slow today, though. What are your plans?"

"Nothing much. If I were me, I'd probably spend the day fretting about the competition tomorrow."

"The competition?" She glowers at me, which jogs my memory. "It involves tables, right?"

"Yes. We're setting a table for tea at Downton Abbey in Hoboken."

"And you can't do it without me?"

She points her fingers at herself. "Hello? My name is on the registration list. I can't very well march up to the organizers and tell them I'm Violet, can I?"

"They'd be very closed minded should they disagree."

"Just help me, will you?"

I have nothing against helping her, but I'm the last person she should bring to a crafting contest. I'd probably end up gluing myself to a centerpiece.

"Can't one of your friends pretend to be you?"

"They're in the competition, too. We've planned our designs together for the last few months, which has been almost as good as having either of them assist me. I suppose not having an assistant is fine, because I'd rather not boss someone around. I'll swing by my apartment at eight tomorrow morning to gather you and the props. It will be fun, I promise."

I have so many questions. My mom used to make my brothers and me set the table for dinner. Fun isn't how I'd describe the experience. "Um, sure."

She ducks into the bathroom and returns with a roll of bandage tape. "Before you leave, let me redo the tape on your arm. I bought two rolls; you should take one home." She tears off a strip and attaches it to my bandage. "I wish I could see my tattoo."

"You haven't peeked at mine, have you?"

"Nope. It doesn't hurt or anything. I can feel the lines, though. The skin is slightly swollen in the exact design. It's a Braille tattoo." Her fingers trace the starburst pattern that lies under the bandage on her calf. "You know what hurts? Ripping out the hair on your leg whenever I remove the tape. It would be easier if I could shave—"

"Nope. Saffron shaved what needed to be shaved. Leave the rest alone."

She says, "Mine are due for a grooming. Sorry."

"And my face is entering its caveman phase." Out of habit, I caress the chin I'm currently borrowing. "Not this face. Smooth as a shark."

"Are sharks smooth?"

"So they say."

Her fingertips slide along her growing beard. "Smooth as a porcupine. It's small comfort the wish didn't make facial hair sprout on the wrong face, I suppose. I promise I won't hack yours to pieces when I have at it with a razor." She pushes herself away from the counter. "On that note, let's keep moving."

"Got it. You need anything, give me a call. Otherwise, I might attend another ballet class. Or find new friends to buy me shots of tequila." I wink at her.

"Don't. You. Dare."

I clutch my still-aching head. "Not a chance."

She drops the tape, my keys, phone, and debit card into a small plastic bag and hands it to me.

Oh, right. I used an alternative pocketbook last night. "Don't forget the tampon case."

"Already inside the bag." Her eyes dart between my eyes and body. I glance downward. I'm standing in the living room dressed in nothing more than a shirt and panties.

"You might need to change into what you wore last night before you leave." She sucks her bottom lip to keep from laughing.

Damn. My first official walk of shame as a woman will involve hot pink ruffles.

# CHAPTER 21
## VIOLET

Well, these last fifteen hours have been... interesting. I toss the shirt Ben had discarded onto the pile I've hidden in his closet. Spending time together outside of work would have melted my brain under normal circumstances, but adding in the entanglements with my friends, the sight of him in my dress being harassed by two men, plus the body swap, and I'm fried.

I keep wanting to be mad at him for trying things I would never do in my body and he wouldn't do as himself. Meanwhile, I'm in full-on Violet mode, cooking, cleaning, and making safe choices. Yes, he made a couple of gargantuan mistakes last night, but I envy him his courage. He's having more fun in my body than I ever have.

Sometimes my friends tease me, calling me Shrinking Violet. Short jokes aside—and with me being the runt of my pack, short jokes are common—the nickname doesn't fit. I'm not necessarily quiet or retiring. Maybe I'm easy to ignore because I occupy less space than most. My voice disappears when others speak loudly. While I'm in a crowd,

I don't bother trying to rescue myself from the invisibility people force on me, accepting it instead.

I often want to be seen. But when I assert myself, I might sound strident. Derek's reaction on Friday morning after I raised my voice because he hadn't heard me implies I come across as unpleasant. Ben hasn't inherited my resentful side. I hope my muscle memory doesn't inflict it on him.

I can't spend my day thinking about him. I need an activity to keep my brain out of trouble. If I were still me, I'd spend the day double and triple checking the items I've made for my tablescape project. But I'm him, and I'm bored.

Today is a perfect day for a walk. His apartment's location puts the Hudson River right at my feet. I could head south to Liberty State Park or north to Hoboken, but I expect both stretches of the waterfront will be crowded because of the holiday weekend. Weehawken it is.

I take the light rail to Lincoln Harbor. By the time I arrive, Ben's stomach has forgotten the lovely meal I fed it only three hours ago. A guy could go broke tending to his appetite. Especially since it has roared to life in the land of expensive restaurants. At least there's a market across from the station. I load a carryout container with a pound of food from the salad bar and bring it to a bench near the river.

Every once in a while, people walk onto the pier where I'm sitting to enjoy the view of Manhattan. Everything is peaceful. No one around me would suspect me to be the freak show I am. It's freeing.

I chug the rest of my iced tea and set off for the Port Imperial rail station a little over a mile away. The sun, directly overhead, beats down on me. Dark moons grow around the armholes of my T-shirt.

I stop in my tracks from a revelation Ben had planted in my head yesterday. Laws about wearing shirts don't apply to me. I tug my shirt over my head and bunch it in my hand. The breeze from the river immediately cools my skin. He wasn't wrong to float the idea of campaigning to permit women to go topless. I resent every day I've spent trapped in a bra and sweaty shirt.

I borrow Ben's swagger as I saunter upriver. It requires a bit of getting used to, but I'm developing a sense of taking up more space than usual. I don't have to play sidewalk chicken; people voluntarily veer to the side of the path when I approach.

Were I to tackle my stack of leads bare chested, with my shoulders back, and my stride purposeful, figuratively speaking, would my contacts respond positively? I have the perfect means of testing my theory. On Tuesday, at my meeting with Ben's hotel client, I will occupy my space with confidence and let things unfold rather than assume the client will ignore me. No shrinking violets here.

Near the end of my walk, I become a little knock-kneed because I need to pee. I could continue north to the ferry terminal to use the public restrooms. But it's out of my way. What would Ben do?

He had jumped into the swap with a list of things he was dying to experience in a woman's body. Sure, I had my fun reaching objects on his upper shelves, but playing Mr. Tall Guy is not on par with him tarting himself up to score free drinks.

I glance at the shirt in my hand. I will forever be jealous of men for being able to disrobe in public. But it pales in comparison to bathroom envy. Between avoiding the long lines and not needing to sit on nasty toilet seats, men lead a charmed life when it comes to peeing in public. Whip it out, take care of business, and boom! Done.

A ferry horn sounds, the lone sign of life on this stretch of the waterfront. A grove of trees separates me from the apartment building behind me. Weeds grow tall in the rocks on the far side of the fence running along the river, providing cover. I can do this, right?

A quick check of the sidewalk for any new arrivals, and I press my fly between two bars of the fence. I turn left and right, maintaining a friendly, Hey, how's it going expression on my face while unzipping and positioning myself. Nothing suspicious going on here. I measure the first burst to confirm the tall weeds mask the stream I've produced. Totally in the clear. Ah! I close my eyes, smiling with relief and the joy of the simple things in life.

I zip my shorts. The sound of the ferry's engine draws my eyes forward. I always prefer riding on the left side because when the boat turns right, it gives me a full view of the city. The passengers on the right side today have the more interesting view. Cameras train on me and fingers point in my direction. I do the only thing that makes sense: behave like Ben, not Violet. I wave at my fans and relish the fact it won't be my face splashed across social media today.

# CHAPTER 22
## BEN

On the ride to Journal Square, I perfect the smile I need to share with the nosy passengers on the PATH train. It's one part *I know I'm wearing last night's dress* and two parts *Aren't you jealous you aren't as pretty as me.* I clutch my plastic bag in my lap and pray the train doesn't come to a screeching halt inside the tube, leading to a long delay. There's only so long a gal can withstand being on display.

Thankfully, we arrive at the station on schedule. I lose my self-consciousness once I'm above ground. In the chaos of Journal Square, I'm another oddball worth ignoring. I hold my head high and make my way to Violet's apartment.

My memory of the state I had left it in doesn't match reality. The damage is worse than I remember. But it can wait until I've showered and eaten lunch.

The fear of caring for Violet's body is less than it was yesterday. The temptation to anoint myself with every available product has abated, and I don't face the burden of having to grapple with wardrobe and makeup today. Get in, get out, get on with my life. This is more normal.

I hover over the kitchen sink, snacking on chips, cheese, and salami while I make a plan for an afternoon of housework. The best place to start is to put away her clothes. Motivated by the image of a clean apartment, I return the chip bag to her pantry and take care to wrap the plastic all the way around the cheese and meat before returning the food to the fridge.

I select a playlist, crank the volume on my phone, and stare at the clothes strewn across her bed and the floor. Cleaning her home would be a whole lot simpler if I could remember where everything belonged. I hang the shirts in the closet despite knowing Violet will have to rearrange everything. Color-coordinating her blouses is above my pay grade. I stuff the rest of her clothing into random drawers and declare the bedroom done.

The kitchen deals a blow to my gut. Yesterday's food has formed impenetrable crusts on the dishes. Comparing this mess to the project I handled under Violet's supervision earlier, I now see the point of cleaning dishes soon after a meal. I grab yesterday's cereal bowl from the stack and reach for the dishwasher door. Hello, dishwasher? Where are you?

It seems wrong to have one in my apartment, given my lack of respect for washing dishes or even using them. Meanwhile, poor Violet, who cooks actual food and eats on plates, has none. I owe her a sink emptied of its science experiments at the very least. But I don't want to!

While I'm inventing ways to delay the inevitable, her doorbell rings. A welcome distraction, yes, but...

I could pretend I'm not home. The bowl slips from my hand and clatters against the stack of dishes. Guess not.

"Coming." I approach the door, hoping it's a package delivery. I'm about to fling the door open until I remember Violet's warning not to trust men. "Who is it?"

"Oh, hey, Violet. You're home. It's Adam."

Adam? Ah, yes. The guy she pretended to be when she answered her phone earlier. I wonder who he is to her.

I open the door. He could be the sort of guy Violet would find attractive. He has a buzz cut, and his brown eyes brighten behind the lenses of his glasses when I smile at him. I bet he works out a lot.

"What a surprise. Come on in."

He rubs his palms together. "I told you I would stop by today to get a preview since I can't make it to Hoboken tomorrow. I'm dying to see your table design. And happy to help you complete a dry run."

Oh, that can't happen. He'll figure out I'm not Violet the second I stumble over which side of the plate to put the knife.

"You're going to kill me, but I decided it'd be bad luck to rehearse. Whatever happens tomorrow will happen."

"That doesn't sound like you. You're the last person on earth I'd expect to wing it. What's gotten into you?" He elbows me and gives me a playful grin.

Violet *does* have a flirty buddy. I knew it!

The thing is, I don't know how to proceed. If they have something going on, he's not kissing me today. Nope. Sorry, dude. If they don't, my abilities to charm could land me in trouble because I'd hate to encourage him. Like I've said, he ain't getting a piece of this.

A third thought floats around my skull. I'm not simply opposed to kissing a guy; I'm not sure I'm comfortable with Violet kissing someone else, either.

Okay, that took me by surprise.

My moment of inexplicable jealousy causes me to forget what we were talking about. "I, um… Can I offer you a drink?"

"A glass of wine, perhaps?" He gazes at me from this moon of a face. His expression is sweet and… Oh, those eyes tell me everything I need to know. Adam has a thing for Violet.

I run my hands along my thighs, which are mistakenly overexposed, thanks to the tiny pair of cutoffs I put on after my shower. "Coming right up."

I scamper—a brand-new action for me, thank you very much—into the kitchen. Now what? Should I call Violet and ask her where things stand with Adam? No, she'd be mad I invited him in.

I pour a glass of wine for my guest and water for me. Alcohol in my system could only make things worse. I take a step toward the door before remembering Little Miss Hospitality would offer her guest snacks. I toss a hunk of cheese onto a plate and scatter crackers around it before returning to the living room.

"Here you go." I set the plate and his glass on the coffee table.

He lifts the glass and slides a coaster under it. Whoops. How very un-Violet-like of me.

"No wine for you?" he asks.

"I overindulged last night."

"Please tell me it didn't involve tequila."

Seriously, is there anyone in Jersey City not well versed on the battle between Violet and tequila?

"Of course not. I was out with the girls and shouldn't have had the third glass of wine."

"The girls? You mean Tracey and Anja?"

"Right. Women, not girls. Which sounds odd, doesn't it? *I went out with the women.* Anyway, yes, we had a great time."

Oh, I need to shut up now. I reach for the plate to slice a hunk of cheese. Shoot. "Hold on. I forgot the knife."

I'm killing it as Violet. Not.

Could I be more tense? Kind of ironic, given how I've been advising her to relax.

I return from the kitchen and hand Adam the knife. "Help yourself."

"Thanks. Just because I'm not rehearsing with you doesn't mean I can't take a peek. Can you show me the backdrop?"

"You got it."

But do I? I have no idea what I'm looking for or where to find it. I open the closet by the front door. It ranks as the neatest space in the apartment since I hadn't yet been in it. It contains exactly what a normal adult would store in a coat closet: coats rather than teacups, silverware, or a backdrop.

I try the closet in the hallway. Someone has magic-markered the top of a cardboard box with the words *Tablescape Contest.* Violet must somehow have intuited I'd need a guardian angel to help me find her supplies. Behind the box is a piece of plywood hinged to another board. I gently maneuver the boards around the box and take a look inside. It might be a craft project. I hope it's the right one.

"Here we go," I say with false confidence.

I lay the boards on the living room carpet. They wobble because of random bits of hardware screwed onto their backs.

Adam bends over them. "Violet, you've outdone yourself."

I stare at the artwork on the floor. Even I can recognize the cast of *Downton Abbey* standing in front of their castle. Violet has glued the photo onto the boards and added bits of feathers and lace to fancy up the people's outfits. The upper half of a man twice as large as everyone else looms behind them. He wears a fedora and holds a teacup between his fingertips. She has highlighted his eyes with shiny blue sequins, which is on point, since the man in the picture is Sinatra. I wonder why he's hanging out with lords and ladies of the manor until I remember tomorrow's competition is in Hoboken, his hometown.

I brush my hand across the surface like a hostess on a game show revealing a prize, and one of Sinatra's eyes pops off. "Oh, shoot! I've ruined it." I hold the sequin in front of Adam, my heart heavier than I'd expect it to be for such an insignificant item.

"Did you destroy your art for my benefit? I've seen you with a glue gun before. No need to showboat by demonstrating your gluing prowess for me."

Oh, duh. Of course, I can glue it. "I'll save it for later. I'd hate to bore you." Or demonstrate my lack of knowledge of where Violet stores her glue gun.

He stands over the picture. "Your piece is fabulous. You used decoupage, didn't you?"

Decoup-what now?

I nod emphatically. "Yes. What else could I have used?"

"And you said you'll mirror the feathers and lace on the table?"

I need to abort my mission before I prove I'm a fraud. I fold the boards and stuff them behind the box in the closet. "Enough about *Downtown Abbey*."

He thrusts his chin forward and presses his lips together. "Down*ton*?"

"See? My brain is so sick of abbeys and Sinatra, it's telling me to take a break from table stuff tonight. And since I don't need you…"

He gulps his wine. "Excuse me? Are you kicking me out?"

"I… uh… Stay as long as you want."

*Provided you don't want to be here any longer.*

"Honey, say the word, and I'll fly home. You know me too well to be shy."

"You're right. The sequin incident kind of has me spiraling. Me melting down is not exactly a spectator sport." Violet would say something like that, right?

He places his hands on my shoulders and air kisses me. "From the state of your apartment, the spiraling began well before I arrived. I can take a hint. Text me pics tomorrow. And we'll celebrate cocktail hour once you're back to normal."

Five more days, buddy. Five more days.

# MONDAY

# CHAPTER 23
## VIOLET

Is it weird that yesterday was one of the best days I've had in months? I'm not me, which would be the simplest way to explain it. Except I am, regardless of the packaging.

No pun intended.

Ben's go-with-the-flow nature is why I had fun. Not just because I peed in public, although I can't help but grin at how stupidly pleasurable it was.

Eating breakfast with him was partly why my outlook for the day changed. Conversations with him might never lead to where I expect, but I'm more than willing to follow him. He's funny and empathetic. While shreds of my general distrust of men have surfaced, he has given me every reason to trust him. And he's...

I grip my skull. Damn it. If I didn't know better, I'd suspect I was crushing on him. Which I'm not. How can I have a crush on a person who is part me?

Things could enter wack territory fast. Whatever I feel for him does not in any way encompass a physical attraction. It can't. Either way I look at it, there I am.

*La, la, la.* I stick my fingers in my ears and sing nonsense syllables to clear my brain. No way can I dwell on such nonsense while I spend the day with him today. I assign myself a single job for the rest of the week: be a eunuch when we're together. Hormonally speaking, that is.

*Ben, your family jewels are safe with me, I promise!*

I—and all his important parts—arrive in front of my apartment's gate on Monday morning at seven forty-five. I haven't been home since Friday night, but it seems like it has been longer. Nothing has changed. The street is quiet because of the holiday but otherwise normal, which makes sense. I'm the one who has crammed an entire, surreal experience into the past sixty hours and brought it home, hidden underneath wrapping none of my neighbors would recognize.

I stare at the welcome mat, waiting for him after I ring the bell. On the first morning, we each woke according to our old bodies' habits, but I've since trained my new body to be an early riser. Ben must have taught mine a new trick, too. Judging from his expression when he opens the door, I'm pretty sure he had been fast asleep a minute ago.

"Oh, hey. Is it eight already?" He ushers me into…

I don't know whether to run or to investigate a potential crime scene in my living room. "What happened here?" I ask.

If Pottery Barn and Banana Republic had digestive systems and had to share a toilet during a round of gastric distress, this would be what the bowl would look like in the aftermath. Droppings of clothing and dishes infect every available surface.

"Oh, sorry. I meant to clean it yesterday, but Adam dropped by."

"Adam saw what you have done to my apartment?"

"Yeah. He didn't stay long."

"Go figure." My eyes twitch. "Wait. You met Adam? Oh, it's too early, and I have too much I need to accomplish for me to handle your news."

"I didn't spill our secret. He's a good guy. I approve."

"Approve of what?" The case of nerves jangling in my belly has switched from reminding me I'm entering a competition today to expecting the worst regarding Adam.

"The two of you." He scratches his head and bunches his left eye. "Or me as you."

"I'm not his type. You are." I point to myself. "But he's in a relationship. Oh, no. Oh, no. You didn't make a move on him, did you?"

Ben steps away from me. "Of course not. Everything was cool between us. He seemed a bit concerned about my housekeeping, but nothing else happened."

"He's my landlord. He and his boyfriend live upstairs. Hopefully, he won't evict me after witnessing the cockroach amusement park you've built in my apartment. We have bigger fish to fry. While you get dressed, I'll call a rideshare."

"Is the hot pink dress proper attire?"

My heart, ready to cannonball into my stomach, instead does a swan dive when he emphasizes his joke with a lift of his left eyebrow.

"You can't be seen wearing the same outfit twice in one weekend. Here, I'll pick out something for you."

The decor in my bedroom shouldn't surprise me, but it still delivers a punch to the gut. I'm a lot fonder of Ben in neater environments.

*They're just objects, Violet. None of this matters.*

I select a denim skirt and a sage-green sleeveless blouse. On second thought, I'd rather not have my bandage on display. I hand him a navy blouse with three-quarter sleeves. He'll be hot, but the competition crowd runs conservative. "Once you're decent, I'll fix your hair. You'll be happier with it in a ponytail today. Meet me in the living room."

It takes every bit of willpower to keep my focus on my punch list instead of detouring into clean-up mode. I pull the backdrop from the closet and unhinge it a couple of inches. Looks like Ol' Blue Eyes is now Ol' Blue Eye. No biggie. I have a bag of blue sequins at the ready. I set the panels by the front door and go to retrieve the box with the rest of my supplies.

I bend to slide it, expecting to tug it from the closet inch by inch. Instead, I careen into the wall behind me from the force I exert exceeding the resistance. I pat my right biceps muscle appreciatively. Forgot about Ben's guns. I lift the box onto my shoulder and set it next to the front door.

Ben joins me in the living room, carrying a comb. "Do you need this?"

"A brush will be better." I lead him into the bathroom. It seems to be a thing with us. Provided he doesn't ask me to wash his undercarriage, I suppose I have no reason to worry.

I haven't done someone else's hair since high school. Braiding a friend's hair is a rite of passage and a bonding moment, but the practice from years ago is meaningless when I'm doing my own hair on the head of a man I may or may not have a bit of a thing for. The hand maneuvering the hairbrush wants to linger, but I rush the last strokes before I become embarrassingly dreamy during the process.

He remains quiet while I fix his hair. I love having my scalp touched. The shampoo is the best part of a haircut. I wonder if Ben's having any sort of reaction.

He jumps from the chair once I snap the elastic around the ponytail. "Thanks. I haven't figured out how to make it neat yet." His eyes don't meet mine, and his energy level has increased tenfold.

I take a stutter step away from him, wondering what I might have unleashed.

# CHAPTER 24
## BEN

The sensation of Violet gently tugging on my hair and the way she'd follow each brushstroke with a pat of her hand against my scalp sent shivers all the way to my toes. I doubt it was the same for her, especially considering that she had walked into the apartment pissed at me because I had overslept and trashed the place.

She stares at her phone while I shove a protein bar in my mouth, proving her disinterest in the inappropriate thoughts I had entertained during the hair brushing.

She looks at me. "Our driver's here."

"How can I help?"

"Why don't you take the backdrop? Unless it's too heavy?"

Too heavy? I had meant to offer to carry the box. "It's nothing."

I stretch my arms to the far edge of the boards. My fingers barely wrap around. It requires the same wimpy, two-handed maneuver I used to drag it from the closet yesterday. I can't see the steps with the backdrop in front of me, and my knees keep banging into it. This would be a breeze if I were me.

Violet waits in the apartment until I reach the sidewalk and then strong-arms the box onto her shoulder before running up the stairs. I can't help but smile with pride for my old body.

*Yup, still got it!*

She shoves the box into the trunk of our car and races back into the apartment. "I'll grab the braces for the backdrop, and we're good to go." She reemerges a couple of seconds later with a pair of legs made from two-by-fours and shaped into upside-down sevens.

"We good?" She nods, and I lock the door.

Holding the front passenger door for me, she asks, "You want to sit up front?"

The backseat doesn't leave much legroom, which means she won't fit here. The smallest member of a group always gets shoved into the worst spot in a car. While it's never me, I assume this is a familiar scenario for Violet. "The back's fine."

We take our seats and close the doors.

The driver turns toward Violet. "What's in the box?"

"Oh, I'm helping my friend. He, uh… Sorry. I haven't had my coffee yet. *She* is entering a competition where they have to set tables according to a theme. Formal settings, lots of decorations. I went… Violet and I attended it last year, and it was such fun."

I cough, ducking my shoulder to hide the finger I hold to my lips from our driver. Is she aware that she's talking like Violet, not me? I have never in my life said *such fun*. Sheesh!

She stares at me, furrowing her brow. "What?"

I mime at her, pointing to my mouth while moving it and then trace a womanly outline with my pointers. My performance does nothing to smooth her forehead. We'd make the world's worst Pictionary team.

She swivels forward again, ignoring me. "Anyway, Violet has spent months preparing for today. I'm rooting for her."

"You guys a couple?" the driver asks.

Violet chokes and slaps her hand across her lips. "Us? No! We're… We're cousins."

I can't say I'm the biggest fan of her vehement denial of us being a couple. Whatever. I cross my fingers, hoping tablescape competitions are swarming with hot chicks who dig women who are men.

I lean against the door and watch Jersey City blur outside the window. For every great moment I've experienced with Violet this weekend, there have been subtle—and not so subtle—reminders that she's stuck with me, a guy she thinks doesn't care whether he succeeds or fails.

Trust me, I'm an expert on the subject of subtle insinuations regarding my achievements or lack thereof. Twenty-six years of being my father's son has trained me to hear every kind of hint aimed at reminding me my efforts are worthless. Violet's lie to a man we'll never see again about who I am to her gives me the sense she wishes she weren't saddled with me today.

She probably expects me to goof off or make a mess of everything. I'm motivated to try hard to help her win. But something tells me whatever I do won't be good enough. This is why caring about results never pays off. It's safer to play it cool.

# CHAPTER 25
## VIOLET

B en lags behind me on the trip from the car to the tent in the park on the north of the Hoboken Terminal. I hoist the box onto my right shoulder and carry the backdrop's braces in my left hand. I can't tell whether he's struggling with the backdrop or avoiding me.

I am making good on my promise to put him out of my mind. Well, to put certain thoughts about him to the side, anyway. Which is why I said we were cousins, the relationship at the opposite side of the spectrum from a guy I might kinda like. Perhaps my lie offended him. I should have said we are coworkers. Or friends?

Focus on the competition, Violet.

My heart gallops upon entering the tent. I'm here! Velvet ropes ring eight rows of two card tables each. I wonder which table is mine. Before the swap, I had wished I'd be side by side with Tracey and Anja, but having to interact with Ben in front of them for a few hours? Yikes!

I march up to a woman with a clipboard. "Hi. I'm... Ben, Violet Pensky's assistant. She's right behind me." I turn, but don't spot him. "Hold on a sec."

I drop the box and braces next to the ropes and retrace my steps to find him. He rests at the foot of the stairs leading onto the lawn with the boards leaning against his legs. "Let me help," I say. "I wouldn't have made it this far in my own body."

Ben narrows his eyes and inhales. "This isn't right. I should be making things easier for you."

"Don't worry. You're a good man stuck inside a minuscule body. I know your heart is in the right place."

Which is the oddest thing to say, because his heart is beating inside the chest my consciousness wears. While I glance at him, his heart does something else, too. It spins slowly and sends caressing waves of tingles throughout my body. There might also be tosses of glitter involved.

I pick up the boards to retrain my focus. "Let's go check in." I lead him inside the tent and point to the woman with the clipboard. "You should take the lead. Introduce yourself, take any paperwork she has for you, and claim your table assignment."

"I'm getting a Dolores Umbridge vibe from her. No offense to her, but I've had my share of witches casting spells on me."

"Now that you point it out, I do, too. Someone should tell her to steer clear of pink suits."

After speaking with the proctor, Ben leads me to a table in row seven of the group. I bet they assign the prizewinners and contest regulars the prime spots in the front. Next year.

He wiggles the card table. "Can I say this is anticlimactic? I expected long wooden tables in a more formal setting."

"Thirty-four inches by thirty-four inches is standard. It doesn't leave much room between the table settings for decoration, which is part of the challenge. The judges pay equal attention to precision as to originality. A misplaced spoon or lack of uniform spacing between place settings would doom my entry regardless of the originality of the design."

The corners of his lips lift. "Yours will be the prettiest table here. I copped a peek at the thing I carried. I didn't know you were an artist."

"I'm not, but give me adhesives, a stack of pictures, and a place to put them, and I'm a happy camper."

"Too bad you don't get to use your skills at work."

"Agreed. I had applied to Heading Up in hopes of landing a position in communications where I could develop content—and maybe make the occasional poster, but I couldn't turn down the promotion into the sales department after Helen in HR offered it to me."

He squeezes his arms against his sides. "Maybe you'll have your chance one of these days. To be transparent, you should know I lack your talents in the crafting department. I can draw okay, but I suspect I'll be out of my element today. Does that make you regret having me assist you?"

"What? Why would you ask such a question? It will be fun, so long as you don't mind me being bossy. Just remember I'm directing my drill sergeant routine at me; it's not a response to you, okay?"

He relaxes his stance. "Of course. Did you become better acquainted with me yesterday after I left?" His eyebrows put a bit of emphasis on his question.

"I avoided an intimate introduction, if that's what you meant. Although you did enjoy a free-range pee on the banks of the Hudson yesterday."

He breaks into a wide grin. "Violet Pensky, you aren't the woman I pegged you to be. Well done!"

"Thank you. And apologies for any photographic evidence of the incident. A few people on the ferry might have spotted you."

"Don't sweat it. It was for a good cause."

I lean against the table, which can't take my weight. Ben and I grab it before it tumbles. "That's one way to get eliminated." The word eliminated reminds me of my pledge to quit my job. "What would you do if you had the choice?" I ask.

"You mean, how would I get you eliminated?"

"Sorry, I jumped back to our previous conversation. I meant what would you do if you didn't work at Heading Up?"

"Can't say. It's an okay job, right?"

"Eh. I haven't determined whether sales is right for me, but I'd hate to give up on the job before I figure out whether I'm any good at it."

Ben's smile pushes a dimple into my cheek. I've forgotten I had a dimple. "I have a premonition I might enjoy my job a bit more now that we've become friends."

His response startles me, and I ram backward into the table, sending it crashing to the floor. My clumsiness is in my favor, though, because it masks the chugging sound of my heart racing with happiness to learn Ben considers me a friend.

I hoist the table onto its legs, becoming aware of a pair of eyes boring into me. Tracey has her arms crossed on her chest and her eyes squinted. Anja is stifling a giggle. I nudge Ben and gesture to my friends with my head.

He turns around. "Oh, good. You guys made it. You had me worried."

Tracey says, "I could say the same thing. We're not the ones knocking over tables. I thought you said you didn't need an assistant."

"Oh, right. Him. Yeah, I inherited one of Ben's old accounts on Friday, and today was the best day for us to discuss it. Might be my lucky break because I bet he has a hidden talent for tablescapes."

Anja wraps her arm around Ben's shoulder. "Who does the lady in charge remind me of?"

I answer for him. "Dolores Umbridge?"

"Exactly! Thanks. She's totally a witch, because we're up by the front. I asked her to switch us to be next to you, but 'We do not make unnecessary changes on competition day.'" She alters her voice into a boomy, stern admonition.

Ben straightens his back. "Speak of the devil, she's staring straight at us. You'd better take your places before she turns you into a teacup."

Anja kisses the top of my head—well, the head she identifies as mine— and drags Tracey to their table.

I check my phone. "It's almost nine o'clock. The contest is about to begin."

# CHAPTER 26
## BEN

Violet, which is to say, her in my body, could not be more out of place in the tent than were she a hippopotamus dancing the tango. Except for us and her friends, the rest of the contestants are decades older than us. Two of the participants are male, but their hands appear more adept than either of ours at fussing around with tiny sequins and feathers. Violet and I make a pair, what with her frustrated attempts to line everything up just so using my sausage-like digits and me, blessed with spindly fingers, unsure of what to do or why I'm even doing it.

She hands me the bag of blue sequins, huffing like a chain-smoker. "Here. I can't grab hold of a sequin. Could you perform eye surgery on Mr. Sinatra?"

"Sure." Fitting, since I poked it out in the first place.

I do a better job of gluing my fingers together, which hurts, by the way, than of affixing a sequin to his face. They ain't fooling by calling it hot glue. Once Frank has two blue eyes (and I have adhered three sequins to places I'm not willing to mention), I reach for the folded tablecloth Violet sets on the card table.

She slides it away from me. "No way you're touching anything until your fingers are clean."

"How can I wash them? There isn't a sink in here." I stare at the graying patches of peeling glue on my fingertips.

She grabs my hand and scratches the tip of my thumb, scraping away flakes of glue.

A woman at the table next to us smiles when she catches my eye, which I had been rolling in response to the indignity of being groomed by a man. "You two are the cutest. How long have you been together?"

Violet says, "Um—"

I interrupt her, not wanting to hear the cousins story again. "Three years. We met at the Hi-Seas habitat in Hawaii."

Violet ratchets her chin to the left, fixing her stare on me throughout the rotation.

"Oh, you're marine biologists?" the woman asks.

I shake my head. "No. We met at a Mars simulation. Ben worked in the command center, communicating with the crew."

Violet does that same smile thing she did in the mirror yesterday, starting it in her eyes and opening her lips before she's ready to speak. She has my attention. "Yes, I did. I could go home every night, unlike the participants in the study. Now, Violet, she was part of the crew who lived out there in…"

"Mauna Loa. I was stuck in the middle of nowhere for a year, dealing with the rocks."

Our new friend nods, impressed. "Ah, you're a geologist."

Violet cuts in. "No, custodian. She raked the grounds daily. It was the only job left. She had applied for the program as a mime—did you know universities in Europe offer degrees in mime? Violet spent two years studying to be a mime in Belgium."

"Mimeology is the exact field of study." I rest my hand on her upper arm. "But honey, you know what a disappointment it was for me to have my application rejected. I haven't been able to mime my way out of a box ever since."

Violet presses her hand to her mouth to prevent herself from laughing. "My bad. I should know better than to mention it." She pivots toward our neighbor. "Can you imagine dating someone for three years and never witnessing their truest gift? We've been in couples' counseling to overcome the issue. Violet had a breakthrough just last week. She waved goodbye to me." Violet runs the knuckle of her pointer under her eye, proving her prodigious gifts in the art of mimeology as she wipes away pretend tears.

I close my fingers into my palm and stare intently at them. "It's no use. I've forgotten how to do it."

"You open your fingers and then close them." Violet's hand mimics her words.

I turn my back on her. "How *dare* you flaunt your abilities! Dr. Flintstone warned you it is my trigger."

Our friend from the next table wrings her hands. "Oh, I seem to have stepped in it, haven't I? Don't let me intrude in your private affairs. Well, good luck with your display and your miming." She busies herself with her table settings, pretending she didn't witness the spontaneous combustion of a fake couple.

I meet Violet's eyes and nearly lose it. "Mime? You took it *out*."

"I followed your lead. What's with the Mars simulation?"

"Ah, I read about it last night. I'd be an okay guy to be stuck with for years in a spaceship, right?"

"From the point of view of a person whose life is currently fused to yours, I'd have to agree." She sucks on her bottom lip and lowers her gaze.

Huh. That was interesting.

# CHAPTER 27
## VIOLET

Between being antsy about the competition and my anger at the state of my apartment, I had been tense all morning. With one silly improv prompt, Ben has eased me out of my head. In a roundabout way, I'm glad he's assisting me today.

I return to setting my table with renewed vigor. "Since our boy Frankie has two working eyes, we can put the backdrop aside." I tuck it under the table and hand Ben the printed instructions for setting the table.

His face crumples. "No offense, but do you really need schematics to understand the placement of a couple of plates and glasses?"

In my head, he has shouted his words of sacrilege for all to hear. I spin around, expecting to witness the horrified expressions of my peers. They continue their labors, unaware. "Shh! You're me, remember? Tablescapes are your passion. We have to keep up the appearance that you know what you're doing. I'm just here to help."

"And to impress the judges. I've noticed Professor Umbridge taking the occasional appreciative glance at you."

"If you meant it to be a compliment, it failed. I bear no responsibility for the man meat upon which she feasts."

His eyes sparkle, instantly making me regret my choice of words. "So, you think I'm tasty?" he asks.

"You've twisted my words. I was just pointing out how she can't keep her eyes off of you, as in your body with me in it."

He holds his right hand behind his head, juts his hip to the side, and places his left hand on his other hip in a pinup model pose. "I'm sure she finds me nearly as irresistible as you."

"Oh, stop it, would you? I have no idea who is who in this scenario, and I'm not the least bit interested in solving the puzzle."

My head swims in the aftermath of our exchange. It mortifies me to have blurted out my stupid *man meat* comment. He must have assumed—correctly—that I've done more than my share of posing in front of the mirror lately and enjoying the view more than I care to admit to either of us. And what's with him advertising his wares? Is he teasing me or admitting he might like what he sees in the mirror, too?

I tap a rhythmic pattern against my thigh to derail my train of thought. "We have a little over an hour left to ensure every detail is perfect. The judges will look for fingerprints or lack of symmetry between each element on the table. A smudge or mislaid knife, and I won't win."

"I've never mislaid anyone. Every customer leaves satisfied."

One minute, his easygoing nature saves me from myself and the next, he has my guts wrapped around my spinal cord in a death spiral. "Keep it in your pants. I don't want to boss you around, but I need you to maintain your focus and commitment to being Violet while I instruct you on what to do."

"Yes, sir. Right away, sir."

I'm ready to throttle him. Which isn't fair. He doesn't have to be here; he's doing me a favor. I pull a pair of white cotton gloves from the box. "You'll be in charge of laying out the dishes and silverware, which means you need to wear the gloves to keep the smudging to a minimum. We need three settings; the backdrop goes against the fourth side. Unwrap the dishes and place them according to the sheet. Same for the silverware. I'll focus on the centerpieces. But first, the tablecloth."

I unfold the Egyptian-blue velvet square and drape it on the table. Many of my favorite costumes from *Downton Abbey* are blue, which made choosing my palette easy. Lady Mary's coat is the inspiration for my table. Made of a similar shade of blue velvet to my tablecloth, it has a taupe fur collar and cuffs and gets buttoned at the side with two large, flat silver discs. No animals had to suffer for my art. My napkins are taupe linen, not fur.

I unspool my tape measure and assure the drape on each side of the table hangs ten inches below the edge. Ben pinches a corner. "You'd kill me if I tugged on the tablecloth, right?"

"Eventually. But not until you've endured eleven hours of torture. It starts with this." I pull an ostrich feather from the box.

His eyebrows dance. "I do approve of a bit of feather play."

"Oh, the feather is not for tickling. I will thread it into your left nostril. You don't want to know what goes in the right."

"You can't tease a girl and retreat. Give me something more vivid to imagine while I'm wearing your ridiculous pair of gloves."

I spike my left eyebrow. "Funny you mentioned gloves. I will insert the pointer finger of your glove into your right nostril."

"Like this?" He threatens to contaminate the only pair of gloves I've brought with me.

"You can pick your friends... No, nothing so simple. First, I shall fill the finger with, let's see... Tuna."

He wrinkles his nose and bobbles his head. "Not enough of a deterrent. What else you got?"

"Three-week-old, sun-warmed tuna, seasoned with black pepper. I will tape the feather and glove in place, sealing your nose. Should make sneezing quite exquisite."

He lets go of the tablecloth. "You savored devising a way to torture me more than the situation warranted. We might have to explore this topic in private."

"Dude, even in jest, our conversation might be slipping into awkward territory. Get back to work."

Stupid ostrich feather! Now I can't banish a different use for it from my head. And yes, it does involve Ben, once he's in his body.

I gently remove the serving stand from the box and unearth the fake morsels of food to display on it. Actual food and live flowers are both forbidden in the competition.

Ben holds a silver plate in front of him, catching his reflection in its surface. "Is having the judges stare at themselves part of your design? Could be an inspired plan if they're vain."

"No. We'll place a white plate on top of it."

"This is way too fancy for me."

"If I win, I'll prepare high tea for you one day. You have to experience it to appreciate it."

*Way to load on the pressure, Violet.*

"You'd better win, then." He unwraps a china plate. "Violet? This one's chipped. I swear I didn't break it."

I hold the plate and examine the bite taken out of its edge, probably a result of me banging it when I pulled it from the closet this morning. "I'm not blaming you. And don't worry. I've packed extras."

It's actually a relief to have an item chip. I had figured a broken plate or cup would mean good luck. I continue to stuff silk flowers and feathers into julep cups.

At ten-thirty, half an hour before we need to stop and ten minutes ahead of my own personal deadline for this stage, Ben and I have placed every item onto the table. With respect to the clean lines of the era, I've chosen basic white china with thin bands of silver ringing the edges. Buying the dishes might have stretched my budget more than I had meant, but at least I can use them after the competition.

I pull out my trusty tape measure again and find the center of each side of the table. "Would you follow me and make adjustments to anything out of alignment? This plate needs to slide one-quarter of an inch to the right."

"I have the impression I'm going to hate this part."

"Sorry. Each plate, cup, and piece of silverware has to be in an exact location to receive full points. Here, line up the silverware so the middle of the fork is on the twelve-inch marker and the knife is on the twenty-four."

I anchor the tape measure with my thumbs, and Ben presses into me to reach the knife. I mean to retract. A twinge of electricity shoots from my arm into my chest, and my body has no interest in moving away from him. Am I attracted to him, or is Ben's body operating on its own?

*Focus, Pensky!*

We repeat the measuring process on the second side and then the third. "Why don't you come around to my right? The teacup and saucer are out of place."

He reaches across my chest. "I can reach it from…"

The sickening sound of china cracking into a million pieces brings every pair of eyes in the tent to us. "Oh, I'm so sorry!" he says. "Do you have another teapot?"

# CHAPTER 28
## BEN

Violet's face folds and quivers. "No. I brought only the one."

I step away from the table. Dammit! I can't believe I've ruined everything for her. "What can I do? Can I buy a replacement?"

I watch her eyes—my eyes—calculate the situation. My face has never contorted with rage or frustration in the ways she's moving it now. It reminds me of the sore muscles I inherited from her a few days ago. She cares about everything with such intensity and wears her concern deep within her bones.

I wait for her to speak, but she remains silent, shaking her head in movements slighter than the adjustments I had made to the placement of the silverware.

I may be to blame for the state of things, but I might also be able to influence the way she deals with it. "You're more than welcome to call me names, stick the tuna finger up my nose, whatever it takes to make me suffer. I deserve all that and more. Why don't I buy a few bottles of wine and arrange them and myself as drunken props? I could surround myself with empty bottles and slump over the table with my right hand extended toward the broken teapot."

She bites back a smile. "You have an artistic bent. But no. The missing teapot will cost me only a couple of points. Provided the rest of the details are perfect, it won't matter. You sweep up the mess—they have brooms and dustpans at the ready for exactly this kind of emergency—and I'll erect the backdrop."

"Glad to hear Little Ben is unfazed by the disaster."

Her eyes narrow and flicker. Slowly, she widens them and groans. "Oh. I said erect. Please tell me you don't call your favorite bit of anatomy Little Ben."

"Not until today. And I take back the Little part of its nickname. I miss Big Ben. I'm not sure you can understand the trauma involved in losing him for a week."

"He's not lost. I promise I've kept him safe. End of conversation." She points to the broom resting against a large trashcan.

The stress of having ruined her table evaporates. Being able to distract her from unhappiness with a joke or two— even at my expense—fills me with a sense of power, a power I only want to use for good.

While I'm bending over to pick up the dustpan next to the broom, someone calls Violet's name. I turn toward Violet, which is dumb, before I search for the source of the voice.

Her friends' table is on the other side of the rope from the garbage can. "Oh, hey, you guys. How's it going?"

Tracey cocks her head. "Apparently, better than for you. Let me guess: your new best friend broke a plate."

"Ah, no. This is on me. I pushed the teapot off the table while I was measuring the distance between the knife and spoon."

Anja lifts the teapot from their table. "Since there's no way we're going to win, take ours. It's okay with you, Tracey, right?"

Tracey reaches to take the white teapot from her friend before passing it to me. "More than okay. We're rooting for you, honey. Make us proud!"

I drop the broom and dustpan to accept the gift. Had you asked me yesterday, I would have said all white teapots are alike. But the one I hold is short and kind of tubby, whereas the one I broke was taller and thinner. And it had accents of silver on its handle and spout. Theirs won't match Violet's china.

"You're the best! But I can't take your teapot. Your table is so pretty, and I bet you have a better chance of winning than me." I hand the teapot to Tracey. "Thank you, though! I'd better get back to Ben before he thinks I've abandoned him."

Broom in hand, I remove the evidence of my clumsiness. Violet had unfolded her boards and attached the wooden braces to the back in my absence. She'd probably fire me on the spot were I to mention it, but the image of it looming over her table reminds me of the fancy movie-themed slot machines in Atlantic City. But in a good way.

I stand next to her. "I snuck a peek at a few of the tables. Except for your friends, nobody else has come even close to matching your design. White tablecloths? Flowers on the cups? What is this, amateur hour? Yours is definitely the best."

"I'm glad you liked Tracey and Anja's design. Theirs is beautiful and classic. As for our design, don't call it mine. You have to pretend it is your table. In case anyone asks, tell them Lady Mary's coat was the inspiration behind your design."

"I might have a chance to practice. Professor Umbridge is making a beeline for us."

The scary judge holds her clipboard at a severe angle. "Miss Pensky, the regulations specifically forbid contestants from using the likenesses of characters from Downton Abbey in their settings. Please remove your backdrop immediately."

I fidget with my hands, because that's Violet's tell for when she's upset. "I apologize. In my excitement, I must have misread the instructions. I'll remove it right away."

"Thank you. Carry on."

I wait for her to clear the velvet rope barrier before turning to Violet. "Thank you. Carry on," I say in a snooty, nasal voice.

Violet isn't in the mood to laugh. "I might as well pack everything up. I'm not going to win."

"Yeah, that's exactly what you should do. I'm sure you've hated every second of planning your design and shopping for all the doodads. Wouldn't be right to enjoy an activity without achieving your goals. You're in it to win it. Anything less, and the effort isn't worth it, is it?"

Her mouth bunches up, and she avoids my eyes. She exhales and faces me. "Fine. I see your point. It's my first tablescape competition. It's presumptuous to expect to win. And I had fun preparing for it." She tilts her head to study the completed project. "It looks okay, doesn't it?"

"More than okay. You have a talent. True, I didn't know setting a table was a talent, but I stand corrected. I'm glad I could be here to help you. And break a few dishes while I was at it."

Our pal Dolores climbs onto a step stool at the front of the tent and speaks into a megaphone. "Ladies and gents, time's up. Please step away from your tables and exit the tent."

Violet hands me the empty box before lifting the backdrop. "I should chuck this thing. It's such a pain in the neck to carry."

"Nooo! Not Ol' Blue Eyes! Can I keep him as a souvenir? I promise I'll do a better job of escorting him home."

"I never knew you were a Sinatra fan. You're more than welcome to him. We'll stash him with the box in the back."

"Thanks. What's next?"

"We have a two-hour break while they judge the tables. Lunch is a definite priority."

"With your friends?"

She holds her breath and studies the ceiling of the tent. "We'd be courting trouble to eat with them." She faces me with a slight smile. "I'm happy to hang out with you, unless you need a break from me." She grows more serious and steps away from me.

It's my turn to grin. "Lunch it is."

# CHAPTER 29
## VIOLET

I can't make sense of the last few hours. Violet from Friday morning would regard having her apartment trashed by a near stranger an insult, the destruction of teapot by said near stranger to be unforgivable, and her failure to review the regulations before pouring her heart into the backdrop to be an unrecoverable offense. But this Violet? The second I let go of expecting to win, I can take pride in what I've accomplished and appreciate the fun I've had along the way. The best parts of the day—joking with Ben, especially—carry more weight, and my mood reflects the pivot in my perspective.

On our way to the storage area at the back of the tent, I glimpse at my competitors' designs. Several tables are clones of each other, little more than fussy china patterns on white tablecloths with basic centerpieces and menu cards. I'm proud of the direction I took.

We drop off Sinatra and the box and reverse course. I continue to assess my competitors on our way out of the tent. A table in the first row is clearly a contender for best in show. Her backdrop resembles a pair of French doors overlooking the rolling hills of Downton Abbey. Blue velvet curtains with silver trim and ties frame the scene. While her tablecloth is white, a foot-wide satin cloth the same shade of blue as the curtains stretches across the table, lying under two place settings. She uses the space where I had placed a third setting to display the menu card and small bouquets that coordinate with the tall arrangement of tea roses in a slender silver vase. The impact of the elements is dramatic, yet cohesive, and the table teaches me everything about marrying creativity with the precision of tablescapes.

"What do you think of this table?" I ask Ben.

"Fine, I suppose, if you believe a tea party requires a teapot and a strict adherence to the rules. I'll take your table over hers any day."

A band of warmth wraps around me. "My guess is you're buttering me up so I'll buy you lunch. The protein bar this morning wasn't enough, was it?"

His hand presses against his belly. A phantom set of nerve endings in mine respond with a flutter. "Yeah, I'm ready for some grub. Gotta feed the beast."

"We have two hours before they'll let us back into the tent. You up for checking out the food trucks at Pier 13? They're about a mile away."

"Lead the way."

"Oh, we have to check in with Anja and Tracey. They're waiting for us by the door. Ditch them gently. Say we didn't finish discussing your new client."

I don't know what I would say to them under normal circumstances if I was planning to blow them off. I hate having to avoid them, but we don't have a choice. We approach my friends, and I stand behind Ben, holding my breath.

Anja glances at me a little too pointedly for my taste. "You guys want to have lunch with us?"

Ben's shoulders rise. "You're going to kill me, but between broken teapots and banished backdrops, Ben and

I never wound up discussing my new client. We need to have a working lunch."

"What's this about your backdrop?" Tracey asks.

"I missed the part in the rules where you can't have the cast of…" His eyes spin.

I butt in. "*Downton Abbey*. You weren't kidding when you said they were dead to you."

He breathes a sigh of relief. "They and Marcel Marceau. So, the rules stated we couldn't use pictures from the show in our decorations. I missed it somehow. Umbridge enjoyed reminding me my backdrop violated policy way more than she should have. She's canceled, too."

Tracey's jaw drops. "No! They disqualified your gorgeous backdrop? Let me at her." She holds her fists to her chest.

Anja grimaces. "Seriously. I would have said something to you ages ago had I known you couldn't have pictures of the cast. Oh, Violet!" She pulls Ben into her chest.

He breaks free from her hug and says, "Who cares? We had fun. Right, Ben?"

I nod stiffly, gleaning the reason Tracey has narrowed her eyes before she says a word.

"You're acting weird. Not as weird as Saturday night, but I swear I don't recognize you anymore. Since when would making a mistake not bother you?"

Ben's eyes dart toward mine. I tap my watch. He says, "I'm trying to lighten up a bit. That said, I'm kind of freaking out over my new client. See? I'm still me. No need to worry. I'm sorry we can't hang with you guys, but we have to keep moving. We'll meet up again after lunch."

We say goodbye to my friends and walk north along the Hudson River. The day is overcast, and the breeze from the river cuts through the humidity. I've walked this stretch of Hoboken on my own my entire life. With Ben by my side, my pace slows. His presence colors the experience. While I've never lost sight of the view of the river and Manhattan on my solo walks, my habit is to focus my energy inward, losing myself in my thoughts. Ben pulls me into my surroundings and out of my head. And pushes me back into it whenever my skin prickles because I'm next to him.

He nudges me with his elbow. "Wanna talk about it?"

I take a stutter step away from him. "Talk about what?"

"The one-two punch I and good ol' Dolores delivered to you. Unlike what I said to your friends, you're bummed, right?"

"No, not really. I guess entering the contest only because I wanted to win isn't enough of a reason to do it. I love crafting, and I enjoyed turning my ideas into my tablescape. No witch and her stupid rules can take the experience away from me. And don't sweat the teapot. I was in your way, so I'm also to blame."

"Yeah, you and my hulking body. Sorry my fingers were no good to you."

"I'm sure they do some things very well."

He tweaks his eyebrows. "That's what she said."

I gently backhand him and glower.

He clutches his shoulder, the site of my blow. "Ow! I'm more delicate than a teapot. And the optics of a man slapping a woman ain't good."

It stuns me for a second to need him to point it out to me. "Whoops. I keep forgetting who I am."

"Me, too, which is silly, because a single week in another person's body couldn't possibly change who I am. I have over two-and-a-half decades of experience of living in my actual body."

"Still, do you wonder whether you'll change, even a little, by living my life?"

He carries on a conversation in his head before turning toward me. "Nope. You?"

I rub my finger over a sharp edge on my thumbnail. Any hope I held of discussing the influence of certain external forces—namely, spending time with him—might have on me fades. "Nah. Funny, though. I walked into the tattoo shop on Friday because I wanted to change. Like a tattoo would accomplish something I couldn't do on my own."

He stops, concern in his eyes. "What did you want to change?"

"Oh, mostly how I handle myself at work. I can't let things continue the way they are. At first, I wanted Derek to see me differently. But I can't change him; I can only change myself. I hoped a tattoo would remind me to be tougher, and he'd notice the change. It's stupid."

"Derek is stupid. Who cares what he thinks?"

"I care. I'll never succeed without him accepting me as a part of the team. But I shouldn't hold my breath. I might need to find another job soon." I continue walking.

Ben runs to catch up to me. "Don't quit. I'd miss you." He bites his lower lip and gazes at me from the corners of his eyes.

I shush my racing heart. We have so little history to support what he said to me. "You wouldn't have noticed my absence had I quit a week ago."

"I would have. But it's not a week ago. We weren't friends."

Ah, friends. That's what we've become. For some crazy reason, I had started to attach a bigger meaning to whatever positive has transpired between us over the last few days.

I loosen my shoulders. "I'd miss you, too. Ooh, the falafel truck is here. C'mon. I'm starving."

# CHAPTER 30
## BEN

I shouldn't have lied to Violet. *One week spent living her life won't change me.* Yeah, right. Three days of being her has me discombobulated. All her body teaches me is she's short and not as strong as me. And that she has tantalizing bits and pieces she has declared off limits to my mitts. Being her in and of itself doesn't impact me; the transformation comes from taking the sum of her conversations and expressions and internalizing them. It packs a bigger wallop than magical tattoo ink.

Is it because hearing her speak through my voice or gauging her emotions as conveyed by my face makes me listen more closely to her than I did when she was one hundred percent Violet? I would have expected the opposite to be true since I'm the last person who'd take me seriously. Somehow, she puts the brakes on my old habits.

I hate how hard she is on herself and am quick to remind her not to care so deeply, yet going along on the ride with her reminds me the value of taking pride in what I do. A grown man shouldn't discard clothing and dirty dishes, pretending they'll disappear once he has no need for them.

The website for my apartment building boasts of being a showcase for modern design. The way I treat my unit, it's a showcase for nothing fancier than a rat circus.

We reach the pier, giving me a chance to silence the voices in my head. "What would you eat if you were me?" I ask.

"I am you. Oh, this makes my head hurt. Violet 1.0 is a fan of the falafel sandwich. How about me or you or whoever's appetite I'm sating?"

"Empanadas? No, forget it. Not for an early lunch. Don't want it repeating on you later. Chinese is a safe bet. Here, let me order for you, and you order for me."

I jog to the Chinese food cart and wait in line, doubting myself for wanting the beef and broccoli. I bet Violet would order something more interesting, like the pork buns. No reason not to get them. True, I won't be eating them. Why do I think it has to revolve around me?

But it does in a way. Violet's right; thinking about who I am hurts my brain.

I grow antsy while waiting for the chef to call my name. Violet paces off to the side of her truck, reading texts. I'm sure she's not entertaining deep thoughts about me. I should take her lead and not dwell on how being apart from her for even ten minutes leaves me with an achy sense of emptiness.

Finally, they call my name. The pork buns smell amazing, and my stomach growls while I carry the pair of crinkly white paper-wrapped treats to where she's waiting for me. "What's your position on these?" I ask.

"Oh, fine choice. I'm kind of wishing I had... Wait a second. They're for me! Here's your falafel sandwich." She's quick to grab the pork buns from me.

My hands find it tricky to manage the overflowing pita she offers me.

"Do you mind eating and walking?" she asks. "I want to make it back to the tent by one to see the judges' results."

I agree, but within a block, I regret every instance where I had asked a woman of Violet's stature to do the same. I struggle to hold the messy sandwich with two hands. Plus, I have to take small bites to accommodate a mouth no longer the size of the entrance to the Lincoln Tunnel. She has a bottle of water tucked into her back pocket. I had figured out at the truck I couldn't carry a beverage, and until I finish my sandwich, I will have to ignore my growing thirst. Shoot. I forgot napkins. Tahini sauce dribbles down my chin. I wipe my lips with the corner of the paper wrapper.

"Um…" Violet points to my chin.

I swat away a shred of lettuce. "Better?"

She bunches her mouth to the left. "Hold that thought." She pulls a napkin from her pocket and tentatively reaches for my face. "May I?"

"Be my guest."

I hold my breath while she dabs at first my chin and then the corner of my lips. The gesture could be either intimate or embarrassing. I choose to consider it the former.

"Thanks. How are the pork buns?" I ask.

"Delicious. And a little easier to manage. I shouldn't have foisted the pita on you. Since I enjoy falafel so much, I have a blind spot for their messiness. I've worn more than my fair share of them in the past. Here. Take my last bun, and I'll finish the falafel."

I feel tiny, unable to keep up with her or to eat my lunch like a person qualified to enter a competition that revolves around table etiquette, which messes with my brain. The truth is I like when she takes care of me, despite an inclination to believe it is my role to protect her.

I finish the last bite and toss the paper in the trashcan near the entrance of the tent. "That was delicious. Would you kill me if I returned your body fifteen pounds heavier because I ate all the pork buns?"

She wipes her hands with a napkin before opening the bottle of water. Offering it to me, she says, "Yes. Yes, I would."

I take a swig and hand it back to her. "Your friends are waiting for us by the tent."

She puffs her cheeks. "We can't ignore them. Apologize again for not having lunch with them but avoid entering into a lengthy conversation."

We approach the two women. My mouth speaks before I give it permission. "It's, like, totally wack. I'm the worst friend ever for ditching you, and I'm going to make it up to you, I promise." I can't explain why my voice has risen three octaves and I've adopted the accent of a fifteen-year-old surfer girl, but surfer girl seems to be the way I have to play it now.

Tracey places her hands on my shoulders. "We've already established you're not you. I don't know what your problem is…" She glances dismissively at Violet and then turns back to me. "You, me, and Anja need to have a talk. Preferably soon. We don't want you making any major decisions in your current state."

"I'm like, super busy, you know, but like totes, we could do something next weekend?" I flick my eyes up at Violet. She gives me a noncommittal shrug. I've probably blown it with the surfer chick speech.

Tracey sighs. "Today would be better, but I don't want to ruin your day. Ready to see how we did?"

Violet wraps her arm around my shoulder and faces her friends. "Yours and Violet's are the best tables in the competition. If the judges disagree, I'll unleash my opinions of them."

Her protector act is turning my insides to mush. Tracey, on the other hand, appears less than impressed. I suspect Violet's propensity to step in to help is a trait she shares with her two best friends. And it's an instinct they're not prepared to outsource to the man they think she is.

My friends are definitely less attuned to my disappearance this weekend than hers. Being cut off from my normal life has this way of intensifying the experience of connecting with her. Which makes me wonder what it would be like to have the help of someone who knows me well enough to coach me through a rough patch.

We drift away from her friends once we're inside the tent. Violet stops at the front table. A blue ribbon hangs from its backdrop. She says, "Yup. I knew it. This is the first-place winner." She jogs toward her table, slowing her pace before she reaches it. Stopping, she thrusts her chin toward it, reminding me it's my table, according to appearances.

Her table doesn't have a ribbon. I grab the white paper sitting on the tablecloth and hand it to her.

She scans it. "Forget it. Who cares about a stupid contest?"

I tug the sheet from her hand to read it. "The napkin is pointing the wrong way? How would they know? This is some serious BS. Dolores wants to torment you? Well, I have a magic trick for her. Watch me remove the tablecloth without disturbing the stuff on it."

Violet covers her mouth, holding in a laugh. Protecting each other works both ways. And if I can keep reminding her not to take defeat seriously, maybe she'll find her path forward.

# TUESDAY

# CHAPTER 31
## VIOLET

Ben stayed until five last night to help pack the decorations after the exhibit closed. I wonder if he's falling for me the same way I'm falling for him. Or am I projecting? If so, who am I projecting onto?

Romance hasn't been on my mind recently. My last relationship ended nine months ago, and work woes this summer have kept me from jumping back into the dating pool. I hadn't expected my last boyfriend to be The One. He's a friend of one of Tracey's coworkers. Nice guy, but we didn't click.

Now, Ben and I, we click. Perhaps it's impossible not to, given our bizarre circumstances. Regardless, I still believe we've made the choice to forge a bond.

I tried an experiment last night based on a piece I had read about a man and a woman—strangers—who, after asking and answering personal questions, stared into each other's eyes for four minutes. They fell in love and got married within months. The scientific explanation is human brains can sync during prolonged gazing.

For four minutes, I stared into Ben's eyes in the mirror. No surprise that our blinking pattern coordinated right

147

from the start. Nobody needs to explain mirrors to this genius. The longer I stared, though, the calmer I became. Of course, I was staring at myself, but taking everything I've learned about him and seeing it in his eyes still had a powerful effect on me.

I need to bring what I've gleaned about him into the office. Whether interacting with our team or meeting with the client, I can't pretend to be the slacker I used to think he was. He cares more than he lets on.

But what about us? I won't want to avoid him. I'm sure having him nearby could reduce the stresses of my job. Unfortunately, I bet nothing would give us away more than spending time together since we don't have a history of friendship within the office.

Ben and I never did discuss the hotel client over the weekend. I had wanted to yesterday, in theory, but our conversations took us to much more interesting places. What fun would asking him to fill me in on his new client have been compared to our imagined time at a Mars simulation site?

So, I'm going in cold. *Buckle up, Violet!*

I arrive at the office before nine on Tuesday. Out of habit, I walk into my cubicle, not his.

"Yo, Harris! You playing a prank on Pensky?" Peter pops his head through the doorway.

"I… ah… I need to borrow her stapler." I swipe mine from my desk and wave it at him.

"Don't stay in there too long. Wouldn't want her bad luck at making sales to rub off on you."

I pretend to laugh, brushing past him on my way to Ben's cubicle. Meanwhile, my stomach is a coiled cobra, ready to strike. The host of questions I wish I had asked Ben regarding his clients pales in comparison to the emotional briefing I should have offered him. I hope Derek, Peter, and Topher go easy on him this week. I'd hate for him to be on the receiving end of behaviors I've learned to ignore.

# CHAPTER 32
# BEN

Typical of any day of the workweek, my team members have formed a tight scrum around Derek's desk on Tuesday morning before I arrive. I saunter over to the crowd, scanning it for Violet, but I can't see anything except for the backs of the last row of my colleagues. Violet always stands here, which is odd because she's never late. Wouldn't she want to stand closer so she could see?

I move to the left flank. She's dead center in the front row, and I jump from a burst of adrenaline upon spotting her. A new scab sits on her jawbone, probably thanks to a worn-out razor blade. I can't verify the age of the razor I left for her to use. Her battle scars must be my fault.

Derek's yammering on about... Oh, crap. It's team building day.

Mid-spiel, he turns toward me for a second, a hostile glare training on me through narrowed lids. Shaking it off, he says to the group, "I'll assign new leads later in the day. Let's use Friday's rankings to form three teams of six. Ben, my man, you are exempt because of your meeting. Go prepare to rocket your sales to new heights."

Violet steps forward and scans the cluster of people from right to left. She smiles when her eyes meet mine. "Thanks, Derek. See you later." She walks to the left and stops next to me, squeezing my arm.

"Lucky you," I say in a whisper.

"I'm excited but scared. Anything about the client I should know?"

"I—"

Derek's face reddens. "Violet, you're gumming up the works again. Ben needs to keep moving."

Violet pivots. "Sorry, Derek. It's my fault. I'm the one who stopped to talk to Violet."

He laughs. "Yeah, right. Get lost, will you?"

I knew Violet would be away from the office for today, but I had hoped to talk to her before she left. Realizing I will be alone for a few hours chills my gut.

Derek says, "Now, where were we? Right. Teams. Sort yourself into three groups: For those whose rank from Friday is number one, four, ten, thirteen, sixteen, or nineteen, you're on Team A. Meet by the kitchen. Team B is two, five, eight, eleven, fourteen, and seventeen. You'll stay here. And Team C is numbers three, six, nine, twelve, and eighteen. Gather at the copier. Check the board; I've written who's on which team to the side. I'll meet with each team to explain the activity in a couple of minutes."

People are slow to break into groups, forcing me to wait until a path clears to let me approach the board to find out my ranking. The noise grows as coworkers celebrate being paired with their buddies. Nobody approaches me to express happiness for me being on their team. Which team would Violet want to be on? I've seen her have quick conversations with loads of people, but I'm not sure she has a specific office friend.

I don't, either. Sure, I get along with everyone. I'll join in on a group activity, but I don't make plans with anyone on the weekends. Everyone's fine, but no one is special. Not special in the way Violet has become. For the umpteenth time today, I wish I could hang with her instead of the rest of these fools.

The crowd thins, and I read the whiteboard behind Derek's desk. Violet came in twentieth place on Friday. I scan the three teams. Each has six people. Her name isn't on any list.

"Um, Derek?" Normally, I approach his desk without trepidation. Between my separation from Violet and Derek forgetting to assign me to a team, my shoulders slump, and my voice fights to produce a sound above a whimper.

"What is it, Pensky?"

"I'm not on a team."

"What do you mean you're not on a team? I made the lists. You blaming me because you can't find your own name on the list?"

My eyes flutter to the board, and I read the names a second time. "You said there are three teams of six, which makes eighteen team members, one through nineteen minus Ben. I ranked twentieth."

"Nobody besides you is to blame for your position at the bottom of the list."

"My rank isn't what concerns me; I'm asking you which team I'm on."

He swivels his chair toward the whiteboard. "Hmm. Someone must have erased it." Without looking at me, he spins back to his desk. "You're on team A. Hustle over to the kitchen, will you? I have a job to do."

All the muscles in my neck and shoulders seize, erasing the efforts I had put into easing Violet's tension over the weekend. Has Derek always treated her unkindly? If so, why hadn't I noticed? I had already pledged to do everything in my power to give her a boost this week. Thanks to our turd of a boss, my mission to carve out a place for her in the office has now taken on even more significance.

# CHAPTER 33
## VIOLET

I glance over at Derek's desk. Most of the group has disbanded, but Ben has stayed behind to talk to Derek. My stomach flops, imagining every demeaning interaction I've had with my boss.

*Quit worrying about him, Violet. Ben doesn't have your history.*

I log on to his computer. A mess of folders with indecipherable labels covers his entire desktop. Thankfully, "Christopher Jersey City" pops up when I type the hotel's name into the search bar. I rename its folder and open it to prep for my meeting. Besides the files with the specs on the building's elevators, it contains a note from Ben's initial conversation on Friday. *Alex Jiménez: sexy voice. Bring brochures.* And that's it.

Did he recommend specific services to her? What prompted her (and I have to guess Alex is female because Ben doesn't strike me as the sort to make a similar comment about a man with a voice like Chris Hemsworth's) to agree to meet with him? I wish he and I had spent the weekend discussing strategies to close the deal instead of flirting or whatever it was we were doing.

His body language while he speaks to Derek reminds me I hadn't prepared him for the reality of my existence at Heading Up, either. The nonsense I endure at work is hard to explain. I'm never sure if I encourage it or have misread a situation. It would have been as humiliating to confess to Ben how much I dislike Derek and my colleagues as it would be to describe how isolated I feel in the office. I hope Ben remembers to be Ben in the event they pull any kind of crap with him.

Since I have only a few minutes to familiarize myself with the hotel, I have to let him find his place on the team without my help while I plan my sales pitch. The hotel has six passenger elevators, two service elevators, and an escalator. They definitely need a contract with Heading Up. They might even have the budget to go for our complete package. I've yet to have sold our four-product suite to any clients.

Dreams of the big sale remind me of my swagger while walking—and relieving myself—along the Hudson River on Saturday. I need to march into the hotel operations manager's office and own my space. Not in a pushy way, but with Ben's sense of confidence and decency. Alex will find him irresistible.

Not that I'm speaking from experience or anything.

I pack the brochures in my bag and prepare to leave. No one has returned to their desks. One group remains at Derek's desk and another gathers by the copier, but I don't see Ben in either place. Oh, well. My last chance for him to offer me advice—or at least a dose of his calm confidence—recedes. I tug the hem of my jacket and head into the great unknown.

# CHAPTER 34
# BEN

I shake my hands, ridding myself of the momentary dose of insecurity Derek had laid on me. I know this guy; he's nothing special. He's never done wrong by me in the past, but every once in a while, I've wondered if he believed in every member of his team equally. My interactions with him earlier confirm what Violet has hinted at: he plays an outsized role in her success—or lack thereof—at Heading Up.

It lights a fire under me to change her luck, but her leads will have to wait until after this stupid team building exercise. I wander over to the kitchen. Peter is holding court as if he had been in the top three on the board. He wasn't. He was tenth.

He raises his eyes to meet mine and scowls. "You sure you're in the right place, Violet? Your name isn't on our list." He whispers something to Topher, and the two of them crack up.

Jerks.

I ignore them and approach Julie. "Hey, how was your weekend?"

At first, she reacts to my question with unpleasant confusion, like I've asked her to donate toenail clippings to my collection. "Oh, not bad. My fiancé and I interviewed a photographer and a florist. Wedding plans." She wrinkles her nose, but I can tell she loved every second of it. "How was yours?"

"It was good. Funny thing, though. I kept running into Ben over the weekend, first at a bar on Saturday and again in Hoboken yesterday. I was—"

Derek pushes me aside to walk into the center of our group. He lays a stack of paper, two rolls of tape, and a mess of pens on the break room table. "Right. For the next ninety minutes, you'll bond over shared memories. Spend fifteen minutes writing individual lists of work-related experiences at least one other person in the group shares with you. Once everyone has a list, I want you to draw the memories on separate sheets of paper. No words, just a scene or an abstract representation of whatever you wrote on your list. You have half an hour to unleash your inner artists. When you're done, stick 'em on the wall, but randomly, so your drawings aren't in the same cluster. Everyone can gather in front of each picture to try to recall the memory. If you do it the right way, you're supposed to have a collective, oh, you know, whatever the suits up on the eighth floor would say. You'll bond and stuff."

Peter cozies up to Derek. "What's the prize?"

"This isn't a 'top of the leaderboard' contest. No new phone or weekend getaways to Florida. But since you mentioned it, our floor stunk it up last month. Worst sales record of all the teams in the northeast. You guys pull lousy numbers again this month, and heads are going to roll. And by roll, I mean—" He makes a slashing motion at his throat and glares at me. "Got it?" The group nods. "Good. Now get remembering."

The idea of having to share memories already had me quaking in my shoes, but Derek's hint that Violet's job is on the line turns me into a basket case. I suppose it's small comfort I'm an okay artist. Instinctively, I look over my shoulder, half expecting to catch a glimpse of the tattoo I designed for my calf.

Julie turns toward me. "Ignore him. I was in last place on Thursday. We all land there occasionally. I'm grateful he didn't inflict a physical challenge on us today. Just my luck to be wearing a tight skirt and heels. I had envied you in your sensible suit and loafers in the event he'd force us to crawl around on the floor or something."

I'm not blind; her outfit had caught my attention. Julie dresses... I can't say it without sounding boorish. You notice her in her clothes. She has a few inches on Violet, strawberry-blond hair she keeps short and spiky around her face, and her clothing reminds all interested parties she has a rack on her. I count on at least one pig in our department drawing a memory picture of her chest; it's been a topic of conversation in our Tuesday drink club sessions. Hopefully, the miscreant won't be a member of our group.

I tug the hem of my gray jacket. Since I hit the snooze button two or seven times this morning, I had no time to decide what in Violet's closet besides her uninspiring pant-suits would be work-appropriate. I wonder whether Derek would change his opinion of Violet if she dressed like Julie.

With Derek gone, Peter resumes his role as de facto boss. "You heard the man. Everybody, grab sheets of paper and a pen."

Topher glances over at me, a tight smile stabbing at his cheeks. "I know what memory I want to share."

I ignore him and spend the first fifteen minutes staring at a blank piece of paper. Even were I representing myself, I doubt I'd have more than an idea or two. Whether any of the memories I conjure would be memories I share with Violet, I can't say. Best to pretend they are. I scribble four phrases on my paper before Peter commands us to draw our pictures.

My first memory is likely to appear on multiple pages. During a team-building activity last month involving large exercise balls, Derek sank into a deep squat to sit on a ball. His pants split right down the back.

I mean to sketch him in profile, modeled after Rodin's *The Thinker* and seated on a ball. The pencil doesn't get the message. Somehow, the hunch of the shoulders rises higher than his head. I don't understand it. My brain is doing all the thinking in Violet's body. Shouldn't it be able to tell my hand what to do?

You'd think, but despite my brain being a rank beginner at ballet, my limbs danced their way through class on Saturday. Still, I would expect a woman who can set a nice-looking table to be able to draw a human who didn't resemble something the cat left behind in the litter box.

I crumple the page and give it another try. The result might bear more of a resemblance to a lightbulb than Derek's ass, but it will have to do. I hack my way through three other sketches, pissed they don't come out any better. Is Violet speaking to me, demanding perfection? I have never cared about my performance whenever we've done these stupid exercises before, but today, I hold Violet's reputation in my hands.

I follow the crowd to tape my masterpieces onto the wall. Everyone keeps forgetting to pass me the tape. I wait around until they step aside. The only remaining spaces lie below the rows of pictures. At least they're within reach.

I drift toward the first picture on the left. Someone with better drawing skills has depicted Derek and his pants mishap. My team members gather in front of it, pushing me toward the entrance to the kitchen.

Peter taps on the page. "Who drew this?"

Ricardo raises his hand. "It's mine. Derek, man."

Everyone laughs, which relaxes me. I kind of hope every picture is of Derek doing something laughable.

They move to the right, and I squeeze in front of Ricardo. The drawing is of someone holding a microphone. Peter says, "You guys remember that night at the karaoke bar? Derek kept singing songs by chicks in a falsetto."

Julie shakes her head. "We're looking for collective memories. The Tuesday night men's club meetings exclude a couple of us." She nods at me.

Peter waves his hands frantically and points to me behind his palm.

I cough. "Relax. I know you go out on Tuesdays."

Topher, who is the biggest tool in the office, snickers. "Since you don't mind us reminiscing about what goes on behind your back, I suppose you won't object to the next picture."

The group moves to the right, and Peter cackles, bending in half from his laughing fit. Julie glances at it and stands between me and the wall to block my view. She catches my eye and shakes her head.

I keep my post at the entrance to the kitchen, waiting until the group moves on to the next picture. Slowly, I approach the third picture in the row. Someone drew a stick figure. Vertical lines on either side of the head serve as hair. She's holding a circle with dots on it in front of a pair of crudely drawn breasts. Above her head, a thought bubble reads, "Oh, Ben. I love you. Eat my cookies."

# CHAPTER 35
## VIOLET

While I walk to the hotel, Ben and Violet fight a turf war in my belly. I'm behaving like me, plotting my every move regarding the meeting within an inch of its life and encouraging my adrenal glands to join the fun. The Ben of it all reminds me he succeeds without trying.

The Christopher Jersey City is several stories taller than the hotel two blocks south, where Ben and I had our adventure on Saturday. It juts into the Hudson River on a pier, extending its footprint by more than a city block beyond its next-door neighbor. Its looming mass speaks directly to the nervous planner in me, emphasizing the importance of winning over Ben's new client. No pressure, right?

The doorman shuffles me over to the service entrance on the north side of the building. The security guard checks my ID and issues me a neon-green visitor bracelet. On the elevator ride to Alex Jiménez's office in the subbasement, I catch my first glimpse of the service records, studying the document posted above the control panel.

Ben's comment about my contact's sexy voice rings in my head. Would he enter her office the same way he'd approach a woman who smiles at him at a bar? I practice the eye-brightening, lips-parting, head slightly off-center move he taught me until the elevator deposits me in the subbasement.

I stride along the hallway, letting the beige walls with a neck-height forest green stripe pass in a blur. When I reach the operations manager's office, I knock on the doorframe and bestow upon her Ben's special grin.

"You must be Ben from Heading Up. Alex." She shoves her hand at me and grips it tighter than my real hand could endure.

Her eyes are a couple of inches below mine, and she must outweigh me—the Ben version of me—by fifty pounds. She's wearing a gray pantsuit with a French blue shirt. I could not be more grateful to be Ben at the moment, because in my Violet body and wardrobe, I would have been her mini-me.

"Have a seat." She gestures to a molded plastic chair in front of her desk.

I open my bag and extract the collection of sales brochures before sitting. "Would you like to have all of them now, or should I hand each to you as I walk you through our services?"

"That's quite a package. I can handle it all at once, though." She tweaks her eyebrows with a smirk.

My eyelids shoot open. Would Ben stoop to replying in kind? While the air in our office oozes with toxic masculinity, I assume he rises above it when speaking to clients. "Here you go." She reaches her hands across the desk. I clench my arms to my sides, barely able to push the stack toward her.

"Sorry if I made you uncomfortable with my joke. I must have judged you wrong during our conversation last week." She peers at my open bag. "Speaking of our conversation on Friday, I was expecting you to lead with biscotti."

"Biscotti?"

"You didn't, by chance, suffer a blow to the noggin over the weekend, did you? You don't seem to remember a thing we discussed except for the meeting time and location."

My good will toward Ben is on the decline. Was it too taxing for him to tell me to bring Alex biscotti and to be prepared for off-colored jokes?

"Forgive me for letting it slip my mind. I owe you one." Maybe I should take her lead on the humor front. "It will be so worth the wait, you'll beg for more." I lick my lips, lifting my right eyebrow suggestively to punctuate my statement.

Her face tightens, and she presses against the back of her chair. "Make this quick. You're keeping me from my job."

In an instant, I've lost her. She made it appear like fun, flirty banter was the way to pitch to her, yet the second I act the way I imagine Ben would, I fail.

I switch into Violet mode. "Absolutely. You've inherited a vast vertical transportation system, and with it, complex service agreements."

"I have no difficulty understanding the contracts. If you're implying a woman couldn't possibly decipher the gobbledygook contained within the documents, then we are done here."

I want to scream, "I understand. I am a woman, too!" Every approach I try with Alex is the wrong method. I don't know who she wants me to be.

"I'm sorry to have led you to believe I was disparaging your gender. Please allow me to explain myself. In my experience, elevator service companies often write contracts that shift the balance of power to their side. Heading Up advocates for the operations manager whose daily schedule involves a host of issues that extend well beyond the banks of elevators. And, as you familiarize yourself with our services, you'll recognize we take our role as your advocate to heart. We want you to spend less time and money on elevator maintenance while ensuring the safety of your guests. We're the good guys."

"Which is probably the same thing our service contractor said. Perhaps we need an elevator systems management team. You've opened a world of possibilities to me, Ben. I'll look through your materials, but I'm going to be honest with you; you haven't sold me on you. I need to do my research. One of your competitors might be a better fit. Thank you for your time." Alex rises and offers me her hand.

"Thank you for meeting with me. I'm reachable at any hour to answer your questions or take care of whatever needs may arise."

She quirks her mouth and gives her eyes a subtle roll. Oh, crap. She must think I came onto her. I hurriedly close the buckle on my bag and leave the office without making eye contact.

I've always blamed my work failures on Derek's lack of support and the abysmal leads he sends me. Given my failure today, I've proven I don't deserve better leads because I am utterly unsuited for a career in sales.

# CHAPTER 36
# BEN

Julie's head whips from me to the group on her right. She appears torn between where her loyalties lie. With a sharp inhale and a quick step toward me, she whispers in my ear, "I'd love to hear your take on the toxic work environment that Derek fosters. Hang behind after we finish our so-called team-building exercise, okay?"

Topher's picture is devastating. I couldn't be more grateful to be witnessing it in Violet's place. Julie is right to want to address the issue, but do I have the right to speak on Violet's behalf? I'm barely familiar with her experience in the office. On the other hand, I have perspectives on the workplace culture neither she nor Julie would have. My urge to protect Violet overrules my impulse to let her make a choice on the matter. "Okay."

I follow the group along the wall of shared memory pictures, pretending I'm fine taking one for the team. My drawing of Derek's split pants is one of seven on the subject. Funny how critical Topher, whose stick figures would rank below a kindergartner's, is of the artistic quality of my pictures. I hope his pants rip while he's guffawing at anything Violet-related.

At ten-thirty, Derek finally ends the session. Julie motions to me to meet her in the kitchen. I glance over my shoulder. No one is paying attention to me. I slip through the doorway. "Thanks for caring about what they did to me," I say.

"How could I not? I'm mad at myself for never discussing Derek with you. We only have a second, so let's get to it. I trust you don't drink with the guys on Tuesdays?"

"I didn't even know it was a thing until Ben mentioned it recently."

"I guess you two are friends?" She draws herself upward, as if surprised to hear me mention Ben a second time this morning.

"I'd say we're becoming friends."

"Nice. Did he mention what they talk about at the bar?"

I should be a font of information on the subject, except I've never previously paid attention to what any of it could mean. I also doubt I could plausibly put what I know into words Violet would share. "Stupid guy stuff, pissing contests and whatnot."

"I hope you mean figuratively."

"I do. Basically, everyone boasts about commissions. And sex. He said a couple of the guys are worse than most. You know. Topher, Peter…"

"Do we come up in their conversations?"

I take a deep breath. Neither woman gets a lot of attention, but what is said is nothing I would repeat to Julie. Or Violet. "Not really. I guess they say things about the women in the bar. They're jerks."

"Trust me: I've had my share of inappropriate comments made to my face. I have no intention of changing my wardrobe…" She eyes my suit. Her shoulders snap back. "I wear what I want to wear. It doesn't matter whether you dress conservatively; the culture isn't inclusive of women. Which leads me to one last question. Does Derek grant favors to his boys or give tips he wouldn't share with the whole team?"

I'm ready to punch myself for being an idiot who dismisses everything in life as unimportant. Just because I'm not interested in learning Derek's sales tips or kissing his ass in exchange for better leads doesn't mean I should ignore how he has stacked the deck against a few employees.

"If he's not inviting members of the team to go drinking with him or if he creates an environment hostile toward the women on the team designed to prevent them from joining him, he can't ethically offer opportunities only to the people he invites, can he? But I kind of get the impression he favors the guys who come out to drink with him." I fiddle with the hem of my jacket, not looking at Julie until I finish.

She thrusts her jaw forward. "I can't determine whether he's violating company policy, but it's worth exploring. I'm calling upstairs." She rips Topher's picture of me from the wall. "May I show the sketch to HR and tell them what you told me?"

My insides are burning and raw. I didn't sign up to fight the system. True, what I've learned this morning makes me want to hurt everyone who has hurt Violet. The surge of anger on her behalf surprises me. I'm lost as to what choice she would make. She has experienced Derek's and the team's behavior before. Why hasn't she reported it?

I scan Julie's face. Hints of rage flare behind her eyes, but the emotion shares space with compassion. Would Violet change her mind if she knew she had a friend in Julie? I bet she would. "Yeah, you can."

She wraps her arms around me and gives me a squeeze. "I wish I had talked to you earlier. But better late than never, right?"

"Right." I respond as Ben, not Violet. I hate myself for having ignored the problems of life under Derek's rule until now. And I hate that it took magical tattoo ink to lead me into my friendship with Violet even more.

# CHAPTER 37
## VIOLET

Earlier, I had hoped Ben and I would spend our lunch break together. Thanks to having to stumble through my meeting with his new client because he hadn't coached me beforehand, I lost my appetite. After I returned to the office, I falsely promised Derek I was well on my way to signing a contract with the hotel. He slapped my shoulders and reminded me the gang would be meeting at an Irish bar a few blocks away this evening.

I had my reasons to avoid Ben, but what excuse did he have for keeping me at arm's length all afternoon? He was skittish around me, not that our paths crossed often. I asked his advice on whether I should go drinking after work, which intensified his expression. After much internal deliberation, he gave me his blessing with the warning to be cool.

What the heck did he mean? It seemed like he had begun to understand me over the weekend. What's more, I thought we had become friends.

I enter the bar at five forty-five alone, having given the rest of the guys the slip rather than walking with them from the office. Since I had told Derek my meeting had gone well, I bet he's expecting me to be loud, animated, and full of myself, everything I am not. I stand inside the doorway of the bar, letting the noise wash over me. Maybe I should leave.

The door opens behind me, and I step to the side. Oh, no! It's Helen, my former boss and the head of HR.

She sweeps the gray streak in her otherwise black hair behind her ear while she scrutinizes me. I know I'm invisible under Ben's exterior, but when her eyes fix on mine, they jumble my guts.

"You're Ben Harris from Heading Up, aren't you?"

I relax my shoulders. "I am." I extend my hand.

"Helen Teague, human resources. I'm not sure we've spoken since your interview."

"You're probably right. I haven't been to the eighth floor since. It's nice to see you. Are you meeting someone?"

She purses her lips and gives her head a slow nod. "I'm here on a spy mission. Rumor has it you're a potential asset. You're a regular member of the sales team that drinks together on Tuesdays, aren't you?"

I grit my teeth. "I wouldn't call myself a regular, but I join them occasionally."

"Is the invitation extended to everyone on the team?"

"Uh… I don't think so? I can't say for sure."

"Do you recall Violet Pensky ever taking part?"

I scan the room for Derek, desperate to avoid continuing the conversation with Helen. Peter's laugh cuts through the din, and my eyes shoot to the back corner table. My coworkers are barely visible through the crowd. Even so, I turn my back toward them, blocking anyone's view of Helen and me.

She stares expectantly at me.

"Um, I'm pretty sure they've never asked Violet to come."

"Hmm. I'm also curious whether Derek ever imparts information after hours that benefits a select few. Would you say receiving an invitation to drink is advantageous to team members?"

"I can't say."

She nods. "I don't mean to put you on the spot. I'll sit by myself and enjoy a glass of wine. Should Derek say anything related to my questions, would you find me and share what you've heard?"

Would Ben rat out his boss? The version of him who has gradually sucked me into his orbit would feel compelled to do the right thing. But the guy who didn't prepare me for my meeting with Alex? He has probably never paid attention to the nonsense Derek pulls and encourages a few of the guys to imitate. He'd shy away from becoming involved.

I'd prefer to emulate the detached version of him. The last thing I need is to stir the pot. I'd also hate for Helen to regret helping me with my promotion into sales after discovering how miserable a place it is for me.

I trust no one at the company more than her. While I believe nothing good could come from having her investigate Derek's behaviors, should she have a reason to investigate him, I can't stand in her way.

"I'd be happy to," I finally say.

"Thank you, Ben. Find me at the end of the bar if you have news." She points to a well-hidden spot on the opposite side from Derek.

"Hopefully, Derek won't give me any reason to visit you."

"It would make my job a lot easier were that the case. Take care."

I approach the bartender and order a pint of ale. My stomach hops and flits, dreading having to face the gang. The last thing I needed was for Helen to increase the difficulty level of drinking with people I revile.

I bring my beer to their table, and everyone greets me with loud cheers. Derek and Peter slide their chairs apart and bring an empty one for me to sit in.

I lift my glass to them. "Thanks. Sorry I'm late."

"What are you doing, buying yourself a beer? Derek always takes care of us," Peter says.

"I was thirsty. Couldn't wait. Hey, Derek, sorry I couldn't close the contract today. My contact wants to spend a day or two reviewing my proposal. I guess since the follow-up paperwork took all afternoon and I didn't make any other sales, I'll be at the bottom of the rankings tomorrow."

Derek wallops my shoulder. "That's not how it works, Ben. When have I ever penalized you for having a down day? You know all of you here tonight are golden. Top ten for you every day of the week."

Excuse me?

I slick my hair back, buying myself recovery time. "I know, Derek, and I appreciate it. What I meant was I'll be sitting in the number ten slot."

"Give it a day. Land the hotel contract, and you'll be top sales for the floor this month. Oh, speaking of rankings, you'll never guess who's number eleven."

"Who?" I ask.

"Violet. Can't figure out what's gotten into her, but she closed on two small contracts today from the toilet list I had given her on Friday."

I want to leap for joy. I'm wrong to fault Ben for not helping me today, especially if he spends the week salvaging my career. Which means I had better persuade Alex to sign a contract as repayment for the favor.

"Cheers to Violet!" I chug my beer and slam the glass on the table.

"Watch your language," Peter says.

Derek takes a gulp of his beer. "Her success spoils my plans. I have a buddy I used to work with in the Morris County division of Heading Up. Funniest guy you'll ever meet. I hoped I could clear a space for him on the team by canning her. If she keeps pulling numbers like she did today, I might not be able to bring him to our team. Same thing happened last June. I recommended him for an opening on the team, but Helen gave us, well, you know who instead."

His plan all along was to fire me in order to bring in a friend whose job he thinks I stole? I'd rather quit than give him the chance to fire me. And I definitely don't want my name—Violet's name, that is—attached to any internal review.

I can't spend another second with these people. Leaning away from the table, I crane my neck toward the bar. I need to tell Helen I'm bailing. "I'm going to grab another pint. Anyone need anything?"

"Dude. Free beer, remember? Here, help yourself." Topher slides a pitcher toward me.

"By grab a pint, I mean get rid of the one I just chugged. I'll be back in a second."

I take Ben-sized strides away from the table, watching over my shoulder as I make my way to Helen. When I reach her, I stand with my back pressed against the wall. "I'm going to call it a night. I'm uncomfortable spying on Derek, and I'd rather not remain involved."

She purses her lips. "Thank you for being forthright with me. I understand that I've put you in an awkward position."

Derek has earned himself corporate's scrutiny, for sure. But there's no reason for Ben or me to help with the investigation. I'll quit next Monday, and that will be that.

# CHAPTER 38
## BEN

I have an excellent track record of leaving the office behind at the end of the day. Today, I blow my streak. It doesn't surprise me to witness Derek and a few team members treating Violet unfairly, but until I had connected to her this weekend, I hadn't imagined how hurtful it is. I hate myself for ignoring how awful they are to her.

Julie has proven herself to be a powerful ally. Violet might not have realized she had anyone on her side. Perhaps her sense of isolation explains why she's let Derek and his henchmen's actions slide. You don't want to be the new girl who causes waves right from the get-go, especially if no one else seems to notice the reasons she should file a complaint.

I hope she doesn't hate me for getting involved. It should be her choice, but for the moment, I'm Violet. I want conditions to improve for her and Julie.

Still, the regret of making the decision without her input kept me from interacting with her once she had returned to the office. Something in the set of her eyes made me worry she didn't want to talk to me, either. Had she heard whispers about what happened during the team building activity?

I have amazing news to share with her, though. Two of the messages she had left her leads on Friday panned out. Both are small buildings with a single elevator, but a commission is a commission. One of the clients didn't believe I was the same woman who had left the message. He mentioned I had sounded like a drunk Meryl Streep.

With a win in my pocket, I've decided Violet needs to stand out for the right reasons. Rescuing her from the basement of the leaderboard is step one. I admire how Julie owns her wardrobe choices. True, I also appreciate how she looks in her clothing, but her clothes aren't merely sexy; they give her a sense of power. I pinch the side seams of Violet's jacket, bending my neck downward. I swear this outfit saps me of my will. It forces me to slump and lower my voice.

After work, I head over to the Newport Mall. I stare at the list of stores near the entrance, waiting for a miracle to guide me to the appropriate store. A leggy blond in a cute pair of shorts struts past me, carrying a large bag. Forever 21, it says. Miracle accepted. I locate the store on the map and set off to buy an outfit for tomorrow.

"Can I help you?" A college-aged woman with an exposed bellybutton and blue highlights in her hair accosts me the second my foot breaks the plane of the store.

"I, um…" I need assistance, but I don't want to throw Violet under the bus by being clueless about clothes, either. "Shopping isn't my thing. I started a new job a couple of months ago. I've been keeping my style conservative, but I'm ready to ditch the pantsuits."

"So, like, you want cute work clothes?"

"Yeah."

"Dresses… skirts… pants…?"

"Um, let's start with dresses."

She leads me to a circular rack on the left. "What size?"

I stop cold in my tracks. "Small?"

Her eyes harden, and she tilts her head to study my body. I clench my arms in front of me to shield myself against her gaze. "Probably a two. Here. Do you like this?"

She holds a dress that is missing what I assume are crucial bits of fabric between the sleeves and the waist. I'm not saying I'd hate to see it on Violet, but even I know it wouldn't be work appropriate. "Let's keep looking."

"You like flowers or solid colors?"

"Simple's fine. Blue?"

I wince from the sickening sound of hangers scraping against the rack. My guide to women's clothing shows me a medium-blue dress with short sleeves. "Like this?"

"Sure. I'll try it on."

"Do you want to keep looking?"

*Almost as much as I want to jog behind a garbage truck.*

"Not unless it doesn't fit."

She guides me to a dressing room and hangs the dress on a hook. "Let me know if you need anything else," she says, drawing the curtain closed.

"I'm good."

I'm not, actually. The back and side walls are nothing but mirrors. I have avoided mirrors since Friday with a vengeance unless I am fully dressed.

I sling my jacket onto the bench. The dress is like a T-shirt but longer. I bet I could try it on over my clothes. I slip my hands through the sleeves and stick my head through the neck hole. My blouse bunches underneath, but I keep unrolling the dress until it hits the middle of my thighs. I'm counting on it hanging longer without the bulk of another outfit underneath. If it fits now, it should be perfect.

Before I wrestle my way out of it, I put on my jacket. It makes the dress look corporate. Maybe a little too corporate. My shoes aren't helping matters, either. I remove the dress and bunch it in my fist when I exit the changing room. "It fits. Maybe you know of a jacket and shoes to go with it?"

The salesclerk beckons me to the back of the store, where she selects a white denim jacket. I try it on. It's not as loose as the jacket I've been wearing, and it ends at the bottom of my ribcage. "Yeah, it's cute. Next, shoes. I can't walk in heels, though."

"Have you tried a stacked heel?"

"Uh…"

"Wait. We just got the cutest shoes. They're black, and they lace up like ballet shoes."

Ballet shoes? Be still, my heart!

"I'll try them in a…"

I didn't think through my shopping trip idea. What woman doesn't know her clothing and shoe size?

She gestures to my feet, recognizing me for the dolt that I am. I hand her a shoe. "Six-and-a-half. Let me check if we have your size."

She returns with a box and a pair of miniature stockings. I stuff them and the shoes onto my feet. Even before I stand, I appreciate the loafers I had worn today. My feet slide inside the shoes, and the ties are cutting off my circulation. I walk with the grace of Frankenstein in the new shoes. The clerk points me to the closest mirror. The shoes definitely up the style quotient, so there's that.

I stuff my feet back into the well-worn loafers, toss the new shoes into their box, and take them and the clothes to the register. I'm psyched to go in to the office tomorrow, which is a first. Between two new contracts and the outfit, Derek will have to take Violet seriously.

# WEDNESDAY

# CHAPTER 39
## VIOLET

Had I actually looked forward to going to work yesterday? Between my budding feelings for Ben and the anticipation of meeting with his client, I had allowed living his life to bamboozle me into believing mine would be better. But I'm still Violet, which the state of my life proves in unflinching detail.

I don't belong in sales, regardless of how Derek treats me. I had entered the job market four years ago with a communications degree and no job experience. My promotion to manager of a chain drugstore led to first my job in payroll at Heading Up and then my promotion in June.

If I blow it for Ben this week, I will give notice before I even send out applications for new positions. But what will a few unsuccessful months in sales qualify me for? Nothing better than my previous jobs, I'm sure.

Ten minutes of wallowing in self-pity before getting out of bed costs me the chance to shower. I slick my underarms with several coats of antiperspirant, slide on the pants I wore yesterday, and crack a slight grin at another positive to being a man: nobody cares what I wear.

I slide into the office a minute before nine, dropping my bag at my desk before joining the crowd in the center of the bullpen. As promised over beers last night, Ben is number ten on the board, and I am number eleven. I've never ranked this high, and now I understand why. Derek has rigged the system.

Speaking of me, where is Ben? I wend my way through the crowd to reach the front.

Topher fist bumps me. "Hey, man. Where'd you go last night?"

I need an excuse. Fast. I waggle my brow at him. "Should have said something to you guys. I ran into a woman—"

"Nice. I want to hear details later." He high fives me.

Pig. Well, I did set the bait.

He cranes his neck to the left. "Whoa. Dude, you gotta see this."

I follow his eyes. Ben has arrived. I press my palms against my nose and mouth, cutting off my oxygen supply.

"Excuse me." I cross in front of Topher and approach Ben. "What are you wearing?"

He's taken aback by my stern expression. "I asked a salesperson to help me select something appropriate for the office. At least I didn't choose a dress cut down to here." His finger lands between his breasts. My breasts. I bat it aside.

The dress clings to him like a drowning victim to a hunk of driftwood. Thank goodness the jacket leaves a few things to the imagination. My ass, however, is no longer a mystery. Nor is the type of underwear I prefer. The outlines of my secure cotton bikini pants stick out in full relief. The scantest of inches of blue fabric covers the tops of my thighs. "I have plenty of work-appropriate dresses and skirts. They're in the hall closet. Why did you buy *this*?"

He rubs his palms against his thighs. "What's wrong with what I'm wearing?"

"For starters, you can't sit in it," I say.

He straightens his back. "I sat on the PATH ride here."

"Did you make any new friends?"

"A man offered me his seat."

"I'm sure he did."

Derek raps his notebook on his desk to get our attention.

I whisper in Ben's ear, "We'll discuss the logistics of sitting later."

He bends his neck, examining his hemline. "Oh, shoot. I get it. I swear it was longer in—"

"Violet, would you like us to wait—" Derek's eyes scan Ben from chest to fetish-wear toes. "On second thought, please come here."

Ben toddles to Derek's desk in a pair of shoes designed specifically to hamper a woman's movements. "Sorry for talking over you," he says.

"Nothing to be sorry about. Let's take a look at you." Derek places his hands on Ben's shoulders and forces him to spin. A bile-inducing chorus of jeers rises from select members of the team. "Young lady, had I known you'd spend your commissions on outfits like this, I would have made it my mission to ensure you always received the best leads." He taps him on the rear. "Take that pretty body of yours back to your spot. And Ben, you're one fast operator! Well done, sir."

A few hoots pierce the air. I turn away from Derek's supporters, who are shooting me their thumbs-up.

Ben's eyes wide, he hunches his shoulders forward. "What have I done?" he asks in a whisper.

"The problem doesn't lie with you. I'll head to my apartment at lunch to grab you a different outfit."

My frustration over his lack of help in preparing me to meet the hotel client dissipates. I fiercely want to protect him from Derek and his wolves.

# CHAPTER 40
## BEN

I'm not a complete idiot. I knew the dress was short when I put it on this morning, but I was running late. By tugging it, I can make it three inches longer. Of course, tugging it means reaching my hands dangerously close to an off-limits section of my body.

I had hoped the dress would be longer without the second outfit worn underneath. I hadn't intended to make Violet overtly sexy; I meant for her to look her age. To project a fun vibe.

The fun vibe is certainly lacking today, though. Half the team ogling me feels worse than confronting the image of Violet in Topher's drawing. I'd give anything to disappear. Will Derek believe me if I tell him I need to leave to meet with a client?

The one bright spot is experiencing Violet's impulse to protect me again. I'd love to encourage her to stay with me after the meeting, especially since we barely said a word to each other yesterday. Julie shadows the two of us while we wind our way to my desk. I need to talk to her, too, but I can't with Violet around.

Julie perches on the edge of the desk and adjusts her skirt to the top of her knees. I'd give anything for an extra foot of fabric on the bottom of my dress.

"Did you go shopping?" she asks.

I hang my head. "Yeah, but I suck at it."

"No. You look cute. I love your jacket, and the blue of your dress is awesome for your coloring."

For the first time since I arrived this morning, a drip of confidence revitalizes me. "Thanks."

Violet can't stop staring at Julie. Her brow wrinkles as she processes the conversation—or perhaps Julie's presence—in my cubicle. "I agree. You look nice. Ignore Derek and the guys. I mean, what do they know about fashion? Derek's tie looks like he dipped it in peanut butter and has been sucking spots of it bare down to the darker brown fabric."

Julie covers her mouth, suppressing a laugh. "You're right." She pauses. "Ben, I hate to ask this, but would you mind leaving us alone? Violet and I need to talk."

"No problem." Violet's hand travels along the edge of the cubicle divider. With a quick glance over her shoulder at me, she heads to my old desk.

Julie hops off the desk and stands behind me, whispering. "You and I should schedule a meeting with Helen."

"With whom?"

"Helen in human resources. Your old boss."

I'd rather relive my encounter with Adam, Violet's landlord, on an endless loop than fake my way through a meeting with someone who has the power to fire her because of my missteps.

"You think? We could let her stew over what you told her yesterday. She'll contact us should she need to ask us more questions."

Julie inhales sharply. "I should have reported Derek long ago, even before you joined our team. I'm sorry to have pressured you to join me in filing the report. It's a lot to ask.

But after what Derek did to you this morning, we can't sit tight while Helen looks into the situation. We need to be proactive, to safeguard ourselves and any other women who might apply for positions in the future. They can't fire us for reporting sexual harassment."

I jerk backward. "Sexual harassment? He only touched my shoulders."

"And, well…" She taps her backside. "Sexual harassment involves more than inappropriate touching. He made you model your outfit for a nearly all-male group and equated the style of your clothing with the quality of leads you deserve."

I stare at my nails. I haven't *not* paid attention when news breaks about some heavy hitter pawing at a female subordinate. Derek bullies Violet, and yes, I work with a couple of guys I wouldn't want to date my sister if I had one. But labeling our boss's behavior sexual harassment adds an element of danger. I can't make such a serious charge against him without absolute proof. The only way I could report him would be for Violet to agree. I don't see that conversation happening. Not until we're ourselves again.

"Can I think it over?" I ask.

Julie walks away from me and holds onto the edge of the wall. "Of course. Let me know when you're ready." She takes a step out of my cubicle and pivots. "I have a pair of leggings in my desk you could borrow should you want them."

The idea of wrestling with another pair of leggings is nearly as daunting as reporting this morning's episode to HR, but one glimpse at the exposed entrance into forbidden territory in my lap convinces me. "Thanks. I wouldn't mind borrowing them."

# CHAPTER 41
## VIOLET

**B**en emerges from the women's room, wearing a pair of too-long black leggings under the dress. He has rolled the cuffs above the black shoelaces winding up his calves. I release my breath, relieved nobody in the office can peek at my privates anymore.

I had entered stalker territory by tailing him to the restroom, intending to run interference in case Topher or another guy wanted to bother Ben, thinking he was Violet. I might not have experience throwing a punch, but so help me, I will if need be.

I follow Ben to his cubicle. "So, you and Julie are friends?" I ask.

He stiffens. "Yeah, she's nice. Aren't you friends with her?"

"Not really. Maybe it's a good thing she thinks she and I—or you, rather—are friends."

"It probably is." He sucks in his bottom lip.

I barely recognize him, and not just because he's dressed like a cast member from *Jersey Shore*. Gone is the sense of Ben existing behind my eyes. The sparkle has been extinguished. He has lost his easy-going nature. Is being me the burden, or is Derek's behavior more toxic and damaging than I had acknowledged?

I wish our cubicles had extra chairs in them. Me looming over him can't be putting him at ease. I copy Julie and alight on the corner of his desk. "We have some items to discuss."

He eyes me warily. "What have you heard?"

"Excuse me? What haven't I heard might be the better question."

"Oh, um, nothing. Go on."

"Right. We'll discuss what constitutes nothing in a minute. First, about Alex over at the hotel. Our meeting didn't go well."

He props his chin in his hand, seemingly relieved to discuss the hotel instead of whatever he had expected me to say.

"What happened?" he asks.

"Not much. She was expecting biscotti, and she—"

"Oh, shoot. Biscotti were an inside joke she and I had. She dreams of having an easy day at work where she can put her feet on her desk, drink coffee, and crunch on a cookie."

"A little heads up might have helped. I never found my footing with her. Alex joked around with me, but the second I joined in, she wasn't having it. I'm pretty sure I left her with the impression I am a sexist pig. Can I tell you how close I came to spilling the beans about the body swap? Anything to save your lead."

His eyes dart to the upper corners of his lids. "But you didn't?" I shake my head. "Is she definitely not signing with us?"

"She wanted to think it over and get quotes from another company."

He shrugs. "You did what you could. Give her a couple of days."

"Would you leave her to make the decision on her own, even if it meant you didn't go to contract?"

"I'm not in the business of telling people what to do. We sell a desirable product. I talk to someone, we get along, and if they need our services, they sign. Not everyone wants to work with me. That's why we go back through the dead leads. Maybe the hotel does nothing with us for the moment. In a few months, Julie or someone else gives Alex a call, and they become best friends. Whatever happens is fine with me."

"I'm responsible for you. It wouldn't be fair for me to blow your commission. I need to make things right with Alex."

"Don't try too hard. Gunning for a win isn't my style." His fingers pinch his dress, pulling it away from his waist. "Speaking of style, are you mad at me for wearing my new outfit?"

"I wouldn't wish what Derek did to you on anyone. I can't be mad at you for what he did." I cock my head. "Did you try the dress on at the store?"

"Kind of?"

"What, you held it up in front of the mirror?"

"No. I put it on over the suit I wore yesterday."

I can't help but smile. Trusting a man with my body has been a massive challenge, but Ben continues to erase my worries. He picked the most modest way to buy a dress. I can't blame him for being clueless.

"I prefer to keep my skirt length to the knee or longer and the fit on the loose end of things, not that I expect you to buy more clothes. Stick with my suits; it's better for Derek to act contemptuous of me for being homely than to sexually harass me when I show him some skin."

"You're not homely. Why would you say that?"

"Because it's true. Why else would you parade around a bar in the most garish dress from my wardrobe or buy clothes at... I'm going to guess Forever 21?"

"You can tell the brand?"

"Not the point. You've tried to change my appearance twice now." I want to fight with him, but I also want to swing back to his comment about me not being homely. He sees something in me, but only when I dress a certain way.

"I didn't do it because I want to change... I..." Ben gnaws on his thumbnail. "I was testing Derek. Julie mentioned he behaves differently around her, depending on the length of her skirt. He fell for my bait. He's busted. She filed a report on his treatment of the two women on the team and the toxic environment he fosters. I gave her my permission to include a story about an incident from yesterday's training session." He glances at me, his eyes wide, perhaps expecting me to laud him.

Helen. This explains why she had me spy on the men at the bar last night. Why would Ben assume I'd be okay with him filing a sexual harassment complaint on my behalf? I'm not ready to fight the system, but I'm the person who will be stuck dealing with the consequences once the spell reverses. I've spent the past ten years hoping never to find myself in this situation again.

"You believe it's okay to share information about something that actually happened to me with Helen before you discuss it with me? You've blindsided me, and now I'm trapped by whatever the repercussions are from your actions. Thanks for nothing."

I'm sure men don't exit a room in a huff, but I don't have the patience to filter my anger through Ben's body. Nose held high and my butt clenched, I take quick, short, duck-waddle steps to my cubicle.

# CHAPTER 42
# BEN

Goosebumps march across my arms. I wish I could undo everything from yesterday: say no to Julie's idea to report Derek; dismiss my lame idea to spiff up Violet's image. She already suffers from Derek's actions. I can't fathom why things would get worse for her after she reported him, but my lack of imagination doesn't mean I'm right. What if ratting out Derek costs Violet her job?

All I can control is how well I do her job for her. I've never tackled a list of leads with the ferocity that is currently building in my chest. I nearly choke on the realization I have to set goals and expectations in order to achieve a desired outcome. My scheme requires the perfect hybrid of Violet's planning abilities and my light touch from my former days of not caring about anything.

Which perfectly describes the time we spent together on Sunday and Monday. When she reins in her tension and I step up to lend a hand, she and I sync. A smile creeps across my face, erasing the terrified mask I had worn in response to upsetting her. Something has taken root in me. Whatever happens this week, I'm walking away a better man for knowing her.

I open the email Derek had sent me with today's new leads. Two hold more promise than the garbage he had handed me yesterday. Progress. I slow my reading pace below my usual cursory skim. It would be worth taking notes. Violet-type of notes. While I have my face planted directly in front of the screen, evaluating the data, Derek walks into my cubicle.

He leans against the outside wall. "What's with the frown? You'd be prettier if you smiled."

I pull away from the laptop with a jolt. My lips stretch a millimeter toward my cheeks but not to form a smile. "The maintenance schedule for the elevators in the building in Union City is no joke. That's all."

"Ah, relax a little. You're always so uptight." He walks behind me and wraps his hands around my shoulders. I clench tight enough to crush a bowling ball. His fingers knead deeper, sending painful spikes into my bones.

I wiggle out of his grip. "Thanks, but... uh..."

He gets the hint and returns to the other side of the desk. My phone buzzes. I slide the text from a friend of mine off the screen. "Sorry for the interruption."

"Hopefully it wasn't your boyfriend." He sputters out an unpleasant laugh.

His expression strangles my heart, making it choke instead of beat. Despite what Violet had said, I have to act, to help make the case against him. I hold my phone under the desk and click the voice memo button.

"Nope. Just a telemarketer." I lean forward, extending the hand with the phone farther under my desk.

"Good. You know, a few of the people on the team think you're kind of uptight. We should get a drink after work and discuss how you can fit in better. I can tell you want to change, you know, to stop being drab, sad old Violet. You're on the right path with your outfit, but lose the tights. People around here don't mind a little bit of leg.

You see how Julie always brightens up the office. And you don't have to work so hard. Nobody needs to see the expression you get when you're trying to use that brain of yours. You come out for a drink tonight, and we'll make sure you stay near the top of the ranking tomorrow without you having to think or work too hard. Sound good?"

"I... uh... I'll let you know later. I, yeah, totally want to, but I'd have to cancel plans with, uh, my parents. If I can't get out of it, we'll make it for another day, okay?" My knees bounce faster and faster. I need him to leave my cubicle before I haul off and punch his stupid face.

"I'll be waiting. Now back to work." He air quotes the last word and heaves a distorted laugh. "And by *work*, I mean engage with the team. Get up and take a walk to stretch your legs."

He exits my cubicle backward, dipping his head, perhaps to catch a bonus glimpse of me from beneath my desk. Thank goodness a slat of wood prevents him from seeing either my legs or the phone.

I count to twenty, exhale, and shakily bring the phone to the surface of the desk. With the volume on low, I hold it to my ear and hit play, wincing with each slimy word that oozes from his contemptuous mouth. If Julie heard my recording, she would march it upstairs to Helen's office. It would be the right thing to do. But imagining what Violet's point of view would be—and caring about her opinion, sharing the recording with anyone might be the opposite of right.

# CHAPTER 43
## VIOLET

I have no play here. Even if I went up to Helen's office and gave a glowing recommendation of Derek, any evidence Julie might have provided to the contrary would reflect on Ben. He'd come across as a wienie with a high tolerance for inappropriate conduct.

All of this provides more impetus for me to quit. Of course, I can't quit until I'm me again. Helen might try to blame Derek for making me want to leave, but it wouldn't paint the most accurate picture. I'm the lousiest salesperson in existence. Period.

Ben converted two of my garbage leads yesterday. Me? I took a prime potential client and unloaded my full toolkit of repulsion techniques on her.

I shouldn't have taken this job. Payroll is a safer place for me. The salary might be low, but it requires a much more user-friendly skill set. The people upstairs are nicer, too.

I take that back. My judgment is so last week, before I became friends with Ben. Or Julie. Although officially, I'm not friends with her; Ben is.

She proved her kindness by complimenting him on his outfit, which helped rebuild his confidence. It was the perfect touch. I previously saw her as being in a different league from me. She might have made an overture or two of friendship toward me when I first came downstairs to sales, but I was too intimidated to reciprocate.

Whether I have work friends now is moot. I'll finish my week, trying my best not to destroy Ben's career, and give notice on Monday morning.

My priority has to be winning the hotel contract. I won't take Ben's advice to let Alex decide on her own. Sure, he has an uncanny ability to succeed without trying, but I'm not him. I do my best when I focus on the desired outcome and take the necessary steps to achieve it.

I walk over to my old cubicle. Ben is staring at his phone. Startled, he drops it and springs upright. "Oh, hey. What's up?"

"Did you say Alex likes chocolate biscotti?"

"I'm pretty sure. Why?"

"I've considered sending her a gift to apologize for upsetting her during our meeting."

He quirks his mouth. "I don't know. She strikes me as someone who doesn't want you to nudge her. You ever try to fix something when it was still wet or sticky?"

"Welcome to the wonderful world of scrapbooking. I use toothpicks to move things around, and Q-Tips dipped in a solvent can remove unwanted splotches. Hiding the evidence is tricky, but I can usually clean up a mistake."

He stares at his fingertips, flipping his hands front to back. "I'm not used to having dainty fingers. Huh. I should try a few maneuvers while I still got 'em. Anyway, when I was six, my mom bought a cake for my dad's birthday. It had swirls of thick chocolate icing around the bottom and top edges. It sat on the counter for a few hours before dinner, and I really wanted a taste. Who'd miss a tiny drop of icing from the bottom, right? Famous last words. I put a hole in it—poked straight into the cake and left crumbs in the icing. I smeared a bit of icing into the hole to cover my tracks, which made things worse. By the time I gave up, I had removed an inch of icing, half of which I streaked across the plate."

"Did your parents catch you?"

"My brothers told on me, and I wasn't allowed to have a slice of cake at dinner."

"Ooh, harsh. I'm sorry. You can't compare me gifting Alex biscotti to a six-year-old pilfering a fingerful of icing, though. I'll send a note with the gift. It will be fine."

He shrugs. "You do what you think is best."

"I will." I pivot to leave only to turn to face him again. "Ben, I want to close the deal for you. Trust me, okay?"

His face glows from within even before he smiles. "Trust seems to be the week's theme."

I linger for a second, wishing it were the weekend again. I liked him—and myself—better without the noise of the office. "Well, I'll see you later."

I return to my desk and search a couple of websites for biscotti. The earliest I could have Alex's gift delivered would be tomorrow. It might be too late.

While browsing the shops in Ben's apartment building before going to the bar on Saturday, I had spotted chocolate-dipped biscotti in bags tied with gold ribbons in the coffeeshop's display case. They'd be perfect.

After making several cold calls, I head to my temporary home at lunch to buy the gift. I race walk to the hotel and leave the treats and note with the concierge to deliver to Alex. My chest fights my efforts to take a deep breath, but I know my attempt to right the ship was worthwhile.

# CHAPTER 44
## BEN

Mid-afternoon, after I make an appointment for Violet to meet with the building manager of an apartment building in Union City next week, I run out of steam. Being more engaged in my job should distract me from worrying about Derek, but I don't have Violet's discipline. My phone sits to my right, taunting me to take action.

I want to respect Violet's wishes, but I can't ignore what Derek has said and done. His behavior impacts Julie. It might also affect his female clients. I send Julie an email to meet me in the bathroom.

A minute later, she passes my desk on her way to the restroom, giving me the slightest head nod. I dig my dress and leggings out of my ass, tug the hem of my skirt as low as it will go, and wait a few seconds before I head to the restroom to meet her.

"Hey, Violet. What's up?" Julie asks, leaning against the wall between the sink and the hand dryer.

"I'm sorry I've hesitated to get more involved. I've only been here for a short while, and I don't have the best sales record. If Derek got wind that I was behind the report, and the investigation didn't pan out, I'd probably lose my job."

"I understand. Isn't it always the case; men victimize women, yet the women somehow get stuck having to answer for their behavior?"

"Yeah. It sucks."

She crosses her arms. "Making a claim takes courage, and I see such a spark in you. You're tough. Ultimately, you have to do what you believe is right. I don't want to pressure you."

I hold my phone between us and hover my finger over the icon to play the recording. "Derek dropped in for a chat earlier. Here. Listen."

Hearing him demean Violet and insinuate whatever it is he has planned for her this evening hasn't lost an ounce of its sting when I listen to it again. Julie draws her fists to her mouth and stares at the phone with wide eyes. At his mention of her, she seethes.

I lower my arm at the end of the recording. "I'm ready to talk to Helen."

Her smile is quiet. "I'll head upstairs right now. Wait a minute and then take the stairs. Okay?"

"Okay."

She slips out of the restroom. I wash my hands and use the dryer, pretending I had come into the bathroom for the usual reasons. I exit the room and scan the bullpen before walking toward the stairs.

"Hello, stranger. Fancy both of us answering nature's call at the same time." Derek toys with his belt buckle outside the men's room.

"I, uh…"

I draw a blank on what to say. Honestly, I doubt there is an appropriate response.

"No need to be shy. We all have the same needs." He puts some English on the word needs, making me want to issue a blanket apology to women on behalf of all men. "How does it look for us to have that drink tonight?"

"Hmm. Yeah, sorry. My mom totally wigged out when I tried to reschedule. We're planning a party for... uh... for her sister this weekend. Tonight's the only chance we'll have to make the decorations. Another night."

"Another night, then. Let me escort you back to your desk." He sweeps his hands in front of him. "After you, m'lady."

Hordes of spiders creep across my skin at the notion of Derek ogling me the entire distance between the bathroom and my desk. I balance against a wall and lean over. "Sorry. I have to retie my shoe."

I had been ready to chuck these instruments of torture, but they give me a handy excuse. My right calf breathes a sigh of relief once I untie the laces that have left deep ridges in my skin. I suspect my heels are shredded and bloody, but I'll wait until I'm seated in private before exploring the damage I've done.

Derek tires of waiting for me and trying to cop a peek down my dress. He leaves, and I hastily retie my shoe. He stops at Topher's cubicle; giving me cover. With a last furtive glance for lurking spies, I plan to sprint toward the stairwell.

Instead, I collide with Violet as she exits the men's room.

"Sorry, Ben, er, I mean Violet." She wrinkles her nose in deference to the weirdness of addressing herself. "Where are you rushing off to?"

I rub my shins. "Oh, uh, nowhere."

"Your shoes are doing a number on you. Why don't you tie the laces on top of the leggings?"

"Good idea, but it won't help my heels."

"I, I mean, you have bandages in the middle drawer of your desk."

"You're a regular old boy scout, aren't you?"

"Preparing for certain contingencies is easy. Here. Let's go take care of our feet. I'm inheriting whatever raw mess you leave me with in two days. It's in my best interest to minimize the damage."

I turn my head toward the stairwell. "They're not so bad. I'll fix them soon."

"Then let's circle back to my original question. Are you going somewhere?"

I puff my cheeks and exhale noisily. "I can't tell you here."

Her lower lip drops, and she narrows her eyes. "Does it concern Julie's report to HR?"

"Derek said some seriously inappropriate things to me this morning. I recorded it. We can't let him continue to abuse you."

She clenches her jaw and shakes her head. "Follow me." She leads me into the stairwell. "Look, I know he is a sexist pig, and he encourages a couple of the guys in the office to take his lead. The sales department is not the most fun place to work."

"Why haven't you said anything to Helen about him?"

"I have my reasons." Her face shuts, denying me from reading her.

"You wonder why you always have the worst leads? It's because he rewards a handful of team members and penalizes the others. I know, because he's told me so. Both when I was me and again this week. That's what I have on my phone."

"You're not telling me anything I don't already know. He reiterated his scheme at the bar last night. It doesn't matter."

"But it does. His behavior involves more people than you. It impacts Julie. Three women have quit the team in the year that I've been here. He's not fit to be a team leader. Something has to be done."

"Complaints of sexual harassment don't magically erase the wrongs a man has committed. Derek has the right to defend himself, and whatever he says, true or not, might wind up hurting me. I told you not to fight the battle on my behalf, and I'd appreciate for you to leave well enough alone."

"It makes zero sense to me to do nothing."

My statement takes me by surprise. I've always assumed my tombstone would read Here lies Ben, who preferred to do nothing.

She puckers her mouth and hardens her gaze. "I don't want to discuss it any further, okay? I have my reasons. Please respect my wish for you to stay out of my personal matters. Erase the recording and go back to your desk. This won't be your problem next week."

She holds the door for me, and we reenter the office. Before I can say another word, she blows past me toward her cubicle.

I disagree with her. With my eyes open to Derek's behavior, I won't be able to ignore him, to let him get away with treating her and Julie like disposable objects that exist for his pleasure. It has become my fight, too.

# CHAPTER 45
## VIOLET

It's Mr. Hartshorn all over again. Tracey and Anja goaded me to report him to the principal after an incident junior year. Heap lot of good that did me. He came away from it smelling like roses, while I received a C in trig. Same thing senior year when I couldn't switch out of his calculus class.

Does Ben think I'm an idiot for not understanding the true nature of Derek's behavior? He's been a woman for a minute and never seemed to have a problem with our boss until now. Whatever he believes he heard Derek say on the recording can't be enough to justify the risks involved in playing it for the HR department. Helen's radar is already buzzing regarding perceived favoritism. She has plenty of issues to address. I'll hand in my resignation on Monday. I have to tell her it has absolutely nothing to do with Derek, because if she thinks otherwise, she might try to talk me out of leaving or at least involve me in her investigation. No thanks. If Julie can make a serious claim about her own experiences, then let her.

I have enough on my plate. I dropped off the biscotti for Alex three hours ago, and I still haven't heard from her. Ben will kill me, but I can't leave anything to chance. I dial her number and reach her voicemail.

"Hi, Alex. It's Ben from Heading Up. I wanted to check to see if you received my…" My throat grows dry, and I cough to clear the tickle. "… um, package. There are more treats where they came from." I cough again. "Say the word, and I'll deliver them. Take care."

The voicemail gives me the option to re-record my message. I should, given my coughing fit. I poke the key on my phone with my honking man digit.

"Message delivered," the voice on the phone says.

I stare at my hands, wishing I had my actual hands. And body. This swap has grown beyond tiresome.

# CHAPTER 46
## BEN

I am more confused than ever. My gut tells me what Derek did and said to me/Violet this morning should be reported. But I have to respect Violet and her mysterious reasons for keeping it to myself. I pick up the office phone.

"Hey, Julie?"

"What's up?"

"Derek trapped me. I can't make it upstairs."

"No problem. Send me the recording. I'll play it for Helen."

"Give me a second, okay?"

I hang up the phone. It's unfair to make her wait upstairs without my evidence, but I need to decide whether to send it to her. I untie my shoes and dig out the laces from my tender flesh. With gentle tugs, I remove the shoes and kick them under my desk.

What this gal needs is a bandage or three. Violet promised I'd find salvation in her desk. The middle drawer does not disappoint. It holds not only gel bandages with antiseptic and numbing creams embedded in them but also a store of snacks, hairbrushes, personal hygiene products, and a Teddy bear holding a squishy, red heart. I hold it in front of me and wonder why she has it in her desk.

We've established that Violet isn't in a romantic relationship. Why would she hold on to a token from the past? Or...? No. Stupid idea. She wouldn't be saving it to give to someone.

I hear a rustle outside my cubicle. I tilt my head to get a view through the entrance. Topher, standing in Peter's cubicle, twists his head toward me. He covers his mouth, but I can still hear him and Peter laughing.

I set the bear on top of the pile of helpful stuff and close the drawer. The stuffed animal reminds me that Violet, like any of us, has vulnerabilities. Derek, by exploiting a few of hers, has created the crappiest work environment for her. Maybe we shouldn't aim to get him fired with our report. Instead, we can put the pressure on him to create a more balanced team for the greater good.

I reach for my phone and share the recording with Julie. My stomach wishes I hadn't, but I ignore it.

# THURSDAY

# CHAPTER 47
## VIOLET

I arrive at the office five minutes early the next morning, which is surprising, given how poorly I slept last night. Hadn't I considered hitting the gym before work a few days ago? Between teaching Ben's body to live the tense life and jettisoning its workout habits, I won't be handing him the body he lent to me. About the only thing I've done right is care for his tattoo. It is thirsty, drinking up the lotion I slather on it after dark each night. Two more workdays to endure, and I'll finally re-inherit the mess that is my own life.

Peter and Topher are drinking coffee in the passageway between Peter's, Ben's, and my cubicle. Topher raises his fist. I tap mine to his, inwardly thanking Ben's friend at the gym for reminding me how to greet men. "'S'up?"

They both smirk at me. Peter says, "Hey, we noticed a secret admirer snooping around your cubicle after you left last night."

"What makes you so sure it was an admirer?"

"You'll see." Topher breaks into an idiotic laugh. Ugh. I won't miss these two clowns after I quit my job.

"The intrigue is killing me." I brush past them and enter the next cubicle.

What the…?

The silly bear Helen gave me last Valentine's Day sits in my chair. I pluck him from the seat and shove him into my drawer. Is Ben trying to apologize for interfering with the HR report? Pretty lame to gift me one of my possessions if he is.

Topher pops his head over the wall dividing my cubicle from Peter's. "Heh? Whaddya think?"

"You've misjudged the situation. The bear is an inside joke. Get out of here, would you?" I fake a laugh for his benefit.

With a shrug, they head to Derek's desk. Ben and Julie enter my old cubicle together. I retrieve the bear and throw him at Ben from the passageway between our cubicles. Probably the best throw I've ever made, and Ben misses. Man, I want to try it again, but from farther away.

Ben picks up the bear. "What's… Why…?" He stops trying to formulate a question, instead gesturing his confusion with his hands.

"You didn't put him on my chair?" I ask.

"No."

"Topher and Peter seem to think otherwise."

Julie takes the bear from Ben and spins it in her hands. "Ben, Violet said she didn't. Can't you respect her word?"

Ben pulls his fists to his chest. "It's okay, Julie. The bear's mine. I keep him in my drawer. Someone must have stolen it from me and played a trick on both of us. Sorry for dragging you into it, Ben. I suppose we should go to the morning meeting. You guys ready?"

I take a step toward the door. "Yup. Oh, I like your dress, Violet. And it goes nicely with your denim jacket."

He's wearing a blue and white floral sundress I had retired to the hall closet in June. The full skirt falls mid-calf. Wisely, he's in a pair of flats today. The edges of a bandage on each heel peek out above the shoes.

He pulls the skirt away from his legs before dropping it and rubbing his hands nervously on his thighs. "Thanks. We'd better get going."

The three of us stand together on the left side of the team that has gathered in front of Derek's desk. I'd be fine with Julie standing somewhere else. She has exerted her influence over Ben the last couple of days and has taken a space of prime occupancy in his life.

Derek turns toward us. "Nice to see our girls getting along so well." He rolls his lips, studying Ben. "Huh, isn't there a correlation between hemlines and the stock market? Yesterday, Violet wore a short skirt. Coincidentally—or not—she rose to eighth place in the rankings, her highest position yet. Wonder what her longer skirt means for her future. We wouldn't want you to tumble toward the bottom, would we?"

Ben tucks his fists between his thighs and hunches his shoulders. "I'm sure the clients can't guess what I'm wearing during a phone call."

Derek guffaws at Ben's answer. "But *you'll* know. Tell her, Julie. You've uncorked the secret formula to dressing for success."

Julie owns the floor. She stands with one leg planted to the side and her hands on her hips. I wish I were tall enough to wear wide-legged trousers. I straighten my back, influenced by her pose.

She says, "I dress for me, and I aim for success through my labors. But enough about clothing unless overnight, we transitioned from an elevator service management agreement company into a fashion house."

Derek chokes for a second before turning forward to continue the meeting. Ben pats Julie's arm and gives her a supportive nod. A competitive spirit ignites in me. Ben and I had grown closer over the weekend, but being in the office has destroyed it, thanks to Julie. It's irrational for their friendship to bother me, but I can't tamp the flame of jealousy.

# CHAPTER 48
# BEN

I had never realized what torture it is to have to play a game of chess with one's wardrobe. The dress code for the men at Heading Up is khakis or dress pants and a button-down shirt in the office. We throw on a tie and jacket for meetings with clients. So long as my shirts don't smell and I don't have weird stains on my pants, I could wear the same clothes every day. For the two women in our office, every fashion choice they make puts the men closer to declaring checkmate.

Violet's pantsuits double as both armor and an invisibility shield. They prevent overt acts of sexual harassment, but because she doesn't give the men what they want to see, our boss devalues her. It took exposing myself yesterday to appreciate how her clothing choices protect her.

Derek isn't the only jerk in the office to show hostility toward the pantsuits; I blame myself, too. Nobody told me to buy that stupid dress. I've cast judgement on Violet's style by wanting her to change.

More than issues regarding my attire gnaws at my gut. I've grown accustomed to seeing Violet in the mirror over the last few days, but being her doesn't provide enough of a connection. The truth is, I miss her. I had falsely assumed working together would mean we'd remain united.

When she had first realized her life was tethered to mine on Friday, she must have assumed I'd ruin everything because I am the world's most apathetic person. And after I put her body in harm's way on Saturday, she would have had every reason to lock me in a cage until tomorrow night to ensure she'd survive the week. Instead, she has protected me and fed me and become a friend. I'd give anything to be with her away from the office.

I suck in a breath and slap my palms on my thighs. Nothing prevents us from hanging out. We need to leave our work nonsense behind and pick up where we left off on Monday. I shoot her a text.

> **Ben:** I hear the crew from the Mars simulation project is having a reunion tonight. Promise you won't mention a certain sore topic if you join us.

> **Violet:** I won't say a word about mimeology or require you to communicate using only your hands. White makeup, berets, and striped shirts are completely optional.

> **Ben:** How DARE you!
> Your place or mine?

> **Violet:** Better we meet at my old place. Don't want you encountering roving gangs of mimes late at night on your way home. 7:00 sound OK?

**Ben:** {silence}

Violet tilts her head to the right side of her desk, affording us a sliver of eye contact between our cubicles. I flash her an okay sign, and she covers her mouth, her eyes brighter than they've been in days.

# CHAPTER 49
## VIOLET

While I'm still holding onto the smile following my text exchange with Ben, Derek raps on the outside wall of my cubicle. "Got a minute?"

I set my phone to the side. "Sure. Come on in."

He leans against a file cabinet. "What's the sitch on the hotel?"

"They don't currently use a service like ours. Alex sees the value, but she wants to compare us to our competitors before making a decision."

"She? How'd I miss that detail? I figured Alex was a dude. Is she hot?"

"As the operations manager, she has full control over the temperature in the building." I hold Derek's eyes for a second, raising my brow.

"Oh, good one, Harris. But seriously, what did you think of her?"

"Not my type. And given the radio silence since I sent her a gift yesterday, we're probably not hers, either."

"A gift?"

"She said she likes biscotti. I left a dozen for her at the hotel on my lunch break."

"That's the kind of thing a chick would do. But I approve. Shows initiative. Ball's in her court now. Too bad your contact isn't a man, you know, someone more decisive. If she's easy on the eyes, I'd say schedule a second meeting just to enjoy the scenery. Otherwise, I guess you're stuck having to wait for her to make up her mind. In the meantime, go push some buttons with your other leads and see who wants to ride along with us."

"On it."

He saunters out of my cubicle, turning his head toward Ben and pausing. Ben must be studiously ignoring our boss, burying his head in his computer monitor or something. Derek returns to his desk rather than enter the cubicle.

I kill an hour by leaving messages for my new leads. It doesn't surprise me I have yet to sign a single new contract for Ben. Being a man has nothing to do with whether I succeed. Neither does the quality of the leads Derek hands me. I never wanted to go into sales, and my short stint in the office proves I don't belong here.

A swish of fabric draws my attention to the passageway. I catch sight of the back of Julie's head, walking into Ben's cubicle. It's petty, but watching them together makes me anxious.

I draw a complete blank in coming up with an excuse to visit him, but my urge to interrupt their conversation propels me from my chair anyway. I grab my folder of notes from my meeting with Alex and walk over to his desk.

"Oh, hey. I didn't realize you had a visitor. I can come back later," I say.

Ben grins at me. "No need."

Julie gives him a warning glare. "Are you sure, Violet?"

"I told Ben about the recording."

She jumps from her perch on the corner of the desk. "You did what?"

"He and I had talked about Derek last weekend. I wanted a guy's perspective."

Julie crosses her arms. "No offense, Ben, but I'm not comfortable having this conversation in front of you."

I wave the file at her. "No offense taken. See you later."

I exit the cubicle to the left, walking toward the bathrooms. I count to five, retrace my steps, and lower myself into a crouch outside the wall of her space to listen to their conversation.

Julie is speaking, "… can't do anything. Helen says the recording is worse for you than for him. You didn't tell him he was being inappropriate, and he said nothing especially damning. Also, for you to come forward with a recording the day after we first reported him could appear like you were trying to trap him. Unless he acts in an unquestionably inappropriate manner, we'll have to wait for them to decide whether they want to take any action. Sorry."

I hurriedly rise until my head is right below the top of the divider. Still hunched over, I make my way to the bathroom, trying to contain a building fire within me.

I ball my right hand into a fist, and the muscles in my back and arm contract. They taunt me to punch the wall. I wrap my left palm around my fist, pressing it into my belly to quiet my energy.

Why did Ben share the recording despite my request for him not to? What infuriates me more is him leaning on Julie for advice rather than me. If ever there was a situation to dictate where his loyalties belong, he and I are living it.

# CHAPTER 50
# BEN

I miss sitting at my desk and pretending to work. I miss not having to form an opinion or experience any sort of emotional response to a situation. I'd love to be my old self, and not just the physical version. The thing is, though, ignoring our hostile work environment should never be an option, regardless of who I am.

What Julie said makes no sense. How can a recording where Derek obsesses over my legs and promises that I'll succeed without trying not be compelling evidence against him? While he was in my cubicle, I should have told him off and established I would not tolerate his innuendos. Not in order to have created a better record of the exchange, but to have defended Violet.

However, something prevented me. While he spoke to me, my body had contracted. I was smaller than ever. My brain had simultaneously whirred, searching for meaning in the encounter, and skidded to a halt. A series of contrasts fed my momentary sense of weakness. Boss versus employee. A man controlling the dialogue in a conversation with a tiny woman. Him standing while I sat.

I defy my impulse to hide under my desk and watch epic fail videos on YouTube for the rest of the day, instead tackling the list of contacts Derek handed me today. The medical center alone would bring in revenue close to the hotel gig Violet is handling for me. My stomach clenches as I leave a message for the operations manager. My formerly simple job has become anything but.

The one bright spot today was my texting exchange with Violet. I try to catch her eye, but since she never takes her eyes from her monitor, I fire off another text.

> **Ben:** Did you hear about the mime who got arrested? He committed an unspeakable crime.

She reads the text and flips the phone over without glancing at me. She can't be mad at me because Julie kicked her out of the cubicle. Yeah, we need tonight. Hanging out anywhere besides the office and talking about anything besides work should do us both a world of good.

I fight the good fight, making calls on her behalf, until five o'clock finally arrives. I stop at her desk before leaving. "Seven's still good for you?"

She takes a second, narrowing her eyes. "I don't know."

"Everything's messed up here. I don't mean…" I swipe my pointer in the space between us. "Everything else. Every*one* else. We were fine before we came back to work. I…" I'm this close to divulging the depth of my feelings for her, but to read her face, I'm pretty sure she doesn't share my sentiment. She seems to find talking to me repulsive. "I hope we're still cool," I say.

She wrinkles her nose and mashes her jaw around. "Oh, I suppose I'll swing by, but just for an hour. We can order a pizza."

I hold my smile in check. "Sounds good. See you later."

The weight lifts. She and I can sort through the mess together and go back to where we were a few days ago.

Derek, Topher, Peter, Julie, and Helen fall away. I hitch my pocketbook strap higher on my shoulder and walk over to the elevator.

"There's my rising star." Derek comes up behind me. His hands knead my shoulders.

I wiggle away from him. "Sorry, I'm funny about people touching me. No offense, but…"

He pulls his hands away, holding them in surrender. "No funny stuff going on here. How did things go with the medical center?"

That was easy. I should have stood up for myself sooner.

I say, "I left a message. Hopefully, I can get things moving with them tomorrow."

"If you do, we'll have to have that celebratory drink you promised me."

The worms wriggle in my gut again. I stare at my shoes. "Maybe Tuesday with the rest of the team?"

He holds a finger over his lips. "Um, I… Sure. Tuesday."

The elevator dings, and the doors open. He holds the edge of the door, gesturing for me to enter first.

My breath refuses to go any lower than the base of my neck, and my palms grow itchy from the blood pulsing into them. No way am I getting into the elevator with him. "Oh, I'm such an airhead. I bought a card for a friend on my lunch break and left it in my desk. You go ahead. See you tomorrow."

He nods at me between the narrowing crack of the doors as they close. I rush into the bathroom and splash water on my face. My heart continues to thump in my ears.

After waiting in the bathroom for five minutes, I take the stairs and race walk toward the PATH station. My shoulders continue to drive upward until I grip a pole and watch the train's doors close.

I slow my pace when I'm above ground again in Journal Square. The rain earlier today cooled the air, clearing it of the humidity. I hope the weather holds until Saturday so I can treat my actual body to a jog along the river.

I reach Violet's house and open the gate. While I dig in my pocketbook for my keys, I nod absentmindedly at two women who sit on the steps leading to the upstairs apartments. And then do a double take.

The woman with blond hair pushes herself from the step and walks up to me. "That's how you greet your two best friends? Sheesh! Tracey wasn't kidding; you are in desperate need of an intervention."

# CHAPTER 51
## VIOLET

I'm a coward. I should have told Ben he can go screw himself. Now I'm stuck having to see him tonight, our last night in the other's body.

On Monday, I had envisioned spending each evening this week with him. Weird as it seems now, I had fallen for him. Where I had once written him off as a guy who coasts through life, thanks to the good fortune of being a man, I had instead discovered he possesses greater depths. In theory, his perseverance in matters pertaining to Derek should speak to his character. An evolved man is a decent man, right? But in practice, I feel like my opinion doesn't matter to him, like *I* don't matter. How is him running roughshod over my wishes any different from the way Derek treats me?

I wait for him to leave the office, making last-minute notes in his active work files in order to appear too busy to react to the mythical five o'clock whistle. Still no word from Alex. My best plan is to leave the hotel for Ben to sort out. Let me guess: one phone call from him Monday morning, and she'll beg for him to sell him the complete suite of services. The day isn't a total waste, though. A building manager of a modest-sized apartment in Hackensack arranged a meeting with Ben for next Tuesday.

The office is quiet, which means I can leave in peace. I step into the elevator. Julie's voice rings out from a few feet away. "Hold the elevator, please."

I resist the urge to mash the close button, holding the door open for her instead. She jumps into the car, breathless. "Thanks."

My lungs vibrate. I stare at the molding running horizontally around the interior of the elevator. Julie's presence grows overwhelming as I try to ignore her. I can't throttle my growing rage; I have to address its source. "Perhaps I'm misreading you, but it seems like you're manipulating Violet."

Her shoulders lurch backward. "I beg your pardon?"

"She's been acting differently, making choices she normally wouldn't make. And coincidentally, you've been by her side the entire time."

"What exactly are you implying? I didn't tell her to change her style. She decided on her own. And, by the way, Derek is entirely responsible for his behavior. Blaming Violet for his behavior is the same kind of sexist bullshit he pulls."

The doors open, and Julie strides into the building's lobby, ready to ditch me.

I run after her. "I'm not talking about the outfit. Violet's been in this situation before. You're not the first person to encourage her to report a man for sexual harassment. She paid dearly for it once before, and I don't want her to suffer again."

Julie steps into the revolving door, isolating me behind a plate of glass. Once she's on the sidewalk, she stops to wait for me. I usher her around the corner, away from the stream of pedestrians.

I lean against the building, and Julie faces me. "She's never mentioned it," she says

I shrug. "She told me the story over the weekend. So, what happened is in high school, her math teacher called her to the chalkboard more frequently than the rest of the students in her class. Her friends noticed him watching her butt wiggle while she wrote on the board rather than observing her solutions to the equations. Violet didn't believe them at first. He invited her to help chaperone a group of third and fourth graders on a field trip to the Museum of Mathematics in the City. The day began with a seemingly innocent mistake of his hand being on the bus seat when he ushered her to sit with him. Followed by a less-than-innocent brush against her chest a little later. She determined none of his actions were coincidences when he created a 3D rendition of a formula that produced an ass-shaped object, which he gifted to her.

"She avoided him the rest of the trip and told her friends. They pressured her into reporting him. He was everyone's favorite teacher, and the principal didn't believe her. And when the teacher discovered she had reported him, he took to marking down her grades. She actually had loved math, but he killed it for her. She had him again senior year. Her GPA suffered, and it impacted where she applied to go to college."

Julie's hand presses against her strawberry-blond hair, sliding it to follow the curve of her neck. "I had no idea. Oh, poor Violet!"

"You can see why forcing her to report Derek would stir up a handful of old memories. And from the little she's shared with me, she hasn't presented conclusive evidence against him. What happens if Derek learns about the report and retaliates against her?"

"Helen won't say anything, I swear."

I press my lips into a tight line. "Why now?"

"Excuse me?"

"Why did you pick this week to build your case? I mean, have you ever approached Violet to discuss the way Derek and a handful of team members treat her or brought up the harassment situation with Helen prior to now?"

"I… ah, no. Topher bullied Violet on Tuesday. He drew a cruel picture. And… It doesn't matter. The vulnerability behind her eyes went straight through me." Her eyes darken. "I regret letting things escalate. I've been here for over two years. You wonder why I'm acting now? I thought I was tough enough to withstand it. I'm not saying Violet isn't tough enough; sometimes it bothers me more to observe what happens to other people. Had I heard her story earlier, perhaps I would have omitted her from my report."

The pressure from the steam in my head releases. Julie isn't the enemy, and neither is Ben. He had his reasons to disregard my advice, having endured the harassment firsthand. Whether he was protecting Julie or even me, it doesn't matter. He meant to do the right thing.

I pull away from the building. "It's obvious she respects you, and she isn't blind to what Derek puts you through. I bet she's a lot like you in that her impulse to file the report was to protect you rather than herself."

"What a kind thing to say. I don't know if Violet told you, but Helen doesn't plan to act on our report at the moment. Frustrating, isn't it?"

"Yes, it is, but maybe, for the time being, the best thing is to let it go and do nothing unless Derek commits a serious offense. Thanks for giving me a chance to share my perspective. I'm not the enemy here. I have Violet's best interest in mind."

She pokes me with her elbow. "Topher and Peter might not be entirely off base about her having a crush on you."

I shake my head with a shrug. "If she does, I'm the last to know. See you tomorrow, Julie."

# CHAPTER 52
# BEN

My stomach turns into Mount Vesuvius. I'm as likely to pass myself off as Violet to the people who know her best as I would be to host a monthly salon dedicated to Hungarian poetry. But I can't spend the rest of the night standing in front of them and drooling, either. "You guys! I swear my head was somewhere else when I opened the gate. My eyes went straight through you without registering who I saw."

I know exactly where my head is. It's on the other side of Jersey City and coming this way in an hour and a half.

Anja hugs me before stepping out of the way to let Tracey have her turn. Her arms wrap around me, and I stiffen.

Tracey slides her hands from behind my back to my upper arms. Gripping them, she asks, "You're free this evening, right? No, don't answer. If you have plans, cancel them. We need to talk." She pinches the shoulder seam of my jacket. "This is new. It's cute."

"Thanks. Bought it on a whim."

"I see. Are you going to invite us in?"

It would be the worst idea ever. Besides the fact that I need them to disappear before I make a fatal mistake, I also had planned to undo the week's worth of damage I had inflicted on Violet's home this evening. "My place is a mess, but—"

Tracey laughs through her nose. "Messy to you means one of the pillows on your couch is upside down. I think we can hack it."

I dread opening the door. Magical tattoos that lead to body swaps have nothing on the new ability I've developed: being able to see dirt and disorder only when I'm in the company of other people. Either I pledge to become a hermit, or I learn to force myself to clean whether or not I consider my home to be dirty.

Tracey's pace into my apartment slows. "Good lord, Violet. What the hell happened in here?"

Anja pushes past her. "You must have taken me literally on Friday when I said we should tackle our goals like we were entering senior year again. With a sprinkling of magic, we've traveled back in time to my room in high school. You hated coming over to my pigsty." She scratches her head. "Or you loved it because you had another room to clean."

"Now you know my dirty secret. Secrets. About me wanting to clean your room plus how my housekeeping habits have slipped a little."

Tracey sweeps a pile of clothing and mail to the end of the sofa and sits in the empty spot. "A little? My list of concerns keeps growing. Care to explain? You, sit." She pats to the cushion next to her. "Anja, fetch the wine."

My shoulders beg for me to release my tension. I'd give anything to unburden myself of the entire week's woes, starting with the incident from the tattoo gallery. I should text Violet to come over and tell her friends everything.

Would I believe any of my friends if they told me they were in someone else's body? No way. Truthfully, it would annoy me to hear a friend yammer on and on, trying to convince me. Violet and I might have a chance with Anja, but I can tell Tracey wouldn't believe me as far as she could throw me.

I bet Violet would mention what's been going on at Heading Up, though. I don't know how to explain last Saturday, or why their friend invited a male colleague to help her with her crafting project on Monday. Better I jump right in with my personal experience. Keep it simple.

I have to deal with Violet first. She can't come over. Not that she seemed overly enthused about it this afternoon. By canceling on her, I'm probably giving her more ammunition to use against me, although I don't understand why I appear to have become her enemy.

"Excuse me for a second. I have to text someone from work." I climb over Tracey's legs.

"I hope it's not the cheesy pickup artist who assisted you at the competition."

"Ben. He's not cheesy. And I'm glad he helped me. He ended up making it fun despite the breakage and the issues with my backdrop."

"We'll explore the Ben of it all later, after you text him and we've gotten to the bottom of what's really plaguing our bestie."

I huddle in front of a cabinet, hunching to prevent Tracey from noticing I use a different phone than Violet.

**Ben:** Problem. Your two best friends ambushed me at my apartment. They are intent on grilling me to explain why I haven't been acting like myself.

**Violet:** Get rid of them.

**Ben:** They won't leave.

**Violet:** I can't come over if they're there.

**Ben:** Talk later?

I wait for her to respond, but she doesn't.

Anja returns to the living room with an opened bottle of wine and three glasses. "I ordered a pie from Larry and Joe's. It'll be here soon. Have I missed anything?"

Tracey pours wine into a glass and hands it to me. "*Some*one had to text her favorite work pal."

"Ooh, he's cute. Vi, if you're not into him, give him my number. I'm in a serious man drought, and he might be exactly what I need to quench my thirst."

This is not helping matters.

# CHAPTER 53
## VIOLET

Are you freaking kidding me? Ben's canceling on me? No sooner had I understood why he agreed to be part of Julie's report and in turn, restored my hope to reconnect with the Ben I had gotten to know last weekend, he's shutting me out again.

My gut instinct earlier today had been to decline his invitation. Sure, he had broken through my defenses with his mime jokes, but the silliness is an outlier. The entire week, he has lived my life according to his rules. Had he been his usual detached, easy-going self, maybe we'd still be okay. Instead, he made choices without me.

We're stuck in the most insane situation, and we can't turn to anyone except for the other for support, something we haven't done in days. He's left me isolated. Am I also pissed because the two people in the world I desperately wanted to lean on this week are hanging with him instead? That accounts for part of what's going on with me, but not everything. Perhaps the most frustrating bit is because I'm stuck in his body, it tricks me into wanting to connect to him on another level. No, thank you.

I throw on a pair of shorts and a T-shirt and head to the gym. My body bristles with energy, compelling me to ditch the elliptical and dive straight into the free-weights. I test-drive a few dumbbells to find which one Ben's biceps yearn to curl. I still can't believe my arm doesn't rip out of its socket when I lift a seventy-five-pound weight.

A man sits on a bench near me, anchoring his elbow into his inner thigh and curling his weight between his legs. It's a pleasing pose, not too in-your-face, I'm-the-strongest-man-in-the-gym. I mimic his motions and escape dwelling on subjects any more intense than counting the numbers from one to ten as I do a set.

After a round with my left arm, I drop the weight onto the mat and massage my biceps muscles. It's not complaining from the effort of lifting the weight, but it is standing up at attention, and my veins have come to the surface to cool the guns. Hmm. I might have had the worst week of my life and can't wait to be myself again, yet I'm going to miss Ben's body.

I'm shallow. Sue me.

I sigh, contemplating what it will mean to leave him behind after the spell lifts and I quit my job.

"Yo, dude. No thinking allowed in here." The guy with short, blond hair who I met last Saturday flicks me on the shoulder.

Steve? No. It was a line from a movie. Uh... Oh, yeah. "Hey Shane. What's up?"

"Not a hell of a lot. What's up with you? You look like your grandmother just died. Either that or the train hasn't left the station in a week." He kneels on the bench behind me and lifts a weight, pulling it into his side while bending his elbow.

"Rough week at the office." I pick up my weight and begin another set of curls.

"You've never talked about work. I figured you were allergic to the topic."

He's right. Ben wouldn't give a fig whether or not he closes a contract. I want to leave his life in the same condition I had inherited it. Acting peevish in front of his buddy makes things messier. What would Ben and Shane talk about? Of course, wondering about their conversations leads me to worrying about what he's saying to my friends.

No, Violet. You can't go there.

I chuckle. "You know what? I let my job get to me. Broke my cardinal rule. Who cares about work? What's going on with you these days?"

"Same old, same old. Still dating Lisa. She's okay. I'm not sure where I stand on taking our relationship to the next level, though. How 'bout you? You said something about a chick from your office a few weeks ago?"

"Uh… Did I?"

Not to put too fine a point on it but, WHAT CHICK?

"Yeah, the woman who baked you cookies?"

My heart has enlisted the other organs in my torso to beat along with it.

"What about her?"

"I don't know. You thought she was nice, someone you wanted to get to know better."

I hold my breath, exhaling slowly. "We've hung out a little. She is nice, but I don't think she's into me."

"Whatever. It's not like you ever struggle to find a woman who is."

"Yeah, whatever. You ready to spot me?"

# CHAPTER 54
## BEN

Tracey leans into the corner of the couch, props her feet on the coffee table, and rests her left arm on the side of the couch.

Would Violet be okay with feet on her coffee table? Probably not. I set my wineglass on a coaster and say, "Make yourself at home, why don't you."

Tracey slides her feet onto the floor with a giggle. "There's the Violet we know and love. The way you've been behaving lately, it wouldn't surprise me to learn aliens had abducted you and sent a clone in your place."

I pat my chest to ease my coughing fit. "Sorry. Wine went down the wrong way."

Anja leans forward. "What I want to know is what's going on between you and…"

"Ben. It's complicated?"

Her hands form wings on either side of her grin as she braces her chin in her palms. "We love complicated. Tell us about him."

"We click. On Sunday—"

Tracey ratchets her head toward me, her eyes fiery. "Whoa, whoa, whoa! You saw him on Sunday too?"

"Ah, he had worried about me in the aftermath of my bender on Saturday night. He slept on the couch. Total gentleman. Not for a second did I fear he would take advantage of me. Anyway, you know how I eat my way back from a hangover."

She shakes her head at me. "You're the only person in the world who can be hungry at the same time she's on the verge of puking. Did you make him breakfast?"

"I did. It's funny; I've known him the three months I've worked in sales at Heading Up, but until last weekend, we had never had a long conversation." I rub my palms furiously against my thighs to sop up the sweat. "None of this…" I wave my hand over the piles of clothes, dirty dishes, and knotted plastic bags filled with garbage dotting every available surface in the living room. "… is about Ben, though. I don't want to discuss him. Well, not in a, er, romantic context. Some stuff going on at work has me totally lost, to be honest."

Anja hops off the chair to my right and squishes against me on the couch, wrapping her arms around me. "Oh, hon. Now you understand why we're here. Tracey and I couldn't believe you hadn't texted either of us in days. That's so unlike you!"

Tracey abandons her glass of wine and hugs me, too. "I couldn't decide whether to be mad at you or worried."

I take another stab at keeping the authenticity factor high. "Well, *that* sounds entirely like you."

She cradles my head and lands a loud kiss on the crown of my skull. "Just as you dressing like a piñata, hitting on strange men, and throwing caution to the wind with your housekeeping are red flags, you'll know I'm in a pile of serious doo-doo if a friend blowing me off doesn't set me into a near homicidal rage. But enough with our reality checks; what's the four-one-one at your job?"

"I…"

The doorbell buzzes. Anja runs to the door to accept the pizza delivery. I am grateful for the interruption and the arrival of food. Even half a glass of wine on an empty stomach has my head spinning.

I bring plates and a roll of paper towel into the living room. Tracey rips a sheet from the roll and waves it at me. "The queen of table settings has resorted to paper towels in lieu of napkins? Please don't tell me not winning the contest on Monday has killed your inner Martha Stewart."

"I… It's a keep-it-simple kind of day. Even Martha takes the easy way out occasionally."

Anja drops the pizza box on a stack of newspapers on the coffee table. "At least when it comes to managing her stock portfolio." She studies me. Does she expect a reaction? I give her a comic pout, hoping I've chosen well. She lightly punches my jaw. "Oh, Violet. You're such an easy target."

She tugs a slice of pizza from the pie, deposits it onto a plate, and hands it to me. I'm ready to shove the entire slice in my mouth and dive in for seconds before they've taken their first bites. With restraint I didn't realize I possessed, I wait until Anja has served Tracey and herself. One taste of my slice, and I'm in heaven. "Man, that's the best pizza in New Jersey."

Tracey creases her brow. "No way. You're finally agreeing with me that Larry and Joe's pizza is better than Rocco's? Anja, she has definitely gone off the deep end. Get talking, girl. What's going on with you?"

I'm sure Violet would share an unadulterated version of her Derek experience with her friends. I sense a depth to their relationships that I might lack in my friendships. Which of my friends would jump in to save me if I were drowning?

Violet. She rescued me from the scum I turned to for free drinks; she nursed me through a hangover. While Julie has devoted herself to protecting the women on the team from Derek in her own style, at the end of the day, I am living Violet's life. Shouldn't I have believed she sought to protect both of us with her advice?

I unleash a tidal wave of confessions on her friends. I divulge every detail that is mine to share. Tracey and Anja set their plates on the table, unable to eat.

Tracey furrows her brow. "It's junior year, redux, with Julie taking my role. I'll forever regret forcing you to report Mr. Hartshorn. You know my intention was to prevent him from ever laying a hand on you again. Had I understood how powerless you were to fight the system, I wouldn't have pushed you."

My stomach turns into a boa constrictor, tightening its grip with a soul-crushing force. Violet had told me yesterday, and in no uncertain terms, she had her reasons for wanting me to remain silent. She had even explained how reporting sexual harassment isn't always a solution. I don't need to know the details of what happened to her, but I owe her the respect and concern she and her friends have shown me. Instead, I've failed her.

Until I can ask for Violet's forgiveness, I have to be the best version of her. I bet she has forgiven Tracey a thousand times since high school. Resting my head on her friend's shoulder, I snake my arm behind her. "I don't blame you. We were teenagers; we couldn't have known the system was rigged against us. Julie meant well, too. I could have told her my story, but it happened years ago. I had hoped I could change the outcome now that I'm older. But no. We still live in a world built for men. Nothing's changed."

Anja laces her fingers through mine. Had she taken my hand on Saturday, I would have been a confused man in women's clothing. Now, I recognize the gesture as much more meaningful than physical intimacy with a potential one-night stand. I need a deep connection with someone. I need to care. While I might have been attracted to Anja a few days ago, tonight there is only one person's hand I wish I could hold.

I pull my hand away and grab a second slice of pizza. "Now what?"

Tracey sucks a noisy breath through her nose, propelling her backward. "You had to put up with Hartshorn for three semesters, and he ruined your GPA. It will be the same with your boss. It sucks for you whether or not you act. It's time to make good on your pledge from last Friday. You have to quit."

My brain is in overdrive. Violet had been planning to quit before the swap? I need to talk with her, but if I can't, I would prefer to be alone than to risk saying the wrong thing to her friends.

"Would you excuse me for a second?" I wind my way past Tracey's legs. Shielding my phone from Violet's friends, I type and erase and type again, praying the litany of Violet-related thoughts and questions—and the emotions churning them out—ricocheting around my skull don't betray me in my text.

> **Ben:** I'm about to send your friends home.
> Should we talk tonight? Oh, A & T are
> awesome, BTW.

I stare at the screen for another minute, willing three dots to materialize. They don't.

# FRIDAY

# CHAPTER 55
## VIOLET

I couldn't think of a response to Ben's text last night. It wasn't his fault I ran around his apartment in a panic upon reading his text. I had experienced a lifetime's worth of emotions in the span of two hours. I wasn't in the mood to let go of the last one—elation at learning he had talked about me with a friend—in the event he was going to unload his defenses for the way he has acted. After I cooled down, I sent him a short text, telling him we'd see each other at the office.

I processed the terabytes of data I had uploaded to my brain while I gave his apartment a final scrub. Both his home and I felt a bit more orderly because of it. In the end, talking about him with Julie and Shane rather than speaking with him yesterday somehow drew me closer to him.

We haven't made plans for the great unveiling of our tattoos tonight at eight. Do we need to be together to break the curse? Does he even want to be with me?

I have nothing more I want to accomplish while being him, although it will be hard to give up the power to reach things on high shelves. And having his face greet me in the mirror. I run my hands against his upper arms. Yeah, I might miss the bits and pieces of him I've allowed myself to stare at this week.

Okay, I'll also miss him for additional reasons, including the moments we've spent together where we connected well beyond sharing bodies. But we'll have no reason to get together once we're ourselves again and I no longer work at Heading Up. While being the world's worst salesperson is reason enough to quit; now that life with Derek has become more complicated, I have to leave. I've been down this road before with Mr. Hartshorn. It won't end well for me.

I arrive at the office two minutes late on Friday morning and hustle to join the crowd at Derek's desk for the daily meeting. Julie stands behind Ben with her hands on his shoulders. I head to the opposite side and stand in the back row.

"Nice of you to join us," Peter says, jabbing his fist into my shoulder.

"Gotta keep the fans waiting. Did I miss anything?"

"Nah. Your girlfriend's back in her pantsuit today. Guess she's given up on trying to tempt you since you told her to leave you alone after the Teddy bear incident."

"I told you, the bear's an inside joke. Now, quit gabbing so I can pretend I'm paying attention to Derek."

I wish I could go to the eighth floor and tender my resignation today. Our department is more toxic than a superfund site. I suffer through the rest of the meeting, smug in the realization I won't have to endure Derek's grating voice, lame elevator jokes, and blatant favoritism for much longer.

Ben escapes Julie at the end of the meeting and runs up to me. My heart takes a heroic leap into my throat despite my intention to keep my cool.

"Hey, I'm really sorry I canceled on you last night."

"You didn't have a choice; when Tracey puts an idea into motion, a volcano erupting between her and her goal won't stop her."

"So I've learned. She told me what happened in high school with your teacher. Now I understand why you didn't want me to speak to Helen. I've been a terrible friend to you. I don't deserve your forgiveness, but I still hope you will forgive me." His eyes widen and plead with me. Behind them, I spot such openness and kindness. He's making it harder for me to prepare for us to part.

"Of course, I forgive you. I've begun to put things into perspective. One of these days we'll explore what happened between us this week."

He hunches his shoulders. "We'll be together for the big tattoo reveal tonight, won't we?"

"Sure. But right now, I have a call I want to make. We'll check in with each other later, okay?"

His face shifts from worried to blank. "Sure. Talk later."

We take different routes to our cubicles. It tears me up to hold him at such a distance, but I have to keep myself in check. I need to move forward, starting with Alex at the hotel.

She answers the phone on the second ring. "Operations."

"Alex, it's Ben from Heading Up."

Her sigh pierces my ear. "You're the sort of guy who can't believe a woman isn't interested in him unless she says it to his face, aren't you?"

Well, that answers my question about whether she'll sign a contract with me. I don't need to dance around her any longer. "No, I'm the sort of professional who would never neglect a client."

"Touché. By the way, thanks for the biscotti. Look, maybe you're a nice guy. And your company has many satisfied customers, according to its reviews. My job would be a lot easier having a management company oversee our elevators and escalator. But the company I hire won't be Heading Up."

"May I ask why?"

"Does Derek Finch still work for your company?"

"Yes. In fact, he's my direct supervisor."

"You could ask him why I won't sign with you."

"I had no idea he had ever been in contact with you."

"Figures. Four, five years ago, he had your job. Cold called me at the Morristown branch of the hotel. Super flirty in a gross way. That's on me. I'm friendly, which might encourage men to respond in kind. You and I: we've joked around, which is cool. But your last message might have crossed a line."

"Excuse me?" I press my hand on my stomach to quiet it's rumblings.

"The suggestive coughing in conjunction with the words *package* and *treat* was a tad off color, even for me."

I wipe my left palm against my thigh to dry it. "Oh, I promise you, the cough was innocent and the word choice unintentional. My apologies for sending the wrong signals. It's the last thing I wanted to do."

"Don't sweat it. My fault for misunderstanding you. And Derek's for making me more sensitive. He had pushed it when we spoke years ago. During the entire conversation with him, I had my hand on my rape whistle, metaphorically speaking. Still, I made an appointment to meet him. He took one look at me, and made a snide comment about how I had deceived him into thinking I was attractive. I won't repeat what his exact words were, but they were the sort of thing I'd consider tattooing on my forearm to remind myself I'm not the person people define me to be."

I rub my left upper arm, imagining what part of me will jump to the fore once I remove the bandage. "I wish I could say I'm shocked, but I'm not."

"You came into my office bearing a bit of the sexist pig stench, and I figured it was a company trait. Now do you understand why I don't want to sign with you?"

"Absolutely. And I'm sorry that has been your experience. There's nothing less persuasive than a person claiming they're not who you think they are, so I won't demean you by trying to tell you I'm a good guy. While you met the very worst of our company, I assure you he doesn't embody the company's mission."

She grunts. "Our meeting was the second chance I hadn't meant to give Heading Up. Who would bat cleanup if I gave you a third opportunity?"

"Are you saying you're interested in meeting with another rep, perhaps someone of a different gender?"

"I haven't written you off completely. The biscotti did their job. Perhaps I'd be amenable to meeting a pair of reps who skew the opposite direction from your boss on Monday. You can be part of the team. Do you have a rep in mind who can, let's say, counter any whiff of the toxic masculinity I'm desperate to avoid?"

Julie is the only woman I could recommend for the job, but I can't say she'd be the right fit. I'm glad I understand her motives better, but I can't forget the influence she wielded over Ben. She also has a more aggressive sales style than him.

I grit my teeth. Saving Ben's commission requires a sacrifice I don't want to make. Straightening my back and setting my jaw, I say, "I have a colleague I work well with. She's definitely cut from a different cloth than my boss. I'll check her schedule."

"Sounds like a plan."

"We'll be in touch."

I hang up, wondering what exactly I've just promised her.

# CHAPTER 56
# BEN

Violet's sitting at her desk, wearing the strangest expression. It's a combination of the alluring smile I taught her in my bathroom mirror over the weekend and, I'm going to say, confusion blended with a bit of hostility. Her jaw hangs open while her eyes squint and roll in a conversation I couldn't begin to translate. With a sharp inhale, she claps her hands, stands, and walks toward me.

"I thought we weren't talking to each other," I say with a laugh when she knocks on the wall to my cubicle.

"I... uh... I didn't mean to give you that idea. We have so much craziness in our lives, I find it safest to compartmentalize. While we're at the office, it's best to put anything personal aside."

"Got it. What brings you to my neck of the woods, then?"

"I just spoke with Alex from the hotel."

"Good news?"

"I know why she wasn't interested in signing with me."

"Why?"

She tiptoes behind my desk. A week in my body, and she still moves like Violet. It kind of charms the pants off of me. Her eyes scan the hallway outside my cubicle. Sensing the coast is clear, she leans toward my ear, cupping it to whisper into it. I'm ready to ignore whatever she is saying, instead savoring the intimacy of the gesture. But one word snaps my mind back to the office.

Derek.

She explains the story. Unable to jump in with a proper way to address the more serious content, I choose instead to focus on the least important detail. "Alex has a sexy voice. I have to confess I had pictured a body and face to go with the voice." He pauses. "So, not a clone of Scarlett Johansson?"

"Why would it matter?"

"It doesn't. Men have filthy minds. Doesn't mean we all act on our thoughts. She was funny. I would have enjoyed working with her regardless of whether I found her attractive."

"You might get your wish. Ooh, bad turn of phrase. She wants to set up a meeting on Monday."

"My day's wide open."

"There's another thing." She clasps her hands in front of her mouth.

"She demands a lifetime supply of biscotti?"

"Wouldn't hurt. No, she wants to meet with a team."

"The Yankees? The local middle school's competitive eating team?"

"Is that a thing?"

"Don't know. Should be. What team did she have in mind?"

Violet's eyebrows push a mass of creases toward her hairline. "You and me."

"Little does she know she's already met with the two of us."

"True." She reverses course with her brow, setting her face into a deep scowl.

This must be the conversation she was having with herself before she came to see me. She doesn't want to partner with me.

"You don't seem particularly enthused at the prospect."

"I… No, that's not it." She waves her hands frantically. "Can two people split a commission?"

"I don't see why not. We can always ask…" I retract my jaw, regretting having to finish my sentence.

She senses my hesitation. "Let me ask Derek on my own. I don't want you to meet one-on-one with him. I'll be back once he's okayed it."

She races toward the door. I still don't believe asking for permission to work together is the real hurdle she needs to clear.

I hold up my finger. "So, tonight. How do you want to handle the swap?"

She turns. "Oh, definitely together. It would be disorienting to be alone."

Thank goodness!

"Where and when?"

She says, "You should go to my place and change into a sleeveless top, and I'll grab a pair of shorts."

"You're sure we're supposed to do it at eight?"

"This again? I'm not saying I'm an expert on the subject, but it seems wisest to do it exactly a week after they put the bandages on."

"The rhyme forbids the tattoos from seeing the light of day for a week. The sun sets a little after seven. Shouldn't we expose them to sunlight to break the curse?"

"The instructions said nothing about it needing to be sunny while we remove the bandages. The when matters the most."

I hold my hands in surrender. "Then eight it is." Thanks to what I've learned during my stint as a woman, my protective instinct kicks in. "I don't want you going home alone. We could remove them at your—"

Although I did my best to restore her apartment to its former glory, the results aren't spectacular enough for me to want to be present for its unveiling. I say, "Let's meet at the rooftop bar we went to last Saturday. I'll make sure you get home safely."

"Promise me you won't drink any shots of tequila before the switch. No way I'm nursing your hangover."

"And you have to promise me... Oh, I don't know what."

"I promise I won't wrap your entire calf in tape, forcing you to endure the exquisite sensation of ripping out the remaining patches of leg hair when you're you again."

"Deal. So, you didn't shave my legs?"

"You'll have to wait until tonight to see."

She wrinkles her nose, grinning as she backs out of my cubicle.

# CHAPTER 57
## VIOLET

I peer over the dividing walls in the office toward Derek's desk. He's not behind it. The tiny bolt of courage I had earlier flies from my body. The Violet in me must dread having to speak with him, and the security of being Ben can't counter my gut instinct.

I hope Monday will be my last day, but it's up to Helen. She might hold me to staying for two to four more weeks after I give notice. If I quit before the meeting with Alex, Derek might pull me from it and assign one of his toadies to help. Ben will definitely lose the contract.

The ideal solution is for Derek to deny my request, forcing Ben to go to the meeting alone. I guarantee he'll weave his magic on Alex without my help. Yeah, I won't oversell the idea to Derek.

While I'm on my feet, I decide to use the restroom. A woman's voice filters through the door in the accessible bathroom. She sounds agitated, probably fighting with someone on the phone. A man's voice rises over hers. I hesitate, straining to hear the conversation.

"I said no," the woman cries.

An electric shock sails through my arms, forcing my hands into tight fists. I throw my shoulder against the door and press the handle. Thankfully, it's unlocked.

I burst into the bathroom. Derek has his back to me, bracing a hand against the wall and trapping Julie on the other side with his shoulder.

She spots me first. Her eyes are wide with terror, but my presence gives her a burst of energy. She throws her weight against the shoulder Derek uses to cage her. He skids an inch on the tiles but doesn't step back or release his hand.

"You can't tell me you don't want me. Why else would you parade around the office in short skirts?" he sneers.

I wrap my hands around his shoulders and yank him away from her. He stumbles, catching himself on the sink.

I lower my voice to a quiet but firm growl. "She said no."

"Butt out of this, Harris. I don't know what you think you've stumbled upon, but you have the wrong impression."

"Julie, why don't you tell me what I'm witnessing here?" I ask.

She tugs at her blouse, straightening it and tucking it into her skirt's waistband. "I came in here alone. Before the door closed, Derek slipped inside."

He adjusts his collar. "Exactly. This is an accessible restroom. My intention was to remind her to leave the bathroom for those who need it."

"A point you could only make while pinning her to the wall and ignoring her pleas for you to stop?"

"I didn't do any such thing. Since when are you a defender of the ladies, anyway?"

"You don't know me." I hold my hand to Julie. "You okay?"

I never would have imagined describing her as fragile, but her nod uses the last of her strength.

I hold the door for her. After it shuts, leaving Derek inside, I say to Julie, "Violet and I will meet you upstairs in a minute."

# CHAPTER 58
## BEN

Violet returns to my cubicle with such a severe expression, I reflexively squeeze the armrests of my desk chair. "Did he say no?" I ask.

Her narrowed eyes and clenched jaw remind me of her coming to my defense on Saturday evening at the bar. All she is missing is a tampon case to use as a battering ram. "Didn't ask him. We need to go to the eighth floor. Now. In the event we pass Derek, pretend he doesn't exist."

"What—"

She holds a finger in front of her lips and then to the ceiling. "Upstairs."

I jog to keep up with her. The memory of my mother dragging me by the hand out of a department store because she caught me playing fort in a circular clothing rack springs to mind. Violet doesn't have the authority to confiscate my Lego sets, but I can't help but fear I have done something worthy of a similar punishment.

We carve a Derek-free path to the stairwell and head upstairs. The receptionist ushers us into the human resource office. Knowing they're expecting us constricts my lungs.

Has Derek discovered the report we filed? Have I gotten Violet fired? She has every reason to hate me.

Julie sits in the human resource office, clutching a mug of a steaming beverage like it alone anchors her to the earth. Helen hovers over her, her hands jerking forward like she wants to touch Julie but thinks the better of it. "Oh, there you are. My word! Ben, you were in the right place at the right time. I'm sure Julie will say this and more, but I cannot thank you enough for acting. Sure, I'd expect any of us would say we would have done the same, but how rare is it for a person with your character to be on hand and willing to step in?"

I fight the impulse to ask, "What? What have I done?"

Helen has been speaking to Violet, obviously. She wraps her left hand tensely over her right fist and glances at Julie from the corners of her eyes. Violet says, "I'm glad I was walking past the restroom. Did he hurt you?"

Julie rubs her upper arms. "No. He had barely touched me before you came in. I'm shaken, but whole."

Helen crosses her arms. "Ben, I will need to hear your version of the story. Julie, perhaps you and Violet can wait in the lobby. If you need anything, the receptionist will take care of you."

The fragments of the story I've heard so far are enough for me to want to swoop in to protect Julie. She might not suspect I'm a man inside a tiny woman's frame, but it wouldn't be right for me to encroach on her personal space. Instead, I fall behind her as she leads us into the lobby.

I sit in the chair at a right angle from hers. She takes a sip from her mug and sets it on a table before finding my eyes. "It never should have happened, but since it did, I'm relieved it was me and not you."

"Derek attacked you?"

"Yes. He followed me into the bathroom. I told him to leave, but he wouldn't, instead saying he'd make it worth my while to let him stay. He also mentioned that he needed to punish me for embarrassing him in front of the team yesterday morning. When I told him to stop, to leave me alone, he trapped me and pulled my blouse from my skirt, ready to snake his hand under my waistband. I shouted no, and I guess Ben heard me. I've never considered myself the damsel in distress sort, but I can't complain about being rescued by a man like him. You were right to trust him."

My heart swells with admiration for Violet. Helen has a point; I hope I would have done the same thing had I been the person to overhear Julie's distress. With a bootcamp tutorial on being a woman under my belt, I would in a second, but before the swap? No use asking because the point is moot.

"And you were right to file a report against Derek," I say. "I've been in a similar situation before. I thought nothing could render a person more powerless than to have their claim ignored. It kills me you've experienced worse. It shouldn't take a physical attack to give credence to our claims of harassment."

"No, it shouldn't." She stuffs her hands between her knees and stares at them.

The conversation doesn't continue, and the quiet becomes purposeful for her. I scan the reception area to relieve her from the pressure of me staring at her. The floor-to-ceiling walls and offices with doors on this floor incite a fit of jealousy. With a sudden realization, I understand how the lack of privacy on my floor and the central location of Derek's desk reflect the power he wields over the department. He has access to us, and we have no barriers to protect ourselves. I hope they can his ass today, because even in my normal body, I never want to experience this level of vulnerability again. More important, I don't want Violet and Julie to endure another second of it.

Helen steps into the lobby. "Security has escorted Derek out of the building, which means the coast is clear. Julie, dear, let's send you home for the afternoon. We'll call you a car. Violet, I'd like to have a word with you."

I stand and face Julie. "I'm here if you need me. You have my work email, right?"

It will go to Violet, not that it matters. She'll be more comforting than me, I'm sure.

"Thanks. See you on Monday."

"Take care."

I follow Helen into her office. "I want to discuss a different matter. Ben, perhaps you can head back to your desk?"

Violet rolls her lips and raises her brow, unsure whether to leave me to handle her business with Helen.

I say, "I'm okay having him stay. Besides, we're friends; I'll end up telling him about our conversation, anyway."

She studies us, a sweet smile spreading across her cheeks. "I'm glad to hear you've made connections downstairs. We adored having you in our suite and were sad to see you leave us, but I understood the payroll salary couldn't compete with the potential commissions you could earn in sales. Although perhaps sales wasn't the promotion you had wanted." She bats her hands. "I'm taking the long way round, aren't I? Let's jump to the main point. We have an opening you might find interesting. We need an internal communications associate. Your role would encompass ensuring our company policies reflect our mission and giving the employees the tools they need to comply both within the company and as they interact with our clients. It involves developing content…" She glances at me, lifting her eyebrows.

Violet's eyes grow wide at the word *content*. She pitches her neck forward, desperate to speak.

What have I learned about her this week? Why is that meaningful? Oh! "Like I'd be paid to craft and design things?"

Violet is one iota too professional to skip around the office, but I can tell she's close.

Helen taps her fingertips together. "I knew that would appeal to you. What do you say? Would you like to return to the eighth floor?"

# CHAPTER 59
## VIOLET

I lock eyes with Ben. "You have to accept the offer. Weren't you just telling me how much you enjoyed life on the eighth floor and hoped a job in the communications department would become available?"

Ben's face is a mix of emotions. For all the decisions we've had to make on the other's behalf, perhaps none has carried as much significance. The pull of his eyes convinces me he's in tune with the answer I want him to give. A spark of excitement brightens his face. But I sense a counterweight.

His spine straightens with his inhale. "The job sounds amazing! Yes, absolutely yes. Except..." His eyes shift toward mine. "Ben had been looking for Derek before the, uh, incident. He has a client whose hesitancy to sign a contract, coincidentally, dates back to an encounter she had with Derek a few years ago. The client is considering signing with Heading Up provided Ben brings someone... well, me, to the meeting on Monday. Ben wanted to ask Derek what the company's position on sales reps splitting a commission is. In light of my new job, perhaps I can't help him?"

Helen says, "Why don't we keep you in the sales department for another week to close your accounts? Work together on the hotel contract. Meanwhile, since you won't be accepting new leads, you can train for the new position in your downtime. Is that agreeable to you?"

I wait for the negative emotion tightening Ben's mouth to melt, but it doesn't. Behind Helen's back, I trace a smile—the one I'm dying to unleash once I'm free to celebrate my promotion—in front of my lips with my pointer.

He rubs his palms together and grins. "Yes, it is." I gesture for him to hug Helen, which he does awkwardly. He pulls away from her a second later. "We've taken up enough of your time. I expect you have an insane amount of paperwork to deal with on the Derek front, so we'll head downstairs now."

Helen pats his shoulder and then extends her hand to me. "We'll need an interim sales leader on your floor. Ben, would you consider throwing your hat in the ring for the position?"

Ben struggles to contain his indifference, reining in a litany of shrugs and nose wrinkling, but I suspect it's just for show. I tilt my head. He gives me a committed shrug to imply he's not committing.

I say, "I appreciate your confidence in me. Can I take the weekend to think about it?"

"Absolutely. You've had an overwhelming morning. First thing Monday will be fine. Once again, I commend you for coming to Julie's defense. And Violet, I applaud your courage to bring your issues to my attention. We have to take measured steps when considering accusations such as yours, and while it might have appeared we weren't prepared to act, we take such matters seriously. Never hesitate to speak with me whenever something doesn't seem right. My job—and soon to be yours—is to ensure Heading Up continues to provide a supportive, inclusive work environment. And on that note, I'll send you on your way.

Your co-workers have been informed of the bare minimum they need to know, which doesn't include who discovered Derek, what he had been doing with Julie, or that he had been under investigation for prior alleged offenses. To maintain integrity, we ask you not to divulge any additional details."

I give her a tight-lipped nod. "Easier done than said. Thank you for everything."

Ben and I descend the stairs in silence. I wish we had permission to go home. Better yet, I wish it were eight o'clock already.

# CHAPTER 60
# BEN

"You're more of a man than I ever was," I say to Violet when we are in the stairwell.

"Are you kidding? You've been protecting me all week. I'd given my teen-aged self permission to talk me into remaining silent about Derek for the last three months. You were one hundred percent right to follow Julie's lead rather than mine. Maybe today wouldn't have happened had I spoken up sooner." She stops mid-flight and leans against the cinderblock wall.

I want so badly to hold her hand or smooth her hair or use any gesture to pull the pain out of her. "Derek, not you, bears responsibility for his actions. Don't you dare blame yourself for anything."

I stand on the step below her and gaze at her. For a week, I've been looking at Violet inside of me, but now, I wonder whether I've actually seen her. Or, how much of who she is I've accounted for versus how many gaps in my knowledge of her have I filled in with my own details. For the first time, I see Violet—as Violet—shrinking under my flesh and bones.

Neither Helen nor I have addressed the impact witnessing the attack had on her because, at the moment, Violet is me, and it's natural to assume encountering a sexual assault would be different for a man than for a woman. Had I been me, I would have punched Derek into the next century. Everyone would have hailed me for my physicality rather than comforted me for having experienced a trauma.

"Hey, Violet?" I reach for her hand and lead her to the landing. "You okay? You witnessed something horrible. Even with the protection of being in a man's body, it must have been devastating for you. You must have imagined being in Julie's shoes."

She crumples onto the step and drags her hands across her cheeks. Propping her chin in her palms, she says, "I haven't had a second to process it. Your hands sprang into action the second I heard signs of distress coming from the bathroom. While your hormones dictated my actions, my brain reminded me not to be violent. I didn't have the chance to fear what could have been. But now that it's over, my body has unleashed a full store of adrenaline. I'm really shaken. Until today, his bullying and inappropriate comments were a known quantity. I knew how to manage them. I had never imagined it was unsafe to work for him. Now? I'm retroactively remembering every instance where he could have hurt me."

I sit next to her and lean my head on her shoulder. She slips her arm behind me. Without a lick of magic, I am, for the moment, me again and she is Violet. We have eight hours before I can wrap my own arms around her for real, but I know, without a shred of doubt, there is nothing I want more than to be the person she turns to for comfort.

# CHAPTER 61
## VIOLET

With apologies to Ben, I doubt I will accomplish anything today. After making an appointment to meet with Alex next week and then zoning out during my first conversation with a potential lead following our meeting with Helen, I call it quits. He'll have to begin his day on Monday by picking up where I left off. He isn't at his desk when I leave for my lunch break, which I plan on stretching until five. I post a sticky note on his monitor, reminding him we'll meet at seven-thirty at the rooftop bar.

I'm of two minds whether I should have invited him to play hooky with me this afternoon. Thanks to Derek, our lives collided together again with the ferocity of wishes made on magical tattoo ink. More than a curse and our shared experiences have bonded us together, though. Despite having been a near stranger a week ago, he has been the ideal partner with whom to navigate the insanity. To walk away from him now, even for a few hours, prickles my skin and enhances my sense of vulnerability and loneliness.

I can tell he cares for me in some capacity. But as I admit to myself the depth of my affection for him, bands of tension squeeze me until I cannot breathe. We could walk away from the experience good friends. Perhaps that's all he wants. It won't be enough for me, though.

Once we're no longer colleagues in the same department, I won't be able to peek into his cubicle. We won't stand beside each other during staff meetings. If he only wants to be friends, we'll fall out of practice of making time for each other.

This afternoon is my last chance to explore what it means to be him in the literal sense. I can't name any activities I want to pursue, but it's like the final morning of a vacation. I'd hate to head home, realizing I had missed half of what the destination offered, so to speak.

At his apartment, I retrace the steps I've already taken. A last workout, another round of laundry, and an un-necessary top-to-bottom scrub of his bathroom. I stock his fridge and and even bake muffins, freezing half of them.

I flick the Sinatra bobblehead I had bought for him and place it on his dresser. I had struggled over what to give him as a parting gift. Ultimately, leaving behind a tidy apartment and a store of food more nourishing than abandoned science experiments seems as on brand as I get.

The edges of the tape on the tattoo's bandage have begun to peel away. I rub them against the skin on his calf. It dawns on me I haven't obsessed over my own tattoo, or specifically, why I got it in the first place.

I had wanted to change, to see myself as tougher than I am. I've spent the past week without the tattoo on my arm. The mark I had hoped would remind me of my inner badass hasn't been mine to tap into. Perhaps I need it less than I did a week ago, but I bet it will mean more to me now for all I've experienced.

At seven-fifteen, I lock the door to Ben's apartment and file away the last snapshots of my temporary home in my mind. My armpits have grown damp. I should have left ten minutes ago. Not that I believe the possibility of arriving late is the source of my anxiety.

I milk my appreciation for the amount of ground I can cover in a single stride for all it's worth. It takes eight minutes to reach the hotel. Unlike last Saturday, I step into the first available elevator. The last thing I want to do is to delay my arrival. The elevator deposits me onto the roof, which is already teeming with patrons. From a spot outside the traffic flow, I scan the bar. Ben has claimed a chair where Tracey and Anja had sat last weekend. A man places his hand on the armrest of the chair facing Ben, leaning casually toward him.

I put Ben's long legs through their paces, devouring the space between us. "Hey, Violet. Hope you weren't waiting long." I place my hand on his shoulder and stare down the strange man in front of me.

He backs away from Ben. "I guess you weren't just feeding me a line about waiting for your boyfriend." He turns toward me, his hands in the surrender position. "I wasn't trying to steal her from you. We're cool?"

"Yeah, we're cool."

I claim the empty seat and slide it closer to Ben. "Glad I arrived before the tequila shots started flowing in your direction. Speaking of which, you have half an hour left to get a man to buy you a drink."

"I've had enough adventures with men, thank you very much." He tugs the blue and white gingham sleeveless blouse he's wearing, smoothing the hem against his jeans.

"Even this man?" I point to myself.

"Present company excluded."

"Then let me buy you a drink."

"Already taken care of." He nods in the direction of an approaching server.

The server sets a glass of white wine in front of Ben and a pint of beer on my side of the table. Ben hands the server cash for the drinks. We wait until we're alone to speak.

Ben holds his glass toward me. I reciprocate. He says, "Congratulations on your new job."

"I've dreamed of landing the position since I applied at Heading Up, yet amid all the craziness, I've barely thought about it since Helen offered it to me."

He takes a sip of wine. "I guess it means we won't work together anymore." He's not simply stating a fact; his tone is hollow, and his eyes are downcast.

"I've kept a secret from you. Before I went to the tattoo parlor, I had decided I would search for a new job. Instead of leaving the company, I'm moving upstairs. Better, right?"

"It is. I guess I knew you had wanted to leave. Your friends had mentioned something about a pledge. Was it because of Derek?"

"No. I had finally admitted to myself I'm a disaster of a salesperson."

"Not true. Alex had every reason not to sign with us, yet she still agreed to another meeting because you persevered. I would have blown her off days ago after her radio silence."

"She's just one client. I'm always at the bottom of the leaderboard."

"Could it be because our boss gave you the dregs of the cold call files and did everything in his power to undermine you?"

I draw my shoulders to my ears. "Maybe? I'll never know."

"I'm guessing sales was never your dream job. Consider the last three months the trial by fire you needed to go through to get to where you deserve to be."

"Thanks. That's a good way to look at it. And you? Any interest in applying for Derek's job?"

"Why would it interest me?"

"Oh, um, maybe to ensure the department returns to an era of fair and ethical practices? Someone has to put Peter and Topher on notice that bullying won't be tolerated."

"I'd have to act like I cared about the job."

"Yeah, no. Your slacker routine doesn't fool me anymore. You're meant to fight the good fight. Derek made it easy for you to do the least amount of work possible, but

I don't believe being indifferent is your true style. Given the opportunity to care, you came to life."

He wipes the condensation from the side of his glass. "Thanks, but it doesn't help with the decision. I'll think about it later; I'm done with Heading Up for the weekend. Let's get to the matter at hand. How d'you enjoy being me?"

"Being tall was the best! I reorganized the top shelves of your closets and kitchen cabinets just because I could reach them without a step stool. I'll miss beasting at the gym. You're crazy strong."

"So, you're a fan of my body?" His eyebrows jiggle.

*I plead the fifth, your honor.*

"It offers certain conveniences…" I say.

"Like taking a leak in the great outdoors." He spreads his hand toward the glass wall next to us. "The Hudson would surely accept another donation should the mood hit."

"I'm good. How about you?"

"A little harder to achieve an accurate deposit in my current condition."

"Smart ass. I meant what did you think of the experience of living in what you generously described as your current condition?"

"Ballet class was a highlight. In general, moving your body felt like a vacation. It's so light and nimble." He flutters his fingers. "Never knew I had talents for picking up tiny sequins until I sported these slender puppies. But on a more serious topic, you can't ever coast, can you? Everything is harder for women. I wasn't prepared to have to be conscientious every second of the day. Who I talked to and what I wore; they've stacked the deck against women, haven't they?"

"I wouldn't wish the worst you had to endure on anyone, but there is something to be said about walking a mile in someone else's shoes."

"It means someone is barefoot and their shoes are a mile away from them."

"That too. But I was talking about empathy."

"Huh, empathy. It was definitely missing from our department. And I have to confess it's an area where I shouldn't have been coasting."

"I disagree. Empathy comes naturally to you. You are quick to feel someone else's pain. Empathy is a combination of compassion and imagination. Most people have the occasional compassionate moment. If they witness a person in pain and recognize its source, it evokes an emotional response. But when they encounter someone experiencing an unfamiliar kind of pain, they won't be empathetic to a person's struggles if they can't imagine what it's like to be the other person. And that means they won't seek a solution to end the suffering. Sadly, for humanity's sake, I suspect imagination is in short supply."

Ben sets his glass on the table and reaches for my hand. It's strange to fold my palm around a delicate hand—my hand. And touching him generates a round of tingles behind my belly button.

He says, "You constantly amaze me."

His words and gaze mesmerize me into silence. I remember his description of my eyes from last Saturday, where he claimed they were calm and deep. I had chided him, reminding him he was seeing himself behind my eyes. The pair staring at me are still pools of gentleness and depth. At the moment they are gray, but I know I'll see the same soul behind them once they turn blue after the curse lifts.

Wait. The curse. I had forgotten we had a deadline. I dig out my phone of my pocket to check the time. "It's seven fifty-eight. You ready?"

# CHAPTER 62
## BEN

Violet breaks the spell she had cast over me while we talked to remind me our week has come to an end. Odd as it sounds, a part of me isn't ready to return to normal. I run my hand over the bandage on my left arm.

I say, "I'm jittery in a 'good excited' way and maybe a little, oh, anxious."

"Are you worried the curse won't be lifted?"

"No. That never occurred to me. We've had to be close this week, to depend on each other. I suppose I'm nervous about…" I stop myself before I blurt out my fear she'll want to walk away from me after the switch. "Sorry, I'm rambling. So, how should we do this?"

"Let's get a head start. Peel away each strip of tape right up to the edge of the bandage. Shoot me if you think my plan is cheesy, but we could count down from ten and pull off the dressings at exactly the same time." She waves her hands in front of her face, erasing her last sentence.

I'll miss watching my body react like a woman's, although it could be in these gestures where I've seen Violet more authentically. If I'm lucky, I won't have to give up such moments.

"Sounds good to me," I say.

We scratch and tug at the tape, contorting ourselves to prepare for eight o'clock. Her hand pressed against the black bandage on the calf that soon will be mine again, she says, "I'm ready. I'm watching the second hand on my phone's clock. Okay, here goes. Ten, nine…"

I loosen one last centimeter of tape. "Ready?"

She exhales. "Five, four, three, two… Rip away!"

Even with my eyes closed, I sense an ocean's worth of luminescent algae twinkling under the surface of my skin. A tingling just this side of numb zips through each of my fingers, across my scalp, and along my ribs. When the sensation abates, I focus on the crumpled bandage in my right hand, which I toss onto the table as I open my eyes.

Violet sits across from me, where I had been sitting. Everything about her makes sense. Her quiet intensity had gotten lost in a larger body. Contained within her smaller frame, it creates a more concentrated blend with her kindness and strength, filling her with beauty.

She twists her head, regarding me from the side. "Are you smiling because you're relieved to be you again?"

"No. I mean, of course, I am. But I'm also smiling because it seems right to see you."

"I was thinking the same thing." Her fingers trail against the violets sprouting on her upper arm. She casts a furtive glance at them and then meets my eyes again. "I'll show you mine if you show me yours."

"That ship has sailed. Although I promise you I never so much as peeked at anything marked private last week."

"Not what I meant." She drags her chair next to mine. "The last time we saw our tattoos, we had much different vantage points. I need a mirror to see mine right-side up, but you won't."

I trace a stem and then the petals of one of the flowers. "They're beautiful from where I'm sitting."

Her shoulders retract, and she has a sweet smile blooming on her lips.

I prop my right foot on the table, rolling the outer edge of my leg upward.

She leans forward. "I love the 3D effect of yours. You could get a gig designing tattoos."

I drop my foot to the floor. "Can't say whether I'd be up for that ride."

She wags her finger at me. "No elevator puns. Being free from Derek's overuse of them is a bonus of your future work experience."

I trap her right hand in mine to stop the playful wagging. She relaxes her arm, lowering our hands into her lap. Her eyes have locked onto mine. I'm finding it difficult to catch my breath. The tickle in my body kicks into gear again, and for a second, I worry by touching her, we'll swap bodies again. Which is stupid. This sensation doesn't involve magic.

I rest the top of my forehead against hers. The fingers on my left hand swim toward hers until they entwine. Our eyes are at the same height, but we have to glance up to find each other. "Is it okay if...?"

She nods, bobbing my head with hers. I let go of her hand and thread my left arm behind her, drawing her body against mine when my hand finds her shoulder. Trust me, I want to jump lips first into a kiss with her. Yet the prickle of waiting, of stolen breaths and flicks of my tongue to wet my lips is intoxicating.

I've moved too fast with each woman I've kissed before, missing the power of anticipation. I guarantee this kiss will be different. First kisses have always come before I've known a woman. With Violet, I have built the case over every second of the last week for why I need to kiss her.

But analyzing a kiss is stupid. With an inhale, I draw her mouth to mine. Oh, yeah. This is what I'm meant to do. Nothing welling up inside either of us is lost in translation. How every move of her lips and tongue can be simultaneously familiar and beyond exciting confounds me. I doubt I'll tire of investigating the mystery.

She rolls her head downward, finding the balance point between our foreheads again. Her pointer pokes the center of my lips. "Just checking that you're still you."

"Wouldn't want to be anyone else."

"Our kiss knocked me for quite a loop. I'm dizzier now than I was when the curse lifted."

"In a good way?"

She nods. "A very good way, although I'm not sure I should operate farm equipment in my current state."

"The harvest will have to wait. How about your feet?"

She kicks her left foot to the side. "They're the feet I know and love. A tad more blistered than I remember, but everything else checks out."

"Sorry I didn't return them in the condition you had lent them. But that's not what I meant. Can you operate your feet for a short walk? I've heard of a charming apartment a few blocks away. I'm betting it would meet even your standards of cleanliness."

"I am well acquainted with the apartment. And yes, it currently is the very model of hygienic."

"Do you really know the apartment as well as you say? I'd love to give you the owner's tour, perhaps starting in the bedroom?"

"I stand corrected. I'm sure I missed a detail or two concerning your bed while I was alone in it."

I point at myself, grinning enough to make my cheeks ache. "Me. Please say what you missed was me."

"What I missed was you and me."

She tugs my hand, and we race away from our table. I doubt her legs will get us to my apartment fast enough. Scooping her into my arms, I run the rest of the way across the bar. I swing her foot toward the elevator call button. She taps it with her toe and beams at me. The doors open. I carry her into the elevator and lower her feet to the ground. She stands on her tiptoes and numbs my brain with another incredible kiss.

# EPILOGUE
# ONE MONTH LATER

# VIOLET

I unplug the smart board from the socket behind Ben's desk. "Was my presentation okay?" I ask him.

He reaches his hand behind him and flutters his fingers at me. I tap the tips but resist intertwining my fingers with his. Touching him for real will have to wait until we're out of the office. It would appear pretty sketchy to his team to watch their boss and the lady who just lectured them on gender biases in the workplace for the last hour getting all hot and heavy.

"You're a rock star. I wish you could have delivered your presentation to Derek before…" He nods toward Julie's cubicle to his left.

"He had sat through plenty of workshops on sexual harassment. Heap lot of good they did him."

"Topher and Peter, too."

"Good riddance to the three of them. Pretty sweet to see a few of the recently opened slots on the sales team filled by women."

"The sales department is more pleasant now, isn't it? I still think Julie should have gotten my gig, though." He sits on the outside edge of his desk and crosses his arms over his chest.

DIANE MICHAELS

"She didn't want it."

"Neither did I."

"Baloney. You had never come to work earlier than you did the first day in the office after, well, you and me... Anyway, I caught you waiting for Helen to arrive to tell her you were going to apply for Derek's old job, so don't feed me your nonsense about not wanting it."

"Busted. Hey, it's time for lunch. Why don't you wheel your smart board upstairs and then take a man to lunch since you're flush with cash from your settlement?"

Julie and I had hoped Derek's punishment would be more severe than simply being fired, but legally, the company—rather than him—bore responsibility for his actions. They offered me compensation for the lost commissions I might have earned during my first three months had he been more equitable with the lead distribution. They offered Julie a settlement, too. Because she loves working in sales and trusted the experience would improve exponentially under Ben's leadership, she chose to stay at Heading Up.

I say, "Today's Friday. You know I have a standing lunch date with Anja and Tracey. You're more than welcome to join us."

"I wouldn't want to intrude."

"What intrusion? You're part of the family now that you've received Tracey's seal of approval."

He buffs the backs of his fingers against his chest. "I told you back when I was you, women never reject me."

I snort with mock disdain. But it's true; Tracey wanted to have nothing to do with me when I was Ben. Now, she thinks he walks on water. As far as she and Anja are concerned, he was the hero on that fateful day a month ago. I'll never tell them about the body swap. I don't mind for a second letting him take the credit, though.

"Do you miss being me?" I ask.

His satisfied grin tells me the answer before he says a word. "I prefer the view from here, thank you very much.

And I'm serious; you need to stash your equipment fast, because if I don't kiss you within the next three minutes, I might die."

That's all the motivation I need. I hustle up to the eighth floor, stash the board in the conference room, and race down eight flights of stairs to meet Ben on the sidewalk in front of our building.

His hands cup my head. He bends over to negate the height difference between us. I'm tiny beside him, but not vulnerable. Secure and never invisible. But now is not the time for deep thoughts. Our lips meet, and the same as it was during our first kiss, every inch of me tingles more than when our lives collided in the tattoo gallery.

Thank you so much for taking the time to read *Inked Together*. I hope you'll share your review on Amazon, Goodreads and/or Bookbub to let new readers know what you thought about this book.

The tattoo ink hasn't lost its power. Experience its magic again in *Found Together*.

**Magical ink. Two wishes. Now Anja and Griffin are searching for a connection.**

Free spirit Anja Lund is hearing voices. And they're spilling the dirt on all the eligible men. Learning their secrets before she falls for them seems like a wish come true. But when every man has a fatal flaw, she chooses to settle for the devil she knows.

Griffin Hull dreams of love. Instead, constant rejections because of his scars turn romance into a nightmare. After he mysteriously loses his inhibitions whenever he uses his phone, he believes he has found his curse's loophole.

Whether he's texting his ex, calling a Hollywood star, or working remotely with Anja, Griffin is learning to trust women again.

Until painful reminders force both Griffin and Anja to rebuild their walls. She alone understands his wish to be seen as more than his scars, but can he trust their friendship to protect him when they finally meet face to face?

# THANK YOU:

Writing Violet and Julie's horrific workplace stories meant I was also writing a human resource department's nightmare. Thanks to my wonderful friend Bill Van Patten, I had a kind, patient, and empathetic guide to lead me through the red tape of reporting sexual harassment in a corporate setting.

I extend my gratitude to Kirsty and Karolyn for once again braving an early draft of my book and helping me to shape it into something publishable.

My sister Heidi has always been one of my biggest cheerleaders. And now she is my favorite cover designer. I loved that our Zoom editing sessions meant we had bonus visits with each other!

I have an endless list of reasons I love my husband. That he is an ally to women is right near the top.

For anyone who has experienced sexual harassment or assault, you are not alone in your journey toward recovery. I wish you the courage and strength to come out of it stronger than ever. For those of you who've helped someone to survive and surmount such an experience, you make the world a better, safer place.

# ALSO BY DIANE MICHAELS

## Novels
**The Inked Together Series**
Inked Together
Found Together
Back Together

**The Empire State of Mind Series**
Splitting Heirs
Last Resort
Home Cooking
Keyed Up
Date Bloomer

**The Ellen the Harpist Series**
Ellen the Harpist
Ellen at Sea
Ellen the Bride

A Christmas Rescue
Pet Peeves

## Novellas
King & Queen of the Bouncy Castle
King & Queen of the Roller Derby
King & Queen of the Bowling Alley
King & Queen of the Poker Game
King & Queen of the Carnival

## Short Stories
Watching the Grass Grow

## Wedding Ceremony Music Guide
From Here Comes the Bride to There Go the Grooms

Visit http://dianemichaelsbooksandharp.com to view her
sheet music for harp.

# ABOUT THE AUTHOR

Diane Michaels is a harpist and author. She balances her fondness for ice cream with her enjoyment of working out and walking through the woods. When she is not spying on the world from behind her harp to collect ideas for her next book, she and her husband make up stories and songs for and about their miniature poodle, Lola.

You can learn more about Ms. Michaels at http://dianemichaelsbooksandharp.com

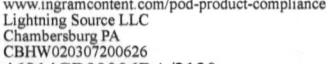